TWIN GENIUS

FAMILY GENIUS MYSTERY #4

Patricia Rice

ALSO BY PATRICIA RICE

THE WORLD OF MAGIC:
The Unexpected Magic Series
MAGIC IN THE STARS
WHISPER OF MAGIC
THEORY OF MAGIC
The Magical Malcolms Series
MERELY MAGIC
MUST BE MAGIC
THE TROUBLE WITH MAGIC
THIS MAGIC MOMENT
MUCH ADO ABOUT MAGIC
MAGIC MAN
The California Malcolms Series
THE LURE OF SONG AND MAGIC
TROUBLE WITH AIR AND MAGIC
THE RISK OF LOVE AND MAGIC
HISTORICAL ROMANCE:
The Rebellious Sons
WICKED WYCKERLY
DEVILISH MONTAGUE
NOTORIOUS ATHERTON
FORMIDABLE LORD QUENTIN
The Regency Nobles Series
THE GENUINE ARTICLE
THE MARQUESS
ENGLISH HEIRESS
IRISH DUCHESS
MYSTERIES:
Family Genius series
EVIL GENIUS
UNDERCOVER GENIUS
CYBER GENIUS
TWIN GENIUS

Twin Genius

Patricia Rice

Published by Rice Enterprises, Dana Point, CA, an affiliate of Book View Café Publishing Cooperative

Cover design: Mandala

Book View Café Publishing Cooperative

P.O. Box 1624, Cedar Crest, NM 87008-1624

http://bookviewcafe.com

ISBN 978-1-61138-641-7 ebook

ISBN 978-1-61138-642-4 print

Author's Note

THE FAMILY GENIUS MYSTERIES were conceived in the tradition of tall tales with a soupçon of satire and a dash of dry humor. Do not expect reality, or even *CSI*.

The timeline for Ana's stories takes place over a period of roughly a year—an election year. Unfortunately, I'm not capable of writing fast enough to produce an entire series of books within that same interval. So the series will not take place in real time. Current events and technology will remain static even though changes have multiplied since I conceived the original concept—and occur rapidly every day that I write.

Anyone with a modicum of political knowledge will realize that ten years after 9/11/01 does not correspond with a Senator Paul Rose—or anyone similar—running for office. All characters are fictional and entirely the product of my warped imagination.

One

Ana gets religion

"AND BLESS THIS COUNTRY in the name of the Lord, our God, Amen," thundered through the attic sound system from my ostensible landlord's desk.

Startled, I nearly dropped the file folder on Graham's antique Persian rug before he hit the sound button. That minimized the prayer, but it was too late for my fractured nerves.

I was accustomed to the silent flash of multiple monitors on the office walls, but our landlord's obsession with spying on the world did not often lead to him actually *listening* to anyone, much less to passionate televangelists. The blaring speakers had to be some form of joke.

Amadeus Graham, secret operative extraordinaire, would be a founding member of Robots-R-Us should such an organization ever exist. Robots do not express emotion, much less pray, and he was not praying now but studying the screen.

I've only seen the man do passion once—and that had been explosive and of a satisfyingly sexual kind that had left *me* intrigued and hungry for more. Not Graham, who apparently did not indulge in normal human appetites—he had not even turned around at my entrance, although he knew I was there.

If only to prove my point to myself, I grasped his wide shoulder and leaned over the back of his chair to place the folder on the console. My breasts pressed into his impressive biceps. He didn't flinch a muscle, and his thick dark head of hair didn't swerve to indicate a break from his concentration on keyboard and screen.

Our one passionate encounter had been when he'd been holed up in a hotel, on the run, over a month ago. Despite all my provocation, we'd not shared so much as a hug since then. That gave me one more reason to want to smack him, but he wasn't even engaging in our tension-relieving kickboxing matches lately.

I returned my attention to the wide screen that held his attention. Other men watched football. Graham watched street corners and public buildings and. . . televangelists, apparently.

"Is that Joshua Arden?" I asked, examining the golden-haired preacher bowing his bare head in front of an enormous outdoor crowd. December in D.C. wasn't precisely warm, and I shivered just watching all those huddled masses in puffy nylon overcoats. The good reverend disdained bulky outerwear. Instead, he displayed his massive former-quarterback's shoulders in a form-fitting cashmere sweater.

"Pretty," I said, acknowledging his good looks since there wasn't anything in the preacher's sermon to hold my interest.

Graham rubbed the wicked scar marring his otherwise handsome forehead. He'd been severely burned and injured attempting to rescue his wife from the Pentagon on 9/11. I'd seen his visible scars and knew they were bad. His inner scars were far worse.

In my unbiased observation, he'd been trying to make up for his failure to save his wife ever since that catastrophic day.

Once, I would have ignored his unusual gesture of self-consciousness. Lately, I'd been softening to the grouch. The contents of the file folder I'd handed him made me downright magnanimous.

"He's *too* pretty," I corrected, studying the perfectly sculpted features filling the screen. Arden's styled and tinted blond hair stayed solid in the brisk wind. The blue of his eyes was so clear and vivid that it was obvious he wore colored lenses. And the golden tan? Give me a break. One does not acquire tans in DC, and certainly not in December. "Pretty is a weakness. Pretty people get noticed too easily. It gives them unwarranted confidence which leads to arrogance. Arrogant people don't have the sense to watch out for themselves, much less others."

Graham's shoulder relaxed a fraction as he scrolled over the crowd. He wasn't watching a public television program but a security camera that he controlled. "Says the arrogant virtual assistant," he murmured, hitting more buttons.

Miffed, I smacked his arm, leaned over his shoulder again, and opened the folder. "I'm not arrogant. I just know what I do best and stick with it. And you will note that, unlike pretty people, I make it a point *not* to attract notice until I want something. Which is now." I tapped the top page in the folder. "Sign this, and you'll be half a million richer than you were last June."

Graham and I had been feuding for six months over the DC mansion we shared. The house had once belonged to my grandfather, Rathbone Maximillian. When he'd died, Max had left his home to his grandchildren—one of whom would be me. Long story short—Max's executor had been scum who'd sold the house to Graham and absconded with the funds before I even knew my grandfather was dead.

As Max's long-time protégé, Graham had picked up the enormous, antique-filled mansion near prestigious Dupont Circle for a pittance. He claimed to be looking after our family's interest. In reality, he didn't want to disrupt this nifty attic fortress he'd established with Max's permission.

Graham glanced at the folder holding all my dreams. Then, as if it were of no moment, he returned to refining his search. Golden-boy Arden was relegated to a smaller screen, and the big one was now occupied with boring cashmere-coated old guys. "I'll study it later."

"You've already studied it," I scoffed. "You snoop through everything on my computer. I'm offering half a mil more than you paid for the place. That's more than fair appreciation and interest for less than a year's use of your money."

"The house is worth ten or twenty times that amount," he reminded me, unnecessarily.

Chances were I might actually be able to pay that exorbitant amount, and he knew it, since he'd helped me retrieve Max's hidden funds. But Graham had also stolen our inheritance by buying it from a corrupt lawyer.

Six months ago, I'd been living in a basement in one of Atlanta's worst slums. Now I—and my half siblings—were worth a fortune. As eldest, I was currently acting as Max's executor in place of his crooked, dead attorney. The responsibility was almost worse than the one I'd once run away from—keeping my family safe in war zones. Money is as hazardous as war to one's health.

"I can't spend the entire family's future for a single house," I argued. "Max meant this to be our safe haven, a place we could all retreat to in times of need."

"Which in your family is pretty much every day of the week. Are you planning on living here for the rest of your life to look after them?" The screen now showed the street of stately mansions outside our front door.

I'd run away from my family and their problems when I'd been young, poor, and helpless, knowing they had better opportunities without me. Things were different now, but still, the money was too new and unreal for me to plan anything except my current goal—making this house mine. Or my family's—same difference.

"That's none of your business, is it now?" I said coldly. "Oppenheimer is still willing to take you, as well as the executor's firm, to court. I was trying to settle this part of the case amicably." Oppenheimer was the shark we'd hired to go after the crooked attorney's law firm.

Instead of answering, Graham zoomed in on a tall, handsome boy striding past the evergreen-decorated light pole on our street corner. The kid looked cold in his hoody, with his hands shoved in his pockets, but he carried his heavy backpack with ease. He kept glancing from side to side, either looking for something or nervous, or both.

Although the young man's clothes looked American, he had a vaguely European cast to his features, and his brown skin was real, not an artificial tan. The coloring could have come from any number of exotic or not-so exotic countries. Our neighborhood consists mostly of embassies, so we see a lot of foreigners coming and going—mostly via limousine—which made the boy look out of place and suspicious for lack of transportation alone. Why did *South African* come to mind?

Wishful thinking, for one.

But suddenly bells and whistles clamored in my head, and visions of Christmas miracles danced like storied sugar plums. Could it be? How could it possibly be? Not lingering to ask, I dropped the argument, forgot the house, and dashed for the main stairs. My brain performed mental aerobics as my short legs carried me down two flights. I'd made wild suppositions in the past, but my current instinctive leap of hope surpassed all logic.

Graham could track my every move on his security system if he liked. Having deliberately zoomed in on the stranger meant he was already a dozen steps ahead of me. That he'd bothered focusing on the boy made my hope at least a tad more reasonable.

The doorbell rang before I reached the last flight. EG—Elizabeth Georgiana, my nine-year-old genius half-sister—had figured out how to change the chimes. In deference to the season, for the last few days, the bell had been pealing some Christmas song I vaguely recognized as having a line about sleigh bells ringing. Chip off the old geek humor block—not that either of her parents had a sense of humor. Our techie half-brother Tudor had probably provided the instructions.

I shouldn't be so excited. A stranger at the door almost always meant bad news. I didn't expect this time to be any different. But my mental gyrations had put two and nine together and reached fourteen, which only made sense to me.

My mother—Magda Maximillian Llewelyn Bullfinch Hostetter, the self-proclaimed Hungarian Princess—had borne eight children. She's Catholic and one of the few church rules she adheres to is the one on contraception, a serious point of contention for us, had we ever discussed it. Which we don't. I assumed, after my father's tragic death, she went looking for love in all the wrong places. Except the men she married or hooked up with were always conveniently wealthy and powerful.

I'd been Magda's live-in babysitter, bodyguard, nanny, and tutor for the half-siblings she dropped like cuckoos into the nests of all her acquaintances. The South African paternal family of her twins had rightfully objected to this behavior and snatched them from my arms when the kids were almost four, and I was around thirteen. I hadn't seen them since. They'd be about twenty now.

Having had them ripped from my young arms had broken something inside me that had been exacerbated by the death of my baby sister in a war zone years later. Sometime after that, I'd refused to be Magda's doormat anymore. I'd survived by living in the moment and not thinking about the twins for years. I'd told myself they were safe with family and better off without us. Only in this past month have I had the wherewithal—financially and psychologically—to dare think about looking for them.

I clattered down the final steps in my Birkenstocks with unreasonable hope choking my throat. Mallard, Graham's butler/aide-de-camp/cook ceremoniously opened the front door as I arrived.

Mallard is barely average height, square, bald, and Irish, but that doesn't really describe his true presence. I was convinced he was former CIA, and he looked as if he were born to the tux-like outfits he chose to wear. He's one imperious penguin.

The tall young man at the door looked just like his distinguished African diplomat father. My smile widened as my hopes rocketed. With gracious proficiency, he flashed his passport at Mallard. Acknowledging the name, Mallard intoned as if in front of a ballroom, "Alexander Khosi Kruger, Miss Devlin. Shall I show him to the parlor?"

Mallard missed the good old days of Queen Victoria. There were times when I wondered if he and the house hadn't been transported forward a century. But I'd just been flung back a dozen years into a thousand both painful and wonderful memories, so I couldn't complain about Mallard's sentimentality.

Ignoring our butler's pomposity, I cried, "Zander! Is it really you?" If he hadn't looked so much like his father, a man I had adored, I would never have recognized this tall stranger.

At his bashful nod to my idiotic question, I gestured at the parlor. "How did you find us? Where's Juliana?"

His hood fell to reveal close-cropped dark curls, and he stared at me through deep dark wells of pain. His shoulders slumped.

My heart sank. Juliana was his twin sister. They'd once been inseparable.

"I was hoping you knew," he replied.

Two

Ana meets her brother

I LET MALLARD SHEPHERD us into the cold, overstuffed Victorian parlor where he'd at least deign to serve warm beverages, and if we were really lucky, baked goodies.

Raised as we had been, our family didn't normally do hugs. I didn't know how Zander and Juliana had been brought up. Since he could scarcely know me, I respected his personal space and let him choose the ancient leather Morris chair while I curled up on the horsehair sofa. "How did you find me?" I asked, as he settled in and took his bearings by studying the parlor.

I doubted that he was searching the room for an escape hatch. Yet. The twins had never been given the dubious benefit of Magda's evasive-tactics training. The rest of us had learned to locate exits and disappear into woodwork as soon as we learned to walk. The twins had spent their formative years in the relative security of a rural area in the Rand.

At the time, Magda had probably been helping the CIA with information from the twins' father, an associate of then recently-released Nelson Mandela. All water under the bridge in these days of mad terrorists and legalized corruption, but in contrast to most of my troubled, peripatetic life, I remembered those halcyon years very clearly.

"Our mother told us where you were," Zander said, staring in awe at the massive oil of our grandfather over the mantel.

I'd found the painting buried in a storage room in the warehouse/garage behind the house. Max had been a stern-faced, whiskered old man even before I'd been born. I thought the portrait added gravity that our flighty family needed.

"Magda knew how to find you?" I asked, thinking I ought to reach through a phone and punch our mother for not relieving my worry about the twins.

He shrugged shoulders he hadn't quite grown into yet. "I called her. *Antie* Hildegarde always had her phone number for emergencies, but she would not let us use it. Only, when Juliana quit answering her phone. . . " He sighed and dipped his head into his big hands. "We knew about our grandfather living here. He helped our father obtain our American passports."

Their father had been dead for some years, I knew. Magda's paramours didn't often lead placid lives.

"Juliana came here?" I asked in confusion, not quite following his thought process.

He nodded. "She thought it would be safe, knowing we had family in this city. She is an artist and not always practical. She loved working with the Americans on the school building projects and wanted to learn more. I think, mostly, she hoped she would meet our mother."

I rubbed my eyes at this combination of his twin's sheer naiveté and pure Maximillian willfulness. "She didn't try to find out if our family actually *lived* in D.C. but simply grabbed some offer to work on a project?"

He nodded. Rummaging in his backpack, he produced a rumpled brochure and passed it over. "They are good people, and the village approved of us helping with this very Christian project. They did not know Juliana's ulterior motives."

His English was better than mine, which gave his speech a foreign accent right there. He sounded vaguely British, although I knew his father's family lived in a tribal village that had once been predominantly Zulu. I assumed private schooling had erased most of his mixed Afrikaans and tribal accents. His father had been a respected, fairly wealthy diplomat before he'd been kidnapped and killed.

I glanced at the brochure. My eyebrows shot up and I studied it closer. *Damn Graham to hell and back.*

The brochure was from Joshua Arden's Christian America Development. My cynicism loved the acronym CAD and skipped right over Arden's name.

"Juliana came here to work for CAD?" I asked, still trying to puzzle out the chicken and the egg. I was still soaking up the joy of seeing the little brother I'd never been given a chance to know.

"We graduated early, at the head of our class," he said in halting explanation, not really looking at me. "We were offered grants to pursue the projects we began at university. Julie's art project involved schools. She created a video that JACAD uses as a promotional tool. She wanted to inspire more people to contribute time and money to supporting education. They invited her to continue her education and join a much larger project here in DC. The grant allowed her to come, and she jumped at the chance."

"Thinking Max was still alive and Magda might be here?" I asked dubiously.

He nodded. "She has always been curious about our mother. She took pictures of her that she found in our father's effects and hid them from our family. *Antie* Hildegard did not approve of Mrs. Hostetter and is wary of all foreigners, so Julie had to plan this trip in secret. Even I did not know until she had her plane tickets in hand, or I would have researched more."

Mrs. Hostetter—how very proper for our very improper mother. None of us called her Mother. In time, Zander would learn the family pejoratives for the Hungarian Princess. His use of the affectionate *antie* spoke of a warmer upbringing than the rest of us had had—a more protected one.

"How long ago did Juliana leave? Did you hear from her after she arrived in DC?" I'm a virtual assistant by trade, a very good one—hence Graham's arrogance crack. It's impossible for me to turn off my brain's focus on details.

"She left in early September. When *Antie* Hildegard found out, she went *bosbefok* and called all father's friends, demanding that Julie be sent back, but of course, they could do nothing." Zander shifted uncomfortably in the lumpy chair.

I could just imagine his aunt going berserk. I'd rather not. She was one crazy lady.

"At first, I received excited text messages," he continued. "She loved where she was staying. She loved the project and was learning much in marketing classes. She was making friends. Then about the beginning of November, it was as if she'd dropped off the face of the earth. *Antie* Hildegard went. . . how do you say it? Ballistic?"

Remembering the furious ebony Amazon who had snatched the twins from my arms, I could imagine that. At the time, I thought she'd snap my adolescent head off.

"Ballistic probably covers it," I acknowledged. "Did Juliana have money to buy a new phone if she lost the old one?"

"She should. She was receiving a small stipend plus her family allowance and living free in what I assume is a dorm, since she has roommates. She was buying new photographic equipment. It is not like Julie to forget me." He made an apologetic gesture. "Until this, we did everything together. Our background is so odd, that we did not fit well anywhere else."

"I completely understand." And I did. My next youngest sibling, Nick, and I had been bonded by fire in our childhoods. It is not easy being the only white English speakers for hundreds of miles. The twins were mixed-race, so their experience wasn't identical, but close enough to appreciate. "So when she quit texting, you did what?"

"Panicked, essentially," he said with a grimace, running his hand over his head. "I called everyone we knew, implored the American embassy to look for her, sent emails to all her friends, left messages all over social media—nothing. The embassy couldn't be bothered, and no one else had heard anything. We enjoy geo-caching, so I sent messages to others in DC to put their phone numbers in caches and send out the coordinates to sites she might frequent. No result."

"So you decided to come here and look for her yourself?"

He nodded again. "But I came prepared. I made Hilda give me the emergency number to reach our mother. It goes to voice mail, but she called me back instantly." His voice cracked as he said this last. "When our father lived, he said he'd sent information about us to Mrs. Hostetter via some network that his enemies could not track, but I had never spoken with her until this. She couldn't talk long, but she gave us your address and said our grandfather had died this past year."

"We call her Magda," I said, worrying at my braid. There was only one good reason I could imagine for her not to talk to her long lost son all these years. "She's trying to protect you, just as your aunt was. Magda has some dangerous enemies."

Alexander nodded wearily. "So did my father, so I understand. He arranged for us to be raised with extended family in a village with better security then he could provide in the city. Still, it was good to finally speak with her."

"I think your parents were very happy together in those few brief years," I said as consolingly as I could. "They simply didn't lead lives suitable for children."

"As my father's assassination proved," he said with a sigh.

"Mrs. . . *Magda* told me that you were here in DC and would help me. It is strange, but you are my earliest memory. When *Antie* Hildegard and the rest of my father's family took us away from you, I remember being very afraid. They were enormous and dressed in tribal attire, most certainly to frighten you because they normally don't wear such things except for ceremonial occasions. Instead of being terrified, you grabbed both of us in your arms and held on and refused to give us up. They had us surrounded. There was no one to help but an old cook. But when anyone approached, you shrilled blood-curdling screams that I swear had lions roaring in the nearest jungle."

I'd blocked much of that day, but his words returned the terrifying moment, and I fought tears. None of Magda's training had taught me how to hide from a tribe of armed natives.

"I had my hands full and couldn't fight," I said with regret. "You weren't big enough to run back to the house."

"You fought," he said firmly. "You fought like a lioness. My uncle still proudly bears the scar on his shin. And my aunt wears the mark of your teeth like a badge of honor. When I told her that you were here, she agreed I might come."

I rubbed at my watery eye as if an eyelash bothered it. "I suppose it was best for you to be raised by adults, but I didn't know that then. Losing you. . . almost broke my heart."

Alexander shot me a look of understanding. "We have often spoken of you, but our father would not say where you were. I think, once our *antie* talked him into letting her keep us, that was when our mother left him."

He was undoubtedly right. Magda had been in a fury when she'd returned and found the twins gone, as I recalled. "I hope you had a good life," I said, because I didn't know what else to say. It was hard to grasp that those impressive warriors had admired my puny efforts to save the toddlers.

"We did. We were raised by the whole village, given the best education my father could provide. When he was killed. . . we were sad, of course, but we saw him so seldom, that life went on as always. Until now."

Mallard carried in a tray of sandwiches and hot tea—his nonalcoholic beverage of choice—and left.

Alexander scarfed down almost the entire platter while I nibbled on a Christmas cookie. Exhaustion lined his face. The trip from South Africa combined with his worry was taking its toll.

"I need you to compile as much information as you have on Juliana—her phone number, birth date, schools, anyone she might know here," I told him as he ate. "If she has a bank account, I need the name of the bank. Any little detail could help."

He gulped his hot tea and reached for his backpack again. "I have done all that. Before I left, I went through all her computer files. I emailed everyone in her address book. I made copies." He produced a thumb drive and handed it over. "I am a financial analyst, not a computer person. Mrs. . . Magda said you might be able to do more."

It made me very uneasy that Magda hadn't jumped right on this herself—or jumped right on a plane. I probably ought to expect her at any minute. Consumed by her obsessions, she wasn't maternal, but she looked after her chicks to the best of her abilities.

I took the thumb drive. "I'll go over this while you get some rest. I'll show you to a bedroom. Most of them have already been claimed by other family members. You'll meet some of them later. It's best to be rested when you do."

"I am very grateful that you are willing to take in a stranger, especially without warning." He heaved his backpack over one slender shoulder.

"You are not a stranger, you're family. This house was meant for all of us," I assured him. "Once I have the title back, it will belong as much to you as to me."

I defiantly aimed this last at the foyer chandelier. Graham had bugs in almost every light fixture.

I wouldn't give up without a fight, and he'd have more than teeth marks in his hide if he didn't give in.

Three

Ana tries not to panic

UPSTAIRS, I GAVE ZANDER the Lincoln bedroom. He studied the immense antique sleigh bed and mahogany mantel, while I lifted the oil painting of Lincoln and plastered duct tape over the camera lens beneath it.

"Respect privacy," I told the floor lamp as I reached beneath the shade and ripped out the bug.

Alexander blinked in surprise when I handed it to him. "We do not need the security device?"

Security device! I almost heard Graham howl in laughter. Except Graham never howled at anything.

"If you feel safer having the spy in the attic listen to your every move, then reinstall it. But this is America. We don't spy on our own citizens." Which was a lie these days, but I didn't want to argue details when he looked on the brink of exhaustion.

That he accepted bugs as a security device said a great deal of the climate of violence he'd grown up in.

"Thank you," was all Zander said as he took the battery out of the bug.

He was a foot taller than me, so I resisted the urge to give him an encouraging hug. I couldn't give him comforting words either, because all my experience said Juliana was dead or in dire trouble if she had quit communicating. I didn't make promises I couldn't keep.

I left him unpacking, and gut roiling, hurried to my basement hideaway. EG would be home from school shortly. After a few harrowing episodes, we'd agreed to let Graham's limo service take her to and from school. I feared we were losing our independence and survival instincts by living in luxury. It was a dilemma my mother would appreciate—security or independence? Paranoia versus freedom? It's a choice we all make.

Magda had run away from this comfortable life when I was just a toddler, after my father died in a bomb attack, along with Graham's father and a few other rebellious young men. As a result, I'd grown up surviving on wits, bravado, and any martial arts I could learn on the run. I'd seen the results of bullets too many time to appreciate guns, so I declined their use. I'd rather die than do that to another human being.

I wanted EG to grow up in a world of peace where she didn't have to make that choice.

Telling myself I could still teach her survival, I plugged the thumb drive into the Cobalt Whiz, the state-of-the-art computer Graham had provided, and went to work.

Graham was far more than a security consultant. He'd once been an aide to the President of the United States, and he still maintained high level security contacts. I wasn't entirely certain they all knew who he was since he'd dropped off the grid after 9/11, but I made use of every resource at hand without questioning.

As I worked, Graham dropped files about JACAD into my computer. That pretty much meant that CAD was already on his hit list of suspicious organizations. We both had a vendetta going for Top Hat, a secretive cabal of tycoons that I blamed for killing Max. They were politically-connected, wealthy men with a right-wing agenda. I didn't like the idea that he suspected Juliana's employer to be involved with treacherous men who controlled financial institutions, oil companies, and the media.

But it was best to know what I was up against if Juliana might have disappeared on JACAD's watch. I skimmed through the files on the development's philanthropic goals—building schools wasn't their only project. Funded by gun lobbies, Christian groups, and a few purely political PACs, CAD had acquired some very pricey land across the river in Virginia.

I almost poked my eyes out when I saw the architectural renderings of the planned project. Not low rent housing for the needy, no sirree. They were building a *Christian amusement park*. If I was making any sense out of these images, the park came complete with the disciples riding around on dinosaurs, and Jesus emerging from an Aladdin's cave paved in gold. I closed the document and wished I could purge my brain and unsee that.

My parents were Catholic—in all senses of the word. I'd attended synagogues and mosques and soaring cathedrals and fully respected those who believed in their faith.

I did not, however, appreciate brainwashing. I'd seen the attempts to remove science and historical accuracy from EG's textbooks in favor of Biblical beliefs. I knew the Top Hat cabal was behind a narrow-minded conspiracy to suppress free-thinking. Their clique hadn't—yet—reached the demonic efforts of the Chinese to control opinion by snuffing those who questioned authority, but once Senator Rose, their candidate for presidency, was in office, I could see that as a very real possibility.

I couldn't grasp the unquestioning absurdity behind those dinosaurs. All they needed was a world-is-flat exhibit with the United States drawn as the only country on the planet. That really would make the rest of the world *aliens*, wouldn't it? I tried to laugh, but I was too worried about my sister.

As I drilled down through CAD's donors, my mouth grew dry. Every dangerous Top Hat fat cat I knew had contributed exceedingly large sums for the development of Joshua's berserk Jesus World.

What the... dickens... had Juliana got herself into? These men were *not* philanthropists, although I suppose they might donate if they thought Joshua would shape the world in their white male image. But even in my cynicism, I couldn't believe they swayed that way.

I pulled myself away from my awful fascination with the cabal's scurvy machinations and returned to searching for Juliana's phone numbers, bank accounts, and credit cards.

Alexander was undoubtedly too proper to hack his sister's accounts. I wasn't. She hadn't even set up on-line access. I thoughtfully did it for her, copying passwords she'd stored from other applications.

Her salary and allowance were still being deposited into her bank account. That was a relief of sorts. Surely CAD wouldn't keep paying her stipends unless she was showing up for work, right? But why would she drop out of her family's sight?

She'd had a field day at a photographic equipment shop when she'd first arrived in early September. The payments on her credit card balance from that spree had been automatically transferred from her bank in the months since. The only other withdrawal was nearly the balance of her account at the beginning of November.

Phone and cash made her the target of every mugger in DC.

EG clattered down the stairs. Nerves on edge, I almost jumped from my chair.

"Who's in the Lincoln room?" she asked as she burst in. "Did Magda come for Christmas?"

I narrowed my eyes at her. "Did you invite her?"

Blithely uncaring of my long-term feud with our mother, she settled into one of my wing chairs. "She said she might come. Tudor and everyone will be here. It will be the first time we've all been together since—"

"Since never," I filled in for her. "They're still bombing people in Iraq, and she wants to come home?" This was said in heavy irony. Magda always ended up in war zones, although Iraq was presumably being decommissioned.

"I know. Isn't it rad?" she asked excitedly, missing my sarcasm. "But shouldn't she have Max's room?"

"Probably, if she were here, which she isn't." Max had died in a bed on the ground floor, just above my basement office. With illness, he hadn't been able to climb the stairs, so he'd had an old parlor renovated into a massive suite containing everything a man could want, including bolt holes to my basement office and secret stairs to the attic for Graham to use. I hated the idea of having Magda staying overhead.

EG glared at me expectantly. She really is too smart for her own good.

"One of the South African twins is here—Alexander," I told her.

"Cool! Does he play video games?"

One good thing about living life out of a suitcase, one learned to expect surprises and make do with what one was given.

"I have no idea, and don't wake him up to ask. How did your English test go?"

She gave a heavy sigh of exasperation. "I wrote an essay comparing the spy cases of the Rosenbergs and Pollard and all she did was correct my commas. I think commas ought to be outlawed."

I muffled a snort of laughter, appreciating the teacher's dilemma at being handed a college-level political essay instead of the few paragraphs on pets she'd probably expected. "Tell Mallard to give you some of his molasses cookies and some hot chocolate as a reward. The cookies are heaven."

She made a face but jumped up, ready to experiment with molasses. "We only have room for one more person. Will Juliana be joining us?"

Snoop. She didn't know the twins, had no reason to even know of their existence—except she snooped, just like Magda. And me. I'd have to check her computer to find out what files she'd accessed.

"We don't know yet." I wasn't letting her know there was a mystery at hand or she'd don a Sherlock Holmes hat and be off to find our missing sister.

I didn't want to tell her that the sister she'd never known might be dead.

NICK DIDN'T SHOW UP until after dinner. I'd texted him about Zander's arrival and that we had a problem, but I didn't want to put too much out there. And none of us wanted to discuss Juliana in front of EG, so he waited until he knew she'd be in bed.

Nicholas Maximillian is a brilliant mathematician, card shark, and diplomat. Like many of our nomadic family, he has dual citizenship. He's the illegitimate son of a British lord, who made sure his son had the education I didn't have. Nick is male model gorgeous: tall, blond, has a firm square jaw with cleft in it, and sharp Slavic cheekbones. I have the same cheekbones, and so does Magda, so there's probably some truth to her claim to being Hungarian. She's about as much a princess as any rich Jewish girl, though. Nick also happens to be gay, although in his diplomat's finery, only the bright blue ascot gave him away.

Zander studied him thoughtfully, shook hands, and slumped into the Morris chair without saying a word.

"Takes after Max, does he?" Nick asked with a grin, settling beside me on the horsehair sofa and sprawling his long legs on what was probably a ten-thousand-dollar antique coffee table. "Magda always said her father could out stonewall a stone wall."

While Alexander attempted to puzzle that out, I plopped a paper file folder on Nick's lap. I loved computers. They're my lifeline to the world and I knew how to safeguard them. But Nick worked for the British embassy and was only vaguely aware of the concept of encryption, so I had to communicate with him by paper. All embassies come equipped with spies, and I prefer to keep our private life just that—private.

"Julie is still receiving her paychecks," I told them, giving them the good news first. I wasn't certain I wanted to involve Alexander in my conspiracy theories, so I didn't mention my real concerns. "I want to experiment with the assumption that she thinks her phone and computer are tapped or otherwise watched, and she's keeping a low profile."

Zander's head popped up with interest. "She's protecting us as Magda protected us? By staying out of our lives? That's *bosbefok*."

I lifted my eyebrows and waited expectantly. He dropped his head in his hands again. "Juliana is very, very smart, but not always logical," he admitted.

"Protecting family is perfectly logical," Nick said with diplomatic tact. "If she knows this address, then she knows she can come here if she's in any danger. That would indicate that she's safe but unwilling to involve us. We need to give her a secure means of communication."

That was a pretty huge leap of confidence, but it made Zander come to life.

"Can you find out if she still has her phone?" he asked eagerly. "I could text her with coordinates and leave a message for her in a cache near where she lives."

"Assuming she still has her phone, if she recognizes your number, will she respond? If she's protecting you, maybe not," Nick warned.

"He could use one of our phones, but would she pay attention to us?" I asked, trying to put myself in her position—which was impossible, of course.

"We have a code," Zander explained. "Once we have a cache set up, I'll text her with just the coordinates. I can do it from an unknown number, but if I make the subject header a Bible phrase, she'll know it's me. If she gets it," he added, gloom descending again.

A Bible phrase, of course. I really would have to wrap my head around having a pair of religious siblings. "We'll go out tomorrow and you can show me what we need for a cache. The address she's using is over in Alexandria. It's not exactly a forest where you can bury things, unless it's in someone's front yard."

"Caches can be creative. We'll find something," he said with assurance.

"Leave her a burner phone in the cache," Nick advised. "They're pretty much untraceable. We'll put our number in it. Maybe she can text us that way."

Provided she was alive. We could assume she hadn't been abducted since there had been no ransom note.

If anyone realized we were actually worth a fortune, then every one of us would be a prime target for kidnapping. I wanted to bury *my* face in *my* hands, but I kept a positive expression and nodded approvingly as they made plans with almost no hope of success.

Four

Ana takes Zander sightseeing

AS USUAL, GRAHAM MADE no attempt to greet our new family member. The only way I knew he was alive was by the documents and demands flowing into my computer. I'd once worried we'd be flung out on our heads if I didn't carry through on all his demands. I have more knowledge of his interests now, so they made me curious enough to follow where they led.

But family came before curiosity. After a night's restless sleep, I sent EG off to school, then prepared for the day's outing. I invaded Nick's old room—he now had his own digs—and found one of his old overcoats.

I handed it to Alexander, who still looked like a scruffy adolescent to me. "You'll freeze without a coat. If you're lucky, Nick left gloves in the pockets. Unfortunately, he won't cover up his pretty hair, so he doesn't wear hats." I could ask Graham, but that was just too intimate, and he'd probably look at me as if I was crazy.

Zander looked dubiously at Nick's tailored Chesterfield coat but obediently donned it. He was as tall as Nick but not as broad through the shoulders. He looked like a kid wearing his daddy's coat, but he was less likely to catch pneumonia than in a hoody.

Brought up the way I've been, I don't really notice skin color any more than I notice fashion. But I am over-protective. A black kid wearing a hoodie through white DC causes eyes to narrow and attracts attention. I'm all about doing what it takes to blend in, unless I *want* attention. Zander's tawny coloring gave him a distinguished look in a tailored coat, but I wasn't sure about the hoodie.

I wore my thrift store faux leopard coat, hat, and furred boots. I'd mapped out our transportation—I drive but I don't have a license—and was prepared to trek out when Graham's voice filled the foyer like the voice of God. Zander dropped his gloves in startlement.

"The limo is returning for you," his deep voice tolled through the chandelier.

"You can follow us in it, if you like," I told him in my most pleasant hostess voice. Once upon a time, I used to beat the tar out of his hidden speakers, but I'd learned to live with the intrusions. Sometimes, they were even useful. Or amusing.

Graham's manipulation of my life was not.

"It will take you twice as long by public transportation," he said in irritation.

"But Zander will learn how to use the Metro. Anyone can sit passively in a car, isolated from reality. We don't follow that path." I'd experienced that isolation the last time the family had been threatened. The suffocating cocoon of the limo had kept me from learning what was really happening, and I hadn't liked it.

I opened the massive carved front door and gestured for Zander to precede me.

He looked bewildered, but that went away the moment we stepped outside. It was snowing. Like a child, he held out his gloved hand in wonder, catching the flakes.

My jaded heart warmed. "I take it you don't go skiing in the mountains."

"We never left the village until we went to school in Johannesburg." He tilted his head back to watch the tumble of flakes from the gray sky. "Now I understand some of your Christmas celebration, even though Bethlehem was a desert."

"I thought it got cold enough to snow in Johannesburg." We trudged down the street. I ignored the limo cruising toward us.

I could list a thousand reasons why it's safer to not hand fate to a driver other than myself, but I only pulled out excuses when I was afraid. So that meant I was terrified for Juliana and retreating to my childhood need for control by not taking the limo. I'd been to therapists. I can talk the talk. That doesn't mean I'll change. Given my upbringing, I needed to be in charge of nasty situations. Otherwise, I'd been known to blow up buildings to reach my family. I was clenching my fists as I once had as a teenager, and we didn't even *know* anything.

"Snow is rare, maybe only forming in a small neighborhood, and it melts quickly," Zander replied. "We have much sun in winter. Juliana and I were still in the village the last time it snowed." He glanced over his shoulder, noticed the massive car turning to follow us, and looked uneasy.

We were only half a block from the Metro now. I stepped up our pace, and we disappeared underground where the car couldn't go.

"If we are wealthy, why can we not take the car?" he finally asked.

"Do you want the full lecture or the abbreviated one?" I asked, studying the overhead signs and moving down the platform through the morning rush hour crowd.

"A car would be safer and faster," he said cautiously.

"A car would get caught in rush hour traffic and be a perfect target. We'd be trapped inside," I countered.

"Do we have enemies?" he asked in understandable horror.

"In my experience, yes. Do you, or do you not, want to learn how to survive in any circumstances?"

His father—like mine—had been killed by assassins. Zander looked thoughtful and didn't question more. We weren't born to parents who lived in peaceful suburbs and pushed paper for a living.

My full lecture would have taken the length of our Metro ride and would have been difficult in the crush. I was relieved that he was intelligent enough to catch my drift without argument.

We only had to run for one train connection and endure the crush before we reached the King Street station. I saw no sign of the limo waiting for us. In this weather, the limo could have been caught in traffic. DC didn't handle snow well, and it was coming down thicker now.

The area we strolled through was decorated in evergreen roping and Christmas lights. We had a real holiday happening, which briefly distracted Zander from his gloom.

"Juliana will love this," he said, gesturing at a brilliantly decorated, wheeling exhibition of Santa's workshop in a store window.

He did not say what I was thinking—*if she was alive.*

"All right, let's find her and make sure she sees it. I want to see the address we have for her. On Google, it looks like an office building." Knowing any snow this time of year would melt off soon, and hoping Juliana was enjoying it somewhere, I traipsed down the increasingly icy sidewalk. People in hats and scarves rushed by, late for work if they had to be there by nine. The fact that we dawdled, staring around us, made us look out of place, but I didn't think that mattered—yet.

I followed the map I'd laid out in my phone, and we located the building with relative ease, if I didn't count frozen toes.

Alexander expressed his dismay first. "*Yoh*, she would not be living in a tower like that! Those are offices, are they not?"

Yup, it was an ugly concrete-and-glass office building towering umpteen stories above us—not the church or school dorm I'd envisioned.

"One way to find out for certain." I dove into the crowd crossing the street and pushed through the glass front doors.

The lobby had no security desk, just business suits waiting patiently for the elevators. I studied the index and found Joshua Arden's Christian America Development with a suite on the tenth floor, about half way up. "They're the only office on the tenth floor. That's not looking residential. They'd probably be breaking zoning laws to have a dorm up there."

"But this is her address!"

"They must pick up the mail here and deliver it elsewhere," I said reassuringly. "If they're working on unfinished projects, that could just mean they don't have delivery where they are."

I'd lived in third world countries where no one had an address. I hadn't traveled the United States enough to know if there were places without mail. I kind of doubted it, but construction projects sounded third world to me.

"She was working on the park, yes, but they have *classes* there as well," he said in despair, staring at the index as if it would produce answers. "Perhaps we could go up and ask."

"A perfectly sensible solution—except if Juliana is trying to keep us out for some reason, we ought to respect that for a little while, until we know more." And if she was dead and CAD hadn't told her family. . . then I really didn't want to be on their radar yet. I'd learned my lesson about barging in and jeopardizing everyone I'd hoped to save. I was into subtle these days.

He nodded uncertainly. "Can we find out what projects they're working on?"

"Only one in the vicinity," I said with certainty, heading back for the street. I'd already planned this next step. "First, we should buy phones. I don't want to traipse all the way out there and not be prepared."

Graham's limo was idling in a no-parking zone outside the door.

He would know I'd head for JACAD'S office first. He'd also know my ultimate destination. But we couldn't explore the grounds from a limo, and we'd be darned conspicuous when I wanted secrecy.

I led Alexander to a store that sold pre-paid phones. He grasped the concept quickly, worked his way through the shelf to find the best deal, and whipped out his credit card. I stayed his hand.

"Family business, family card." I added a second phone to our purchase and swiped a card made out to the trust that our lawyer had set up for our funds. The trust had an innocuous name that wouldn't lead directly back to us without a lot of research and prying into secure documents in a lawyer's office.

I had Zander open the annoying plastic packages and charge up the phones with the mobile charger I carried in my faux-Birkin bag. While he was doing that, I opened my cell phone and hit a new app I'd downloaded last night. Then I led him into a Starbucks so we could warm our hands on hot tea—or in his case, coffee—until the anonymous Uber driver arrived.

With our warm drinks in hand, I waved at Graham's limo driver, then climbed into the back seat of a Honda Civic. Zander was starting to wear a perpetual expression of perplexity.

"Can you take us to the entrance of Jesus World?" I asked.

"I can get you close. The road isn't finished yet," the bearded driver said. He looked a little rough around the edges, like a man who'd seen things he'd rather have not. I pegged him as ex-military, out to make a few bucks for Christmas. I approved of the entrepreneurship of the new company and the driver. So, call me an anarchist for being cheap and supporting independence.

"Close is excellent." That meant unfinished areas with no nosy housewives watching us while we looked for a place to cache the phones. "Do you know anything about the project? Know anyone working there?" Another benefit of locals over limo drivers—the locals gossip.

"One of the guys I went to high school with drives a dozer for them. Says they pay good money, but the work keeps getting held up and is moving slow," the driver obligingly informed me.

"Any work is good in this economy." I sipped my tea and waited. I checked his name and number to store in my files.

"Tell me about it." He went off into a rant about jobs going overseas, and I tuned out.

Ignoring the driver, Alexander cuddled his hands around the hot cup and watched the city pass by. "And what do we learn by taking this car instead of the other?" he whispered into a lull.

"That we don't need a limo to get around. They're not always available when we need one," I said in satisfaction, glancing over my shoulder to see the long black sedan following far behind. By now, I was mostly annoying Graham for my morning fun.

Zander looked impressed when I showed him the app on my phone. He figured out my hotspot, pulled out the burner phones, and added the app to both. As I'd hoped, my little brother was naïve, not stupid.

By the time Zander had phone numbers and apps loaded into both burners plus our normal mobiles, the driver had taken us into the countryside and stopped at a gate. Only the name of the construction company adorned the locked gate on the park's chain-link fence, but in the distance, we could see the monstrosities rising.

Mostly, the so-called *attractions* were wood and metal skeletons, now covered in a dusting of snow, creating spectacularly eerie gray images rising from what appeared to be open graves for giants. It was impossible to tell a dinosaur from a disciple. But we could make out the foundations of a merry-go-round, the steel of a roller coaster, and the remains of an old-fashioned Ferris wheel with only three seats. Apparently the park wasn't averse to acquiring used equipment.

I assumed they'd be adding camels and donkeys to the merry-go-round, and the roller coaster would someday be a fun ride across the Red Sea. I wasn't sure how one transformed a Ferris wheel.

The Uber driver rolled away. The limo was nowhere in sight, thank heavens. Graham's driver was an older man, like Mallard, and trained to be discreet.

"Trailers," I said, nodding in the direction of a row of tin cans on wheels and a concrete-block store, complete with showers and propane tanks for sale. "The park will probably have a fancy campground when the project is finished instead of the hotels they have at Disney World."

So, I'm a bigot like the rest of the world. I despise ignorance, and it was showing in my spitefulness. I actually approved of camping over high-rise hotels, but I was scared and wary and didn't have anyone to punch to make me feel better.

Zander shivered in his dress coat and studied the rough piles of dirt, equipment, and materials being buried in a blanket of snow. Then he turned to examine what remained of the trees on what had probably once been a lovely farm. "The cache first?" he suggested. "And then I send the coordinates?"

"You're learning." Not seeing any good excuse for climbing the construction fence, I trudged with him into a copse of half-dead trees, trying to figure out how anyone could find anything in a jungle of dead vines and bare branches. I'd lived in cities much of my life, occasionally a desert or two. I was as ignorant of the countryside as Zander was of DC. "I didn't think they had forests in South Africa. How will you know how to create a cache?"

"We have trees in parks in Johannesburg. They are not like this, however." He studied the vine-covered stumps and limbs. "If I send the coordinates only to Juliana, I don't think it matters that we find a clever cache. We just need a place of concealment."

He glanced at the plastic bag from the phone store. "Will this protect a phone from the wet?"

I pulled a gray waterproof envelope from my bag. "I came prepared."

He wrapped one phone in the store bag, then in the envelope, and folded it until it wouldn't fold more. It wasn't exactly a small package, but flat enough that it shouldn't be too difficult to conceal. I was starting to get the picture.

We traipsed through the meager woods, scuffling paths in the snow that gradually filled behind us. Alexander finally focused on a clump of saplings around a lightning-savaged tree trunk. Pulling out a pocket knife that should never have been allowed on whatever plane he'd flown in on, he pried off the rotting bark around a crevasse in the trunk. The gray envelope blended in with the old wood beneath the stripped bark, and he dug at the crevasse until it was deep enough to hold the package.

When the saplings fell back in place, the hole was completely concealed. We recorded the coordinates of the location from our phones, then hurried back to the street. I checked, and the snow continued to fill our footsteps. Somedays, I seriously believed in a Great Spirit watching over us.

Graham's limo was waiting out on the main road. Figuring Zander had learned enough, I opened the door and climbed in. Zander's hands were practically shaking, whether from the cold or anxiety, I couldn't say. I politely tried not to watch as he composed a message on his new burner phone.

"Home, miss?" Sam, the driver, asked.

"Yes, please," I said, already mentally listing all the directions my research needed to take when I got there.

I heard Zander's message send and prayed that Juliana still had her phone.

"Can you also email her? Is there anywhere else you can leave a message?" I asked as he clasped the phone between both big, bony hands as if praying over it.

He nodded. "I brought my tablet, but should I do it from a neutral computer?"

"Yes, from a new email address under a different identity. If you mean to use social media to send messages, you need to start new ones with the new address and keep logged out of your usual ones. I'll set up my laptop in the library and you can connect with our internet."

I'd used the library as my office until I'd appropriated my basement hideaway. The aging library was as dark, cold, and inhospitable as the parlor, but it had a gorgeous table that could hold dozens of computers. And it was on the first floor where I could keep an eye on him, if needed.

Traffic had cleared out by the time we cruised the streets toward home, and we made reasonably good time. It wasn't lunchtime yet when the limo let us off in front of the house.

I raised my eyebrows at the figure sprawled on the front step, backpack cluttering the three-inch lawn. Tudor was so engrossed in his tablet that he didn't look up when we approached.

I kicked his combat boot. "You could have told us when you were coming."

"I flew stand-by." He reluctantly shoved his computer in the pocket of his old army coat and stood up. Coming from the UK, he was at least appropriately dressed for the weather.

Tudor Bullfinch is our sixteen-year-old computer genius half-brother. His father is an Australian shipping magnate married to his third wife who prefers to keep the peace by sending his son by his first wife, Magda, to boarding school in London. Tudor has his father's carrot-red hair and like everyone else in the family except EG, stands taller than me.

"And Mallard refused to let you in?" I inquired, taking out my key and opening the door.

"No one answered the bell," Tudor replied. "I didn't think it polite to sneak in through the tunnel."

I fought a frisson of fear as I unlocked and opened the door to our secure cave.

The house echoed oddly empty. A cold chill crept down my spine. In these last months, I'd become accustomed to coming home to Mallard's greetings and Graham's snark. They hardly ever left the house together. Where had they gone?

Five

Juliana does something dangerous

JULIANA LABELED THE GRAPHIC of the pyramid granaries, and Baby Moses in his basket among the reeds, and sent the image to the mainframe. She wondered why mummies were stored beneath grain but history and science didn't interest her. She was here for one purpose only—to learn to build schools. If the cost of that education was working on Reverend Arden's park, she would happily pay.

But if there were hidden costs, as she feared, she needed to know about them. Before opening the next screen, she looked around at the other student interns bent over their keyboards, working on their own tasks. None of them were watching her.

Pretending to stretch her back, she glanced up. The office manager usually slipped out for a smoke about now, although no one was supposed to know that. She hid her relief—Mrs. Overcamp was nowhere in sight.

Furtively, she went on-line, called up last night's surveillance videos—both hers and the park's—saved them to a cloud account, and deleted her history. She wasn't certain when she would have time to watch all of the footage. Security was tight, and she had reason to believe she was watched.

Retrieving a dead-tree document from her desk in-box, she opened a comparable form in her computer. She kept that screen large and visible while she opened a smaller screen. Typing in her password, she checked her online email notifications. She knew the account wasn't secure, but she couldn't help checking once a day. Mostly, it was spam these days, and she could ignore the box.

She almost closed the screen on what appeared to be spam from an unknown sender—until the subject clicked in her tired brain—Revelations 3:4.

Yet you have a few people in Sardis who have not soiled their clothes. They will walk with me, dressed in white, for they are worthy. Geeky Zander loved to tease her with that quote when she wore white. Zander would use Tardis when he quoted it, of course.

Verifying no one watched, praying IT wasn't sophisticated enough to store keyboard strokes, she opened the message, and her heart raced a little faster. Embedded in the quote were the capitalized letters N and W, with numbers inserted as if they were verses. Could Zander be sending her coordinates? To what?

The message *had* to be from Zander. How? She didn't recognize the address.

Memorizing the combination of numbers and letters worked into the verse, she deleted the email without reply. With luck, the Bible code would prevent anyone from understanding what Zander was telling her. That was unnaturally devious for a straight arrow like her brother.

Could she hope he was here in the States? She couldn't imagine it, not with his new job, but perhaps he'd found help nearby. She didn't know if electronic listening devices could tell what she was doing if she were to use her phone with the GPS tracker to test this location. Best not to try.

She knew the instant Mrs. Overcamp returned because the stink of cigarette smoke preceded her. Why did smokers think they could conceal their habit? Couldn't they smell themselves?

The general contractor, Mr. Gregory, arrived to inspect some document on Mrs. Overcamp's desk. He was a burly man, smelling of the outdoors and dressed for the cold, alien to the indoor students bent over their desks. The presence of authority made her nervous.

Julie hastily cleaned out her history again. She would make them work to find out what places she visited.

Plotting how she could copy an image from her cloud account without revealing her use to security, and where she could find an unbugged phone, she returned to rendering artistic images of what she now thought of as tombstones.

Ana frets

"TUDOR, YOU'RE HOME!" EG cried happily as she returned from school the afternoon of Tudor's arrival. She dropped her colorfully-decorated purple backpack next to Tudor's grungy one in the foyer. The shabby modern bags looked incongruous beneath our grandfather's antique

Waterford chandelier and polished Sheraton table.

Mallard would have a fit, if he were here. He wasn't.

Nervously I set down a tray of hot chocolate-filled mugs on top of the glossy magazines laid out decorously on the coffee table. Tudor and Zander were playing video games and getting to know each other, and the parlor was the most comfortable location. Mallard would have had a conniption at my serving food in his precious parlor. I was almost begging for him to emerge from the woodwork and sniff in disapproval.

There had been no sign of Mallard in the kitchen. We'd made our own lunch.

Worse, there had been no missives from Graham waiting in my inbox. Graham worked 24/7. I couldn't remember a time that he hadn't been pouring documents into my box, even when he'd been in hiding.

Six months ago, this lack of intrusion would have made me deliriously happy. Now—I was frightened.

I'd had plenty of years of therapy to recognize my abandonment neurosis. I didn't want to admit it. If I started including Graham and Mallard in my family circle, I would never know peace again. I refused to go to the attic to check on them—which was probably even more neurotic but believing they deserved their privacy was my way of dealing with paranoia.

"Now we can find a Christmas tree," EG cried excitedly. "Can Nick come with us? What about Patra?"

A Christmas tree? Where had that come from? We'd never ever had. . . . *Oh.* They'd never had Christmas, so of course they wanted one.

I glanced at the boys. They looked up expectantly, then at my expression, ducked their heads and returned to their games.

Were they hoping for a real old-fashioned picture-book family Christmas? That thought terrorized me almost enough to drive out my worries over Graham. I had absolutely, utterly *no* experience at holiday celebrations.

Dang it, Nick had agreed to help me with this family business. And Patra was expected to join in now that she was in town. I didn't want the responsibility for everyone's happiness—as well as their *safety*—on my scrawny shoulders.

"I'll call them," I said neutrally, making no promises.

But even I had to admit to a degree of anticipation at the possibility of a real Christmas tree. This old Victorian parlor would be perfect. . . .

If I started thinking of this place as home. . .

Growing up, I'd had too many expectations dashed to allow my hopes to rise. Mallard and Graham's disappearance and my fear for Juliana easily damped any incipient excitement over a silly holiday.

I would have to buy *gifts*. Well, I'd already stored one or two for EG. She was just a kid. But a tree. . .

Deep breath. "There's not a lot of room in here," I said, looking around as if they'd asked for a TV—which would, no doubt, be next.

"We could push the sofa down the wall and put the tree in front of the window," Tudor suggested offhandedly—which meant they'd already discussed this, and he'd been thinking about it.

Email made it easy for them to gang up on me long distance.

"We don't have decorations," I reminded them.

"Mallard said we have old ones in the storage room. And we can make our own," EG cried excitedly. "Popcorn strings and sugar cookies!"

If Graham wasn't here. . . I tried to think positively: my workload would lighten considerably. I'd already quit advertising my availability as a virtual assistant weeks ago so I'd have more time for EG and for Graham's projects. If I didn't have Graham's work to do. . . I would go stark raving berserk. If Mallard didn't arrive soon, I'd have to tackle Graham's lair.

"Drink your chocolate before it cools," I ordered. "I'll talk to Nick and Patra."

Patra Llewellyn is Magda's daughter by her second husband, my father being her first. Our mother had married at seventeen and been widowed at twenty-one, so she had some excuse for going through husbands like bottles of wine. The affairs in between. . . were none of my business.

Patra had recently graduated journalism school, helped break a major scandal involving a notorious media mogul, and had just taken a new job in DC. I didn't entertain sentimental notions that she did so to be near us. She had her eyes—and other body parts—set on Sean O'Herlihy, a hot investigative reporter for our local newspaper.

Coincidentally or not, Sean's father had died in the same car bombing that had killed mine and Graham's. We came by our conspiracy theories honestly.

I left the boys rearranging the furniture while I trotted back downstairs to my basement office. Mallard would walk out on us again should he ever return and see what we were doing to his museum. He revered my grandfather and preferred to leave everything as it had been in the good old days—like last spring.

The chances of actually reaching Patra and Nick by phone were almost nil, so I cc'd them both on an email explaining what I wanted—saved me the trouble of explaining to two voice mail boxes.

Then I returned to hacking Juliana's phone account. Her phone bill was still being deducted from her funds, and it was sizable. Surely she'd bought a U.S. chip when she'd come here. If she wasn't calling family, how could she be running up a bill that high? I finally located more passwords buried deep in the documents Zander had copied from her computer. Holding my breath, I opened the website for her carrier and typed in an ID and a password that looked promising.

The account opened on the first try. After studying her bills inside and out, I had to admit defeat. She was paying for unlimited data, which was very expensive. There were no extra costs for phone calls out of the country. Her biggest charge appeared to be for cloud storage. I'd need to crack that next.

What I really needed were phone records to see who she'd been calling, and when and where, but that information doesn't appear on statements. For that, I needed Graham and his illegal resources.

I checked my mailbox. Still nothing from him. If he was in danger, did I really want to know? I told myself that if he had Mallard with him, he wouldn't be anywhere unsafe. He was just being his normal secretive asshat self, and I really needed to smack him for being so inconsiderate, but I wasn't his keeper.

I tried every ID and password on Juliana's list and none of them opened any account in the cloud storage website listed on her bill.

Frustrated, I glared at the screen and heard my stomach rumble. Lunch had been whatever leftovers Zander and I could scrounge. We would have to go out for supper. It wasn't as if I ever fixed my own dinner, much less one for four people.

Fortunately, feeding a family wasn't as fraught with anxiety as fighting terrorists.

Family—I had a family again. I didn't know whether to celebrate or weep. It just needed Magda's arrival to push me over the edge, and I'd pack my neuroses and vanish into the snowy night.

I texted Nick and Patra of my dinner plans. Patra actually called back.

"Can Sean come too or is this a super-secret family do?" she asked without greeting.

"If you wish to inflict your entire family on him, sure, let him tag along," I said wearily. I'd have to start considering adding in-laws to the family table. I was feeling overwhelmed.

"Entire family?" she asked warily. "Magda is here?"

"Not yet. Want to place wagers on when?"

"Christmas morning, guilting us for not buying her anything by arriving with her arms full," she replied without hesitation. "I get your Berkin bag if I win."

I didn't tell her it was a fake, because she was undoubtedly right.

Ana does dinner

WE MET AT A Moroccan restaurant off the beaten path to keep down expenses. I refused to feel guilty for not buying thousand-dollar dinners out of our family funds. We all needed to learn to manage our new-found wealth and channel it for good instead of wasting it.

So far, I hadn't received a lot of resistance to my stinginess. Of course, so far, they had no idea of how incredibly wealthy we were. Our grandfather Max had been a wise investor and a bit of a miser. I could relate to miserliness when money was short, but not when people were starving and homeless, and he had funds to spare. I had some philosophic processing to do.

Patra arrived on Sean's arm. She has our mother's tall, buxom good looks and extroverted personality. Sean is a Pierce Brosnan look-alike who caused heads to swivel. They would make an elegant pair—if they hadn't still been wearing the jeans and cheap nylon coats they'd worn to work. Despite Patra's tacky clothes, the waiters still raced to help her with her jacket—she's that gorgeous. With that figure and face, she belonged on TV news, but she had a mind of her own, and her heart belonged to her daddy's profession of investigative reporting.

Nick and I had already decided he would stay after dinner to explain Juliana's disappearance to Patra and Sean. It wasn't a subject we wished to discuss in front of EG and Tudor. EG was already prone to gloomy predictions, and Tudor could be a mercenary cynic. They needed to see happiness and healthy relationships to give them more positive outlooks.

"How do you plan to carry a tree to the house?" Sean asked in amusement when he heard our request. He had grown up in DC and knew more about this tree stuff than we did.

"Your MG obviously won't carry it," I said. I had unpleasant memories of flying down the interstate in that antique convertible abomination.

"There's a tree lot only half a mile away," Tudor said through a mouthful of saffron pilaf. "We could carry it."

I quirked a dubious eyebrow at him, but he was too engrossed in his food to notice. *He* wouldn't be the one pounding city streets with a tree on his head. The skinny geek couldn't lift a box of ornaments.

"If the snow had lasted, we could have made a sled," Zander suggested.

"Wagon," EG cried. "We need a wagon."

As ideas went, that wasn't a bad one, better than suggesting the Metro anyway. "And we'll find a wagon where?" I asked. "And if we manage this feat, how do we set a tree up in the living room without it toppling through the window?"

"The leaky, thousand-year old window," Patra added unhelpfully.

Zander almost gained some color as he joined the family discussion. For a few rare minutes, he was enjoying himself instead of worrying about his twin.

None of them knew to worry about Graham and Mallard.

When it came time to pay the bill, I used the family credit card. They all watched in awe as I signed away the extensive meal for seven people with wine for four. Even in the out-of-the-way places, DC is not a cheap place to dine out.

"Will Oppenheimer send us statements on the trust?" Nick asked, referring to our trust lawyer and checking the numbers on the bill as I hadn't.

"He can, although we'd be better off hiring a financial manager now that it's almost finalized." The house was the big sticking point. It needed to be in the family trust as well—except Graham's name was still on the deed.

Zander glanced up from the burner phone he'd been checking all evening. "Investing is what I do, although for a firm in South Africa. Perhaps I could have my employer recommend someone here."

Nick and I shared a look. As the eldest, we'd been the family money managers for years. Since we'd never had enough money to lose, Nick's brilliance with math had led down the dangerous trail of gambling. He'd saved our hides more than once with his card sharping. Neither of us had any reason to know anything of investments.

"That's an excellent idea," I agreed noncommittally, but the mental gears were grinding. I much preferred a family member overseeing family funds, but Nick and I were lousy at it.

"You need to set financial goals," he said in all seriousness. "I can help with that."

Patra and Sean were donning their coats. Tudor and EG were scarfing up leftover desserts. They listened, I know. They were just signaling disinterest in money management. I knew the feeling.

Nick nodded almost imperceptibly. With his approval, I was free to distract Zander from his twin with our finances, or some small portion of them.

"Come along, lovebirds, I'll buy you drinks in this new dive I found down the street." Nick straightened his cashmere scarf and gestured at Sean and Patra, leaving me with the under-21 group. I didn't care that I was missing out on adult conversation. I had my family working together and safely in one place—except for one. I needed to get back to my office to find her—that was the only Christmas present I needed.

We took the Metro home. The earlier slush had frozen to ice. No one had thrown out salt on our doorstep. I could feel the house deteriorating already in my inept hands.

No one had turned on the lights or lit the parlor logs. Entering a cold dark house, I felt abandoned, which was ridiculous. Gritting my teeth with determination, I located switches, ordered everyone to take their coats to their rooms, and followed them up as if I meant to go bed, too.

I worked at my laptop in my room until I heard the house settle down. No messages had appeared from Graham in my absence.

When I was assured everyone was in bed, I grabbed a flashlight and started up the stairs to the attic, terrified I'd find it empty.

Six

Juliana meets the boss

SITTING AT HER DESK in the empty office, nervously editing the dangerous photo on a phone she'd "borrowed" from a sleeping security guard, Juliana sent the image fragments to her cloud account. She prayed that neither IT nor security had the imagination to piece together a dozen puzzle pieces, especially since her files were already full of images and designs. Mostly, she prayed they didn't know about her cloud account.

Until she had the photo printed, she wouldn't risk contacting Zander.

"You're working late, Miss Kruger," a familiar voice chided.

She fought a guilty start, hid the phone in her skirt pocket, and reached for her purse. Her pulse beat anxiously. "I was just leaving, Reverend. Hunting for the right image is time consuming, and I feel guilty doing it on company time. Could I help you with anything?"

"I was just checking to see that the snow hadn't caused any harm and saw the light. I don't think you've taken a night off since you arrived. Don't you want to go out and learn more of this country?"

Joshua Arden was a handsome older man with the powerful build of the football player he'd once been before a knee injury had ended his career. He had a megawatt smile that could light a room. She'd heard him preach and knew he could persuade as convincingly as he could bellow condemnations. Tonight, however, he looked like a weary man on his way home after a day's work. A baseball cap bearing the sign of a cross covered his famously golden hair.

"I'm more interested in learning all I can about bringing education to those who crave it," she said honestly. "I won't be staying in this country where you have so much, so I don't want to become too attached to your ways."

He nodded understandingly. "You're young and still believe you can single-handedly change the world. We need that energy. But part of *your* education should be learning the larger world around you, meeting people who can help you."

She knew that, but the privileged attitudes of the material world offended her. Still, she couldn't tell Reverend Arden that she'd never be able to network. "I'm sure you're right, sir," she answered obediently.

"One of our sponsors has given us tickets to the symphony for tomorrow night. I insist you take one, Miss Kruger. It's a holiday program, and I think you'll enjoy it."

She liked that he took the time to learn everyone's name. She had been thrilled when she'd learned the school often offered free concert admissions donated by the park's charitable founders. She had hoped one day to be recognized for her hard work and offered this kind of opportunity.

Her soul longed for the beauty of music, a glimpse of soaring architecture, and paintings from a world she'd never visited.

Instead, knowing what she did now, her spine froze at his command. She tried to tell herself that he was simply trying to reward her hard work. But as far as she was aware—and she'd studied the matter closely lately—those coveted tickets only went to women: young, pretty, and *white* ones. She would like this gesture to prove she was wrong, because she was darker than Zander and very definitely not white.

"That's so kind of you," she gushed. "I would grab one in a minute, but I promised to sing for First Baptist tomorrow. Evan over in accounting loves the Messiah, and he's been a bit homesick lately. Why don't you offer a ticket to him?"

Was he looking at her with suspicion or approval? She could never tell with this man. His smiling public persona hid whatever he thought behind a mask of assurance.

She hoped he wasn't the monster who stalked the campus, but she couldn't imagine anyone else in his organization who had his power to kill and get away with it.

Ana looks for Graham

FINALLY GIVING IN TO curiosity, I climbed the stairs to Graham's office later that night. Entering, I contemplated the blank monitors on his office wall with a degree of relief. At least this time he hadn't moved them out. A month ago, Tudor and I had discovered this room scoured clean, all trace of him gone, and I'd almost had a panic attack.

Now, Graham's blank monitors were like monuments to dead computers. Maybe Graham had family—or a girlfriend—he'd gone to visit for the holidays. He could have given Mallard the weekend off.

I didn't play boyfriend games, mostly due to lack of experience. As my therapists had told me, I was too emotionally distant for close relationships. But had I wanted one. . . No point in going down that path. Graham was making it quite clear that he was even less available and more damaged than I was.

I searched for evidence that he'd left his cat behind. My allergies were already kicking in, so it had been in here recently. I didn't find so much as a bowl of water or a flicking tail. Where could he have gone with a cat?

Refusing to worry about a man who lacked the courtesy to inform me of his departure, I took the hidden stairs down to my office. I had come to rely too much on Graham's resources. I needed to go back to developing my own.

Opening the Cobalt Whiz, I dug around online, then sent out a few feelers to people I thought might help me crack phone records. I didn't hold out a lot of hope, but I refused to feel helpless without Graham's speedier access.

Graham was the covert center of a highly credentialed security agency. I had no clue how far his web reached, but it included a satellite connection or two, and back doors into various government agencies and police records. He had full access to the computer I worked on, whereas his was completely encrypted. My access to his feeds had been cut off. I was on my own.

And I didn't like it.

Returning to primitive Google searches and human contacts was like a step back in time to a different century. It frustrated me that he would disappear at a crucial moment like this, when one of my family could be in jeopardy.

I couldn't even sic Tudor's hack program on Juliana's cloud account since I had no inkling how to get into her specific information. Frustrated on all personal levels—I even dug into her email and social media without success—I started back on JACAD. I'd already discovered connections to the shady Top Hat sponsors

I'd encountered unpleasantly, some months before.

CAD's corporate board included Archie Broderick, head of a media conglomerate, and the Goldrich who ran a nationwide mortgage company. Both of their monolithic companies teetered on the brink of collapse after they'd been caught in corporate wrong-doing of a gargantuan nature. They had more on their hands than a Jesus park, so even if they were on the park's board, I didn't see them as an immediate threat.

Neil Hammond from Hammond Oil was related to EG's father and another of the corporate sponsors. I didn't know anything bad about him except oil companies are notoriously corrupt. So I've already admitted I'm a bigot. It happens.

George Paycock and Tony Jeffery were on the park's board. CFO and CEO of General Defense, respectively, they represented an enormous weapons company. I thought that made them strange bedfellows with a religious community that presumably preached the pacifist views of the New Testament, but I'm not much of a church goer. I've just read the Bible.

I had to look up the last member, Edward Parker III—a professional dilettante with a trust fund.

Maybe I could have Zander dig deeper into the board and their financials. I wanted a smoking gun. Tonight, I went for a broader approach.

I started with newspaper files on both the Reverend Joshua Arden and his community development organization. Joshua had his own church, his own TV network, and numerous other enterprises, most of which he'd inherited from his retired evangelist father. I didn't have the resources to investigate all of them. Since Juliana had gone to work for CAD that was the one I concentrated on.

The good reverend preached an ultra-conservative spiel that appealed to the far right-wing religious fanatics who believed people of other faiths were infidels, traitors, and worse.

As a citizen of the world, I recognized that most folks preferred living in a familiar community, one they understood, such as a church of like-minded people. Unfortunately, one simply cannot force the entire world's population into one's own narrow image, no matter what your creed.

Joshua's church believed in strict adherence to the Bible—

apparently they liked the idea of the world being created in seven actual days, ignoring all the scientific impossibilities involved.

I couldn't quite figure out if they thought the Garden of Eden was populated with pterodactyls, but that was their problem. I just needed to understand why Joshua had poured so much money into building a dinosaur Jesus park near *DC,* one of the most expensive, sophisticated, educated, international communities in the world.

For one thing, I surmised as I studied photos of the groundbreaking, he'd caught the attention of a lot of conservative politicians who were the fronts for extremely wealthy lobbies, corporations, and gazillionaires with their own agendas—few of them holy. Joshua's predominantly rural and poor congregations had votes and used them—and they swung conservative.

The park itself seemed as harmless as a Disney production.

Joshua's ambitious effort to spread his word through schools in third world countries was naively misguided, but he wasn't the first and wouldn't be the last to propagandize in the name of education. If Juliana wanted to build schools, more power to her.

I found an article describing how CAD brought in promising young people from around the world. They employed these student interns in different areas, on different projects to round out their education. Along with the downtown office, they had buildings at the park and scattered around the city. It seemed to be more like on-the-job training combined with programs on how to raise money, find teachers, encourage communities to provide school rooms, and most importantly, convince them that children needed education.

I was totally on board with education being the solution to many of today's problems—teach a man to fish and he'll never go hungry made sense to me. Hand-outs merely taught people to stick their hands out, although there was room for helping those who couldn't help themselves, I supposed.

I was tired and going in circles.

At the very bottom of my search list were some tiny articles that didn't even include CAD in the headlines. I almost skipped them. But I'd been trained to never leave a task unfinished, so I opened the first one.

It contained a small column from the local paper about a girl found strangled near the Potomac at the beginning of November. She had quit working for CAD a month prior to her death.

Except for the date, that wasn't enough to set off alarms about CAD. Cities were dangerous places. From everything I'd read so far, CAD provided secure quarters and working conditions. They couldn't be blamed for a student who quit and went astray.

That Juliana had quit communicating at the beginning of November could be coincidence.

Not until I opened the next article did I experience a frisson of fear.

A family had reported their daughter missing after she'd been with CAD for a few months. That had been eight months ago.

One dead, one missing, and Juliana not communicating—not a good track record for a religious community.

The third article reported a man's remains discovered in a shallow grave by CAD workers on the Jesus World grounds during excavations in October. He'd been dead since spring.

I pictured the huge empty construction site filled with mounds of dirt, deep excavations, and the steel bones of preposterous creatures rising from cement foundations.

I have an active imagination and too much experience in death to see anything except a graveyard for victims in that image. The church as the new mafia. . . I shuddered, even though the possibility seemed preposterous.

Now I really had a reason to worry. I'd have to start planning an invasion of CAD headquarters or sic the cops on them if Juliana didn't respond to Zander's message soon.

Ana makes breakfast

MY CULINARY TALENTS EXTENDED to making French toast. Egg-dipped bread and syrup might not be the gourmet delight Mallard produced, but it satisfied all the hungry mouths around the kitchen table on Saturday morning.

"We found a platform wagon on Craigslist," Tudor reported as he shoveled soggy bread toward his mouth.

Without Mallard to scowl at us, my family had spread out like the undisciplined louts they were. The table was covered in tablets, newspapers, books, hats, and other debris.

"There's a Christmas tree lot just a few blocks from here!" EG reported. "Nick said he'd help us. We can go through the storage rooms in the basement and look for decorations!"

For all I knew, Max had stored dead bodies down there. I sipped my tea without immediately replying.

Zander had bags under his eyes deep enough to bury tree and wagon. He'd evidently been up half the night, searching for his sister or sending coded messages to every media in existence. I had to find Juliana alive just so I didn't have to inform him that she was anything else.

"Zander and I will hunt ornaments," I decided, bringing EG down off her dictator high. "You and Tudor can choose the tree, keeping in mind that the ceiling may be twelve feet tall but we have no ladder, and Nick does not have the strength of giants. Under six feet should be plenty."

"You just don't want us in the storage rooms," EG declared, quite correctly.

"I don't want you staggering around with boxes containing what might contain priceless glassware or Magda's childhood memories," I countered. "And if you want a tree, you have to work for it by helping Nick."

"Where's the attic chap?" Tudor asked. "He could carry a tree without blinking an eye. And there's that motor out in the garage. Wouldn't it hold a tree?"

Tudor had worked hand-in-hand with Graham the last time he'd been here. I'd had foolish hopes that Graham would keep Tudor's cyber-terrorist bent reined in.

"He and Mallard are off on holiday," I blithely lied. "And only Mallard can drive the Phaeton." Another lie. Nick could too. But Mallard really would behead us if we dared stick an evergreen out the window of the old limo, while dripping pine sap and needles across the antique seats. The Phaeton would remain sacred from our disasters.

"We should get a tree for Graham's office too!" EG announced, as if she hadn't heard a word about hauling heavy trees around.

She was nine. In her head, *Santa* probably brought trees. Not that she'd been brought up to believe in Santa, but the whole world was some kind of magic to kids who understood little of it.

"If Graham wants a tree in his office, he can buy one. And if he wants us to decorate it, he'll let us know. Let's stick to one task at a time." I didn't mind being the practical bully, but once in a while, it would be nice to be the good witch.

Nick arrived to steer the two youngest on the tree hunt. He seemed quite enthusiastic about the project, especially since the snow had cleared away and left behind a beautiful blue sky. "Red and gold ornaments," he informed me as the kids wrapped up. "We need a theme and as long as we're stuck with those hideous heirlooms, red and gold works." He jerked his chin in the direction of the parlor with its maroon velvet draperies and gold horsehair sofa.

"You'll be lucky if we find broken glass. We make no guarantees." I turned to Zander. "Are you good with helping me hunt through storage or would you rather go out in the fresh air and tree hunt?"

"I would like to explore the house more, please," he said. "And you will need help carrying boxes."

We sent the others off into the crisp winter air. Without Mallard to serve us, the teapot lingered in the kitchen where we'd eaten. I poured myself a new mug of tea, Zander made a cup of coffee for himself, and then I stole Mallard's key ring from his cubbyhole office.

Since this was ostensibly Graham's house, I'd not gone where I hadn't been invited except in case of emergencies. My definition of emergency was pretty broad but hadn't yet included most of the basement storage rooms. They were locked, for one thing. I respected locks, up to a point.

We'd only recently learned that the coal cellar contained a hidden door to a tunnel leading to the garage on the street behind us. Either Max had been a secretive bastard, or this house had belonged to a speakeasy in the past. Or both.

Since Mallard had been the one to mention ornaments in storage to EG, I counted that as excuse enough to go looking. I unlocked the first set of double closet doors and pushed them wide.

Mallard was organized, I'd give him that. Floor to ceiling metal shelves lined each ugly cement and concrete-block wall, with two aisles of shelves in the center of the low-ceilinged space. Each one was filled with neatly labeled cardboard boxes. I found a switch that lit overhead fluorescents, but I handed Zander a flashlight, just in case.

"If you find anything labeled *dead body*, don't tell me, okay?" I headed to our right, leaving Zander to start on the left.

I thought I heard him chuckle. Or maybe that was wishful thinking.

"These appear to be linens and clothes," he called a few minutes later.

"Draperies and towels over here. We could start our own Goodwill store." I considered opening a few to see what condition they were in, but there were more shelves and another closet to examine.

"Glassware," he called back. "Dishes, candlesticks and knick-knacks."

"Honestly? He stored and labeled a box of knick-knacks? Did they never throw anything out?" I ran my flashlight over dusty labels of ancient household items. If the money ran out, we could start an antique mall or at least a thrift shop.

"This aisle contains boxes that all start with *Magda*," he said uncertainly.

Crap. That proved they never threw out anything. "Skip that one." I had a burning curiosity but no masochistic tendencies.

Not finding anything blatantly labeled *Christmas*, or even *holiday*, we moved on to the next closet. The shelves in this area were made of heavy wood and covered in a century of dust. The boxes were wood, also, similar to the tangerine crates they have in grocery stores this time of year, only much larger and with lids.

The overhead light was a dangling bulb.

"Okay, I'm gathering this place hasn't been touched in a while," I said, wiping my hand through the thick dust.

Zander flashed his light over the nearest crate. The label had turned nearly brown, and the ink had faded to chicken scratches. "How long did our grandfather live here?" he asked in awe. "I'm pretty sure this label says 1901."

"He wasn't that old. I haven't done the research. I thought he'd bought it, but maybe his parents lived here first?" I moved in the other direction, running my flashlight over more browned paper with fading ink. If I had anything to hide, this would be the place, except it would be difficult to do without disturbing the dust.

"It is very strange to think that this represents the home of half my family," he said in awe. "I am so used to my father's village being my family, but here. . ." He let out a sigh. "I am not even certain who I am anymore."

I'd seen his father's family. They were one generation short of a Zulu tribe. The one time I'd seen them, they had worn bones in their hair and loincloths and had been huge and terrifying—no doubt deliberately to scare the white-faced city kid. Modern financial analyst Zander with his pale brown skin and skinny shoulders had a lot of our mother in him. I could see where he'd be conflicted.

"Our ancestors ground us, they do not make us," I said, repeating some idiocy I'd probably heard from a therapist. "I'm pretty certain Max was no better than he should be. People don't become humongously wealthy by abiding by laws, so don't idealize this side of your family, please." I was thinking we probably had bootleggers on our family tree if this house had belonged to Max's family. That would explain a *lot*.

"What was our grandmother's name?" he called from behind a distant dusky stack.

"Antonina. I used to think my name was some corruption of hers until I recognized Magda's predilection for naming us after royalty. Why?"

His head popped out from behind a stack. A gray dust-coated cobweb dangled from his neatly cropped dark hair. "There are boxes here labeled A.M. Do you think these are hers?"

My grandmother had died when Magda was still little. I knew nothing of her beyond that. I was curious about our past—but we had all we could do to handle our present.

"Possibly. I don't suppose any of them say anything obvious like *A.M.'s ornaments?*"

"No, but judging by the level of dust, they were all stored on this shelf at the same time. How long ago did she die?" His voice was muffled as he ducked down to examine the bottom shelves.

I performed a few mental calculations. "She died when Magda was six, I think, maybe about 1970. Do they have tests to determine if that's forty years of dust?"

"No, but the labels are less faded than the ones where you are, if that counts. The handwriting is illegible however. Would it be all right if I pull out this one that seems to have straw sticking out of it?"

I grimaced. "What happens to straw after forty years?"

"Mold most likely. Everything down here is probably ruined. But ornaments from that long ago would have been very thin glass and require packing."

I heard him haul a box off the shelf without my giving him the go ahead. Fair enough. The boxes belonged to him as much as they did to me. Just because I'd spent my first few years in this house, and his had been spent in Africa, didn't change the family genes.

I heard grunts of disgust. Unable to contain my curiosity, I wandered back to see what he'd unearthed.

Disintegrated straw, dead spiders, filthy layers of dust—and crystal globes so delicate I feared they'd shatter if we removed the crud. I'd seen Czech crystal like this in museums. These ornaments were far older than the 1970s.

On top was a crystal oval framing an old color photo of a young couple and a toddler girl—our grandparents and mother. I'd never seen my grandmother. She wore the hideous bouffant hairdo of the time. They actually looked like a normal 1970's suburban family—

And not like the Machiavellian characters I knew at least two of them to be.

Seven

Juliana on Saturday afternoon

"REVEREND ARDEN GAVE ME a ticket to tonight's *Messiah*!" Maryam waved one of the coveted pieces of cardboard as she bounced into their shared mobile home.

The words struck Juliana with a wave of guilt and fear. Unable to reveal her unproved, incomplete theories, she could only smile to share her roommate's excitement. "You have only a few hours to prepare. What will you wear?"

Maryam had a colorful collection of *shalwar kameez*—pants and shirts—that she wore every day, but she also had an enviable collection of heavily embroidered Punjabi dresses. If Maryam hadn't been one of the shortest people on campus, and Juliana one of the tallest, she would have borrowed any of Maryam's outfits in an eye blink. They both had dark hair and eyes and brown complexions, so they favored bright reds and golds and blues—a fact that gave her pause now.

As far as she was aware, even though the students working at JACAD were both male and female and predominantly people of color, only girls with light skins had received tickets. Juliana had wanted to believe that most of the lucky ticket-holders came from English-speaking families like hers and were better able to communicate. But she'd seen blond German and French girls who barely spoke English receive the coveted symphony and theater tickets before she had been offered one. Again—that could be a notion developed out of offended feelings of rejection.

She'd only recently switched from offense to concern after realizing that the girls who received tickets often started dating the men they met outside the school. Several were long-time students who had given up their studies and not been seen again.

The roommate she'd had when she'd first moved here haunted her. Esther had been one of the second year students. She'd been dating a wealthy older man whose identity she kept secret. When they'd broken up, Esther had been angry for weeks. Then she'd packed her bags and said she was going home. Why hadn't she let Julie know she'd returned safely home as she'd promised?

Julie would like to believe that Maryam receiving the ticket was evidence that her observations of prejudice over the tickets were incorrect. And if the tickets brought Maryam in contact with wealthy older men, then Julie hoped her friend was sensible enough not to fall prey to temptation.

That did not mean she should send her friend out completely unprepared. Juliana prayed silently as she helped her roommate choose the perfect outfit, but at the same time, she was building an emergency kit in her mind.

"How will you go to this place?" Juliana asked.

"They send a car," Maryam said with relish. "I am so tired of that rattily old bus! I know I am to aspire to a life of poverty, but the bus stinks."

Like Juliana, Maryam came from a fairly well-to-do, educated family and was accustomed to a higher standard of living than an aging trailer park. Her much older brother worked at the embassy, but so far, he'd been too busy to bother taking Maryam anywhere.

"Do you know if there will be others with you?" Juliana hunted through her trunk for the items Zander had insisted that she bring with her to this country.

Studying their tiny wall mirror, preening with the gold embroidered shawl she'd flung over her thick dark hair, Maryam shrugged. "I've not heard of others. I guess I will find out. It does not matter. For a change, I will see the rich and glamorous part of DC, and enjoy real music! One needs the occasional reward. I'm sure you'll be offered one soon."

Juliana didn't say that she'd already turned it down or she'd ruin her friend's pleasure in the moment. "I'm sure you will have a lovely time, but it is a big city, and you are unfamiliar with it. You should not go unprepared. Take your phone, some money, and a credit card. Zander gave me this whistle flashlight. It can serve as an alarm. You are not large enough to fight, so if there is trouble, run and cry for help."

Maryam looked at her as if she were crazed. "What kind of trouble would there be in a concert hall? And how could I run in these?" She held up one foot bearing her favorite pair of high heels.

"I would suggest wearing the gorgeous gold slippers instead, but you could pack them in your purse, just in case," Juliana urged. "What if there was a fire? Or a terrorist attack?"

Her roommate rolled her eyes. "This is America. We are safe here."

Not from the kind of predators Juliana feared. She packed the items into Maryam's gold purse. "Take them for me, so I can sleep while you are out having a good time. Do you have 911 programmed into your phone?"

After much good-natured arguing, she sent Maryam into the world as prepared as was possible.

Now, she had to find a printer for her photo and some way of locating the coordinates Zander had sent. Sneaking and stealing weren't her favorite pastimes, but she'd been left with little choice. Perhaps she should have gone into DC and slipped away, but then she wouldn't be able to come back here. And if she couldn't work here, she would have no means of uncovering whatever was going on.

Because her fears for her missing roommate Esther were based on her terror of what the photos on her video cameras had revealed.

Ana helps decorate

I ADMIRED THE EVERGREEN fragrance of the tipsy tree framed by our large front window. "It's fat," I said dubiously, studying the thick layers of long needles.

"I vote we wrap an apron around the bottom and put a hat on top and call it Mrs. Frosty Claus," Patra said, sipping at her coffee and tilting her head to the angle of the tree. She looked as if she'd just dragged out of bed and pulled on leggings and Sean's sweatshirt. She'd stacked her heavy chestnut hair on top of her head in a precarious knot. I tugged my own plain black braid self-consciously, knowing I could never achieve Patra's casual glamour.

Maybe I should have tried. I quickly shut out the wayward thought of Graham's empty office.

EG sent Patra an evil look and dug through the box of ornaments.

Zander and I had unanimously voted to rewrap the delicate

ornaments in a stronger box and had bought "learner" sets of plastic and wood from a drugstore. We'd gone a little crazy, so there was roping and tinsel and blinky lights. We'd torn them out of their packaging and repurposed one of Magda's dusty boxes to hold them. Until this moment, EG had accepted them with delight.

"There's no star," EG said with a pout after she'd spread the loot across the priceless Persian carpet.

"No angel either?" Nick asked, occupying the Morris chair. Nick didn't do casual. For our Christmas tree experience, he was wearing gray pin-striped trousers and a pink dress shirt with contrasting collars and cuffs that matched the stripes of his trousers. At least he wasn't wearing a tie.

So, I wasn't proficient at decorating trees, and Nick wasn't educated in choosing one. I hadn't known a star was required, and he hadn't known to check the trunk. I sipped my tea and dismissed the critics in favor of action. "I don't suppose there's any way of making it stand straight?"

We all studied the crooked trunk nailed onto a rather rickety cross of two-by-fours.

"We'd need a saw to cut off the bent part, and then we'd have to saw off the lower branches." Tudor pointed out the obvious. Garbed in his usual grunge, his auburn curls needing a cut, he had his ever-present tablet in hand and was poking at some game while keeping up with the conversation. Sixteen was an awkward age. He didn't want to appear childish like EG, but he was as interested in the production as any of us.

Graham and Mallard still hadn't returned. I was convinced that if Mallard were dead, he'd come back to haunt us over the destruction of his parlor. I studied the mess EG had created.

"I'm guessing we start with the lights," I suggested. "And we can look for a star or angel later. It probably ought to be something special to celebrate our first Christmas together."

EG accepted that. She tugged out a string of lights and looked expectantly at Nick, who just grinned at her and shoved a cookie in his mouth.

We'd spent some valuable family hours bonding over cookies before we started on the decorating. The results were predictably disastrous but edible. Luckily, we didn't have high standards when it came to our own cooking.

Zander took the string of lights, studied the crooked tree, and drew the coffee table up to it. I watched in trepidation as he stepped on the expensive antique, but the sturdy legs held up to his weight. He carefully clipped a light near the top, and wound the string as far as he could reach. Almost as tall as Zander, Tudor finally dragged himself up to grab the string and wind it around the back.

The rest of us threw out various instructions on where and how to fix the lights, and Zander and Tudor cheerfully ignored us. We were a masterpiece of international holiday good cheer and incompetence.

"Those are perfectly hideous ornaments," Nick murmured as I perched on the arm of his chair and watched EG hang the first red ball. "If you want to hide the real stuff, you could have at least bought from somewhere besides *Tar-zhay*."

"Not enough time. When we have more time, I think we ought to make our own, or hang ones that have meaning to us." I pulled the oval frame from my sweatshirt pocket and showed it to him. "Or you could hang this if you're feeling really sentimental."

He took the frame and studied our mother and her parents. "I see where we get our cheekbones and why Magda calls herself a Hungarian princess. That looks like pearls on her little round neck, and our grandmother is wearing a fortune in rubies. I don't suppose you found a box labeled *jewels*."

"No, but you're free to search for yourself. Bring spider spray, a vacuum cleaner, and an army of dust mops." I left him with the frame and went to help EG hang a feathered hummingbird toward the top of the tree. I had no idea what birds had to do with Christmas, but it was red and gold, as specified.

I needed to be researching those articles I'd discovered last night, but I'd promised EG a Christmas tree party, and I couldn't renege on that. I'd spent a few hours early this morning looking for information on the girls in the articles, but without Graham's access to police records, I was stymied on the crime details.

I was almost desperate enough to start tracking Graham— almost, but not quite there yet. I was holding out hope that Juliana would respond to her twin's pleas.

Finally, the tipsy tree was dripping with festive glitter. We drew broken cookies to determine who got to turn on the lights. Everyone made certain EG got the smallest one. Proudly, she plugged the string into the extension plug we'd had to run under the sofa to one of the room's few sockets.

I waited for something to explode. Instead, the colorful strings lit up the evening shadows, casting a magical rainbow over the gloomy parlor. Smiles broke out around the room. I tried to store this moment in my heart, with my family all together, safe and happy—except for Juliana.

Later, after we'd consumed our makeshift dinner of store-bought cider and sushi and sat admiring our blinking tree against the night sky, Zander's burner phone finally beeped.

Juliana—Sunday morning

JULIE CLUNG EXCITEDLY TO her new, unbugged phone, her brand new lifeline to the outside world. Whoever she'd texted last night— she hoped and prayed it was Zander—couldn't possibly have found the photo she'd hidden in the cache yet, but she was counting the minutes. Unless they really were magic, the genie who had provided this link to safety would have to wait until daylight to find the heavy burden she'd been carrying these last weeks.

Following the directions in Zander's code last night, she'd barely been able to make her way through the woods in the dark and cold. She'd almost given up several times, until she tried to think like Zander. He'd always been good at natural hiding places.

Zander was here, she knew it. Her hopes would soar—except Maryam wasn't home yet, and the sun was almost up.

She tried to pray, but the knowledge that if anything happened to her friend, it would be her fault, blocked all else from her mind. She should have said something, reported something, taken the ticket herself. . . .

She returned her gaze to the phone. She could still call for help. Maybe it wasn't too late. But what would she say? *I saw them bury a body and Esther has gone missing. . . .* But she didn't know that the body was Esther or that Esther hadn't simply been too angry to let the school know she'd left.

And if it turned out that gangs were using the park to bury their victims, the park might be shut down, the reverend's good work could be ended. . . .

At last, as dawn lit the clouds, she saw Maryam trudging down the muddy path to the trailers. Her lovely gown looked bedraggled, her gold slippers were tattered and mud-caked, and she had only her shawl to cover her shoulders.

Juliana tried not to panic. She put on more coffee and ran outside carrying the cheap down coat she'd bought from a departing student.

She wrapped the coat around a shivering Maryam and let her rest some of her weight on her as they trudged back to the trailer. Fretting, she wished she was strong enough to carry her friend.

"Do I need to call a doctor?" Julie asked, not knowing what else to say.

Maryam laughed hoarsely. "No, not unless they make bandages for stupidity."

Julie tried to feel relieved, but Maryam looked as if she'd been through hell. She sent her to the meager shower, turned their propane heater on high, poured coffee, and set the mug on the bathroom counter.

Maryam looked a little more herself when she emerged from the shower wrapped in the thin cotton robe she'd brought from home, her hands hugging the hot mug. "Thank you. I thought I'd never be warm again. I'm not sure I'm made for this weather."

Julie dropped the coat over her shoulders again. "I have some battery-operated warming socks someone gave me. Let me fetch those."

Maryam didn't argue, so Julie knew she was badly shaken. Maryam always argued. Finding the socks and watching her put them on, Julie finally demanded, "Now tell me what happened, all of it, even the stupid parts."

Maryam grimaced. "Simple, I became scared, I ran, and as you predicted, I knew nothing of where to go because I was too stupid to learn how to travel without a hired driver, and I forgot to charge my phone."

"Start at the beginning," Julie warned. "What scared you?"

"It is silly," she insisted. "The symphony was wonderful. The Kennedy Center... awesome. And the people! So many people, so many cultures, it made me feel as if I was at the center of the universe."

Julie longed to see such a place, to be part of such a scene. Her few brief forays since her arrival in the States had only been around suburban Alexandria and a school bus tour to the Smithsonian, with a glimpse of the Capitol. "So you arrived safely enough," she said, hoping to urge her on.

"A lovely black sedan, a smooth ride, I am just stupid," Maryam repeated mournfully.

"You are not stupid. You saw a beautiful place, heard beautiful music, but you were alone, were you not?"

Maryam sipped her coffee and hesitated. "I arrived alone. The usher took me to my seat. The people around me... They wore diamonds and expensive suits. I did not belong."

"Now *that's* stupid," Julie rudely pointed out. "Your gown is woven with gold thread and cost as much as an Italian suit. You could have worn gold had you not chosen to leave it at home. You belong in that place as much as anyone. Were there not people there in jeans and sweaters who looked much more out of place than you?"

"Possibly." She sighed. "But I couldn't tell it from where I was seated. All around me were wealthy people. The women wore furs. I did not even bring a coat."

"Because you don't own one and won't wear mine," Julie said, hoping the only problem was Maryam's class consciousness. "The lack of fur did not scare you."

"No," she said sadly. "It was the gentleman sitting beside me. I finally realized that everyone around me was part of a couple, and the gentleman on my right was treating me as his date, even though he did not know my name."

"Okay, that's creepy," Julie agreed. "He must be one of the sponsors who donated the tickets, though. He could have just been being friendly, knowing you were from the project."

Maryam wrinkled her nose. "He did not ask about the park. He asked if women wore diamonds and furs in my country. He made one of the women show me her ring. I was very uncomfortable. And then when the lights went down and the music started, he tried to hold my hand."

She visibly pulled herself together while Julie tried to imagine how this could be so terrible.

"I shook him off and put my hands in my lap. But when I was caught up in the music again, he put his arm around my shoulder and groped me. That's when I got up and left. The driver was waiting at the door, as if he'd been summoned." She took a deep drink of her coffee and finished wanly, "I feared they meant to kidnap me, so I ran for another exit."

Eight

Ana's Sunday morning

I THOUGHT I'D HAVE to put a leash on Zander and tie him to the bedpost after he read the anonymous text from the burner phone we'd left for Juliana. He wanted to head straight to that copse of saplings in the middle of the night, and I'd been the one to stupidly show him how to do it. He'd reluctantly agreed that we couldn't do much at midnight, but I could hear him in the hall already this morning.

"It's not even dawn," I yawned, opening my bedroom door. "It's Sunday. The Metro won't open until seven. If Juliana wanted you on her doorstep, she would have texted you her address."

"She's *alive*," he said stubbornly. "She's out there and alive and frightened."

The text from the burner phone had merely said I'M GOOD. CHECK THE CACHE.

"She's alive and paranoid or playing reindeer games," I corrected with impatience. I really hate games. "Go start the coffee. By the time I'm dressed and we grab a bite to eat, the Metro will be open."

"I can call this Uber thing and be there faster," he argued.

"And you will pay him with what? That's a long, very expensive ride." Teaching moment. Mostly, I had no intention of traipsing through fields at dawn when his sister had just told him she was fine, but he had to forget this instant gratification business. "And before you suggest it, the limo driver deserves his Sunday off."

His face fell. He checked his watch. "Coffee, then," he said with a huge sigh.

So very young. I was only ten years older and felt as if every one of those years was a decade.

I closed the door and hunted warm clothes. I was nearly walking on air, knowing that my sister was alive. I couldn't convince myself all was well yet. If Juliana had simply lost her phone, she could have *called* one of the numbers we'd left her, instead of texting. She'd chosen not to, and that irritated the dickens out of me—probably because it was so very like Magda. Our secretiveness must be genetic—born of centuries of royal hanky-panky, if our mother's fairy tales were to be believed.

Nick and Patra had gone to their respective homes last night. Mallard still wasn't back. If we went out now, we would be leaving EG and Tudor alone. I didn't like it one bit. I texted both Patra and Nick that we were heading out, hoping they'd check in on the kids later. Then I left detailed instructions for the sixteen-year old and the nine-year old, telling each of them to make sure the other didn't get into trouble until we got back. I set out boxes of cereal on the kitchen table. They knew how to find milk.

Without Mallard, I would have to go grocery shopping soon. I shuddered.

Zander ripped viciously at a bagel. I took the coffee he handed me and thought with regret of the magnificent Sunday brunches Mallard prepared. I might miss him even more than Graham.

Probably not, but I was feeling particularly murderous as we trudged out into the cold dawn. I suspected the limo driver was with Graham, but I simply couldn't make myself disturb anyone at this hour on a Sunday morning. I wasn't raised in a privileged status and while I was learning to adapt, I doubted I'd ever make a very good arrogant snot.

I could probably work myself up to grouchy curmudgeon pretty fast, though. I liked the image of sitting in a magnificent library with a roaring fireplace, tea and newspaper in hand, snarling at anyone who disturbed me. If I sat on the relatively-empty train, deciding what books I'd allow on my library shelves, I wouldn't have to worry about Graham and Juliana and the state of the world for oh, more than a minute or thirty.

We repeated most of the routine from Friday, taking the Metro and hiring an Uber driver. If nothing else, the platforms weren't crowded, and we could sink into our thoughts without disturbance.

The car let us out on the road near the construction gate. I noted an armed guard there now. I wanted to go in and pound on trailer doors and look for Julie, but the guard didn't look friendly. And a couple of burly, officious guys stood arguing inside the gate—not a good time to intrude. They didn't even look up as we sauntered down the highway as if out for a morning walk.

But I had time to read the names on the construction company's signage. William Gregory was listed as the general manager of Gregory Construction. JACAD was listed as the development company—nothing unusual there, but I saved the manager's name and number in my phone.

Zander was looking as murderous as I felt. He hadn't shaved, and I saw him more as the man his influential father had once been. One of these days, he'd be a formidable foe.

We tramped out of sight of the gate and entered the copse through a field. Limited light filtered through overhead branches and vines. I was wary enough to expect graves as I stumbled through wet leaves.

Using our phones, we located the tree again. Pulse pounding, I watched Zander reach in and pull out the same envelope we'd left there. Had Juliana left the phone? What kind of crazy was that?

The envelope had been opened, of course, since we knew that she'd used the phone. Out of the envelope, Zander produced an 8x10 black and white photo of a dozen square blocks of dark and light. I turned it around in my hands, trying to figure it out, while Zander checked to see if there was any note of explanation. Nothing.

"This is Julie's work," he said gloomily, taking another look at the photo. "At least we know she has a phone and can call us."

"Is she into drugs?" I had to ask. Before we'd left the house, I'd scribbled a Christmas card with a message to call Ana. I had nothing better to put back in the envelope. I pulled out a pen and added *Call or we're coming after you.* But I didn't expect her to return here unless we told her to.

Zander snorted in disbelief. "Holy Julie? Hardly. This is her art. Her photographs always have messages. Usually, the ones like this will evolve into how she feels about black and white and shades of gray. But this isn't complete. She usually has several shots that she fits together seamlessly into a completely new image."

"Sepia works better if she's making a statement about race," I said with a little more acerbity than he deserved. "People really aren't black or white."

Since he was more familiar with her work, I let him study the photo as we trudged back toward the main highway. I'd seen a bus stop down the road.

Zander complained about waiting for the bus, but I pointed out that we couldn't find Julie if she didn't want to be found, so we weren't in a hurry. He probably had chilblains, but I'd checked the schedule and figured we wouldn't turn into popsicles in a few minutes, and the bus would arrive sooner than a car. The bus came soon after, and he shut up.

Once we had a seat, I took the photo from him. "This looks like a jigsaw puzzle. If we cut out these squares, could we piece together the original image?"

"With Julie's work, it's hard to tell. She started out that way, but now she has a vast collection of images she can draw on." Zander leaned over to study it again. "Although if I had to say, this looks like one photo, taken at night."

"That looks like the blade of a dozer." I pointed to one silvered square. Remembering the article about a dead body buried on the park's grounds, I fought a shiver.

"One of those cement foundations in the park?" He pointed at a corner of gray.

If so. . . an awful feeling of dread crawled over me. Zander hadn't read the articles influencing my imagination. I pointed at a limp gray blob with whiter spots in strategic places tumbling in a fall of what appeared to be dirt. "And this?"

He sat silent as he studied the small image. He took it from my hand and held it up to the window's light. He gave it back to me and looked away.

"A torso. I cannot tell if it's a man or woman."

TUDOR AND EG WERE in the front parlor with the tree lights blinking when we returned. I urgently needed to dig deeper into CAD and maybe even Graham's disappearance, but it was Sunday. EG was dressed for going out. Even Tudor had on boots. Sunday was family day, the day I didn't work.

"We need to go Christmas shopping," EG informed us the minute we walked in the door. "The tree needs presents under it."

Zander sent me a despairing look.

"I don't suppose either of you started the laundry?" I asked, stalling.

From their guilty expressions, I gathered not. "And we need groceries, unless you want to eat your cereal dry all week."

"Mallard's coming back sometime, isn't he?" EG asked in suspicion.

"You think he'd abandon his elegant wardrobe?" That was sarcasm. Mallard only wore black suits and boiled shirts. "Give me time to check a few things first. Get the laundry started. Maybe start on a grocery list. Zander, come into the library and let me show you what we need to do next."

After years of bossing the kids around, then living alone, I would have to adjust once more. I was still bossy, apparently, but I couldn't do everything myself with this much family around.

Zander didn't exactly look relieved, but he followed me out of the hearing of the younger two. "I will call her," he said as soon as the library door shut.

"That's an option," I said cautiously. "But think it through first. She must have a reason for not talking to us. She may just be saving phone minutes for emergencies. Or. . . consider this seriously. . . someone may be watching her. If she's photographing bodies, then she's in some deep manure."

"All the more reason to pull her out of there!" he said in frustration.

"Agreed, but just imagine yourself in her place," I said, placatingly, knowing how my over-intelligent family worked. "If you saw something bad happen, even photographed it, but feared it would reflect on a community you respected, what would you do? What if terrorists buried a body in your village and you couldn't trust the authorities?"

"I would find out who did it so I knew which authority to trust," he said gloomily. "Our father taught us that one year when bad things were happening. *Everything is not as it seems*, he told us. Evidence is required."

He dropped into a faded wing chair as if the weight of the world rested on his shoulders. "I have a job I must return to. I need to know she is safe!"

"We are none of us safe ever. A bus could run over us tomorrow. You have to believe your sister is as capable as you are. You have given her what she needs to communicate, when she's ready to do so." I settled behind the library table and booted up my old laptop. "I downloaded financial statements for JACAD. In my experience, following the money will give us an idea where the problem lies. Do you want to dig around and see if the organization is as above-board as it seems?"

His eyes didn't quite light, but he was listening. "Financial statements are what the board makes of them. Even audited ones can hide things unless we have the books."

"True, and this is a non-profit without need to file with the stock exchange. But often, because they think no one is paying attention, there are clues there to be found. I'll show you some sites I've bookmarked as useful. I'm no financial expert but even I've managed to find interesting connections, although you might not recognize them. So research anything you see, and feel free to search my files."

He came over to study the computer screen. "We are doing this why?"

"Because bodies don't get buried with bulldozers without the exchange of money, and Juliana won't be hiding from you because she thinks you won't like her hair. Something is going on out there. If nothing else, look into their expenses and see if they make sense."

"I am not a forensic accountant," he informed me stiffly. "I can look at statements and decide if a company is worth investing in. Non-profits are not investments."

"But the sponsors for this one are huge investors with giant corporations behind them. If you haven't found anything by the time we return, we'll take another tack." I was really biding my time, praying Graham would return so I could have his resources again. I didn't want to tell Zander about missing girls or he'd freak.

He reluctantly took my seat. "Is this the sort of thing our mother does?"

I snorted. "She never met a computer she liked. She does her spying the most dangerous way—in person."

I walked out before he could question. He didn't really need to know the big bad world of spies and diplomats that Magda walked between—although his father had probably been both.

And if we continued down this treacherous path, we could be accused of the same. Every day, I came closer to walking in Magda's shoes—which was why I was taking EG and Tudor shopping instead of hunting for Graham and researching missing girls.

I suspected Magda's goal in life was revenge. I preferred a more positive goal—I wanted to make the world a better place, even if I had to bring down a few asshats to do so.

Nine

Ana reads the papers

WHILE WE WERE LOADING our grocery haul into the refrigerator, Patra texted me to check the day's headlines.

Thinking she had scored a front page byline, I waited until we had everything put away before trotting up to read the paper. It took me a minute to scan the headlines, realize Patra didn't have a byline, and go back to figure out what she wanted me to see. It was buried under a headline about a George Paycock, a scumbag who'd apparently been accused of embezzling funds from General Defense, a major weapons manufacturer. Old story, apparently—because this one was about Paycock having gone missing in October, about the time an audit was requested.

I'd seen Paycock's name on JACAD's board. He'd not only acted as CFO for General Defense, but as treasurer for the board. He would be the one in charge of CAD's accounts—which was what this story was about. Because of Paycock's fraud, *CAD's accounts were now under investigation.*

We just might be on to something.

I sat down and read more closely. Laura Jeffrey, a VP of General Defense Industries and daughter of the CEO, had called for an in-house audit of the company's accounts earlier in the year. The audit had uncovered a scheme of transferring funds to cover losses. The article didn't list details like what losses or what funds. Apparently an accounting firm was now going over the details.

But Paycock had gone missing, along with the funds, over two months ago.

I whistled and trotted the paper into Zander. He was frowning thunderously at the computer. That seemed ominous, but EG and Tudor were waiting for their reward of a gift-buying binge, so I pointed out the article and left him reading.

I ran back down to the kids, who were considerately loading clothes into the washer and dryer.

"Budget of a hundred dollars each," I told them. "Tar-*zhay* or mall?"

They discussed it on the way to the Metro, throwing surreptitious glances over their shoulders to make certain I was behind them and not listening. I hid my grin. Even worried as I was, I couldn't help a glow of pride that I'd made the Hacker and the Evil Genius work together on a positive project.

My grin was a little weary many hours later as we dragged back in at dark, carrying our loot. We'd hit both Target and the mall in pursuit of bargains. A hundred dollars apiece hadn't half begun to cover our purchases, and the crowds had left this introvert battered and in dire need of isolation.

But EG was singing carols, so it had been worth it. Tudor had pragmatically bought himself a new backpack and stowed all his packages in it. We'd eaten lunch at the mall, and I felt guilty about abandoning Zander to forage for himself.

I shouldn't have. The Maximillian survival genes were strong— the library table was covered with the remains of whatever feast he'd prepared. And he had stacks of papers piled along the table in some order I hoped to figure out. "Anything interesting?" I asked, hoping I could make an easy escape to my basement hideaway.

"I think," he said, glancing up. "Give me a little more time. How did you obtain these links? I'm inside some pretty high-end organizations, and I'm pretty sure I shouldn't be."

I wasn't ready to explain Graham's resources yet. On this machine, I'd saved sites that didn't require satellite connections since the laptop wasn't networked with his system. "I'll explain later. Send me anything you think I need to see immediately. I'll be downstairs working a different angle."

He nodded. "I left mujadara on the stove. I became hungry."

"Bless you! Send the kids to the kitchen if they come hunting for me."

I filled a bowl with hot lentils and rice and headed for my office. Once upon a time, I'd eaten like this all the time. Mallard had spoiled us by feeding us regular meals, forcing us to sit at a dinner table like a real family. I knew I needed to establish that routine again, but not now.

I opened up my Cobalt Whiz—and blinked in startlement.

A screen saver of an ostentatiously dressed crowd at an extravagant buffet table glittering with silver and candelabra flashed at me. Tuxes, evening gowns, even a few tiaras adorned the beautiful people drinking champagne. *What the heck?*

Graham was back.

Fighting overwhelming relief, I growled in irritation at his high-handed invasion of my computer and apparent sarcasm about rich people—like me and my family. We definitely were not champagne and tiara sorts. I retaliated by switching to EG's screensaver of pink unicorns and green elves and imagined them blinking across Graham's giant monitors.

I wanted to shout hallelujahs. I wanted to kick his brains out his ears. The best I could do was pink unicorns.

"Dammit, Ana, pay attention!" the intercom yelled at me.

"The hell I will," I shouted back. I hadn't used so many swear words in years as I had this weekend. I am only just learning to deal with family again. Graham's playing hooky had left me walking a tight rope without a net. "You walk out without telling me, and you think we have any kind of collaboration happening here?"

To make my point, I ripped the intercom out of the socket and flung it across the room. I hadn't realized how much he'd scared me by disappearing like that. And because flinging inanimate objects didn't ease my fury, I shoved a chair under the bolt hole in the ceiling. It wasn't any more than a reinforced square panel in the ceiling that opened into my grandfather's bedroom closet. But that closet contained stairs to Graham's lair. I had just pulled myself into the closet and stood up when I saw his long legs coming down.

I froze. He dropped down in front of me. This was a closet. We would be nose to nose, except I'm short and wasn't wearing heels. It was more like nose to neck, and Graham's masculine throat smelled of a spicy aftershave that made me drool. Even a large closet was too tight for both of us.

"You *want* me out of the house," he reminded me in a snarl. He was all muscle-bound male in tight black t-shirt and jeans, and I'd only hurt my fist if I punched him.

"You want my family to get lost and leave you alone," I countered, clenching my hands on my hips. This close, I could practically hear his heart beating.

"The lot of you are dangerous together!" he roared. "You can't expect me to keep up with a dozen human IEDs waiting to go off. And *you* quit paying attention when they're around. Did you even *look* at that photo I sent you? Do you have any idea what your damned sister has got herself into?"

Patra? Or Juliana? I hadn't thought he even knew about Juliana.

Before I could reply, he grabbed my shoulders and smashed his mouth down on mine.

Once upon a time, we would have taken our tempers out on each other in the gym. Since our last encounter in a hotel room, our fury had a new outlet. I grabbed his muscled biceps and lifted myself into his crushing kiss with way more enthusiasm than the wretched man deserved.

We were pawing at each other, stumbling out of the closet in the direction of Max's grandiose bed, when the doorbell rang its Christmas carol.

Graham swore beneath his breath, glanced down with avid interest at my half-opened buttons in the darkness, and set me aside. "Magda," he said. "That's what I was trying to tell you. She's mixed up in this."

He departed through the closet, leaving me gasping and cursing at the chiming carol.

The chime stopped. Someone had answered it. I prayed it was Mallard, but he was probably having a heart attack at the mess we'd left in the kitchen—or the tree in his precious parlor.

Was he telling me Magda was out there? Of course, he was. EG had *invited* her. And if she was mixed up in Juliana's school. . .

I couldn't greet my mother until I'd pulled myself together. I dropped back into my office just as a knock timidly hit my door. I didn't have enough creative obscenities in my weary brain for this.

I buttoned my Henley and yanked open the door. Zander stood there, looking like a bereft waif. Not half an hour ago, he'd been an intelligent man focused on a goal. Magda had turned him into an adolescent simply by crossing the threshold. There was good reason I didn't want to face her.

I gestured Zander toward the wing chair I'd just climbed down from, closed, and locked the door. EG and Tudor could handle our mother for a while. I could hear EG shouting excitedly and the low rumble of Tudor's deepening voice.

"I've never met her," he whispered.

"You used to call her Ma-ma." I sank into my chair and tried to calm my rattled nerves. "She called you sweet bumpkins. You're allowed to hate her for abandoning you, if you like."

He shook his head. "It's not that. We have always understood that she left for our own protection. We knew she was available if we needed her, and she was, when the time came. But most of our lives, we didn't need her. We had half a dozen *anties* in the village to look after us."

"All of them probably better mothers than Magda," I pointed out. "Don't get me wrong. She's a brilliant, dedicated woman, but she's a crappy mother. The Catholic Church did the world no favors when it told its believers to go forth and multiply. Why that was one commandment Magda obeyed is beyond my comprehension."

He made what sounded like a snort. "The world is already too populated, mostly with people unfit to take care of it. But we were supposed to take care of each other," he said despondently. "And I have lost my sister. Our mother will be horrified and think me a bad son."

I crossed my arms on the desk and leaned forward. "Listen, and listen carefully. Magda knows *everything*. Magda can very well have sent Julie here. Magda believes the world revolves around what she wants and needs. She uses people. Stand your ground and do not let her bully you. This house belongs to *us*, not her. She is *our* guest." It was a good thing I'd ripped out the intercom or Graham would be grumbling about now.

My mind slid back to our all-too-brief encounter, but I yanked it back from fiery kisses. I would try to work out what he'd been telling me later, not while Magda threatened my nest. And yeah, that was part of what Graham was telling me—I put family before him and my work.

Zander took a deep breath and swiped at his nearly non-existent hair. I wondered if he used to wear it long and bushy before he went to work at a stuffy finance office. As toddlers, the twins had been adorable with their identical frizzy curls.

"I am a failure at following in my father's footsteps," he finally admitted. "I was supposed to go into politics, but I hated even running for student government."

Ah, there was an interesting insight. I liked him better for it. "It requires a certain temperament for lying to people on a regular basis," I said cynically. "I do not consider it a failure to be honest."

He offered a slight smile. "That's one way of looking at it. Mostly, I don't like shaking hands and making wild promises and remembering names. I am not a salesman."

"Another point in your favor. Let's go up, and I'll introduce the two of you. Magda will shower you with kisses, then disappear tomorrow. Pretend you know nothing until you can trust her. She's not here because EG invited her, I promise."

That really raised his eyebrows, but he intelligently refrained from questioning. He rose and opened the door for me.

The moment we arrived in the foyer, Magda fell into her lost chick routine. We all stood back and let her exclaim over Zander, admire his height and how he'd turned out just like his father, yadda yadda.

Magda was still gorgeous, of course. She'd had me when she was barely eighteen, so she was only in her late forties. Her naturally blond hair changed colors upon occasion, but she'd gone for light highlights on this visit. She was tall and willowy like Patra. High cheekbones and long, up-tilted sloe eyes gave her an exotic look— our Hungarian background apparently. She'd flung her fur coat over her luggage to reveal a red form-fitting cashmere sweater and black leather slacks that only a model should wear—but Magda pulled off the look well.

I yawned. Tudor and EG went back to the blinking lights. We'd bought wrapping paper on our outing, and they had been busy scattering ribbons and bows all over the carpet. We now had cheerfully messy gifts under our eccentric tree. We waited for the reunion to end and the real message to begin.

"Where are Nick and Patra?" Magda cried, finally releasing an embarrassed Zander.

"They have their own places." I only partially lied. Patra had a room upstairs, but she worked downtown and spent most nights in Sean's condo near their office. I would let Patra explain that.

Mallard arrived, looking as if he'd just stepped from a fashion plate for royal butlers. "Madam, shall I escort you to your chamber?" he intoned, while shooting me a nasty look that said I'd be made to pay later. For what, was anyone's guess. My faults are numerous.

"Mallard, you old sweetie. It's good to see you." Magda patted his plump cheek and made him blush. "Daddy's room again?"

Thank goodness Graham and I hadn't made it to the bed!

"Come along, Ana, help me unpack. We have a lot to catch up on." She gestured commandingly as Mallard gathered her luggage.

I picked up the fur and flung it at her, then lifted some of the smaller bags. She really had packed heavily for this trip. That was ominous on many levels.

She caught the fur without complaint, swung on her spiked heels, and clattered down the hall to Max's suite—the only one in the house that had been updated to modern specifications. The rest of us figured it was haunted by our grandfather's strong presence since he'd most likely been poisoned in that bed, but Magda didn't have an ounce of sensitivity in her nature.

Of course, if Graham and I had done the deed on that mattress, it might have changed the whole flavor of that room in my head. Too late now. I sighed in impatience as Mallard dragged out luggage racks and lifted the heavy cases so Magda could better open them.

"Dinner will be delayed until eight," he said in that sonorous voice he had to have copied from a monk's chant. "There has been a minor disaster in the scullery."

The *scullery*. I rolled my eyes. "We already ate. Zander's mujadara was delicious. Have a taste before you throw it out." I smiled brightly, letting his criticism of our kitchen capabilities roll right off me. Now that I was pretty certain we couldn't be thrown from this house, I had to learn to deal with Mallard. He had a temper and had quit before, but he was a sentimental sucker.

He glared and stalked off.

"You shouldn't be so hard on Mallard, dear. He's had a difficult life. He used to be a general in the IRA, if you could call that confederacy of hotheads an army. He lost his family in the riots. He's the reason your father came to Max." She blithely began unpacking her suitcase and hanging things in the closet—the one with the hidden stairs.

While I'd once adored Magda's fairy tales, they were often just that—tales to suit whatever she was doing at the moment. I tried not to encourage her. I could read newspaper archives and knew for fact that my father was an erudite statesman who represented Irish Catholics and sought congressional support for a just cause. I also knew from less reliable sources that he was a weapons dealer for an illegal army of rebels—some malformed descendant of Mallard's original IRA. My father, the diplomatic gun dealer—black and white do not exist in my world.

"We're in contact with Juliana," I said bluntly. "She's fine. You have no need to hang about if you have better things to do."

"That's cruel, Ana." She sent me a disapproving look. "My family is here for Christmas. Would you throw me out in the cold?"

Oh wow, I was starting to see this house from Graham's viewpoint. As long as we were here, Magda would feel free to use it. She could decide to retire and live here for the rest of her life—because none of us would throw her out. That frightened even me. Graham was probably packing his bags again.

"Of course not," I said, spinning out the lightbulb in the bedside lamp and removing the bug.

Magda repeated the act on the lamp on the other side and popped out the battery. "How jolly, just like old times! I trust Graham will have turned off the security cameras in here?"

"Trust away," I shrugged. "He calls them security. I call them an invasion of privacy. You're free to hunt them down and tape them up."

"I'm sure he was simply looking after your grandfather, but I can take care of myself. Men have difficulty understanding that." She dug out her own duct tape—I'd learned from the best—and began hunting under the various paintings on the walls.

"Pardon my doubt," I continued once all the bugs and cameras were disabled. "But you've never bothered to visit us for holidays before. I'm assuming there is a reason this year. And please don't underestimate my intelligence."

She sat on the edge of the bed, propped her chin in her palm, and studied me. "You're hard, Ana. I suppose I made you that way. I can't say I'm sorry, because you needed to survive. You had the worst of it growing up, the times when we were poor, and I was still learning my way around. You need to let the past go now. You're in the lap of luxury. Relax. Enjoy life."

Really, it ought to be permissible to murder one's mother. Relax, right.

"I'd be tense if I *wasn't* working," I said pragmatically. "Somehow, it's difficult to relax when my family keeps dropping in on me unexpectedly, needing things that only I can provide. But if you're here to enjoy your children and have a real holiday, you're welcome to join in the festivities. EG wants popcorn chains."

That last was pure sarcasm. We both knew that wasn't why she was here.

"Shouldn't EG be in school?" she asked, not giving away anything.

"Today, but she's off a few days before Christmas and until after New Year's. Tudor's already on holiday. They'll enjoy having you to take them shopping. I'll leave you to primp before dinner. Maybe Graham will come down to join you." I walked out before I said anything really *cruel.*

I loved and admired my mother, but she'd never completely outgrown the spoiled princess persona of her childhood. Sometimes I just wanted to shake her until her brains rattled. It was simpler to agree to disagree and move on.

Applying that realization to my relationship with the spy in the attic, I knew that I couldn't endure a similar level of passive hostility with Graham. We either had a meeting of the minds, or we battled it out until one of us lost. Since there was no way I was able to concentrate on my work after what we'd just done, I figured it was time to take a big stick to his head.

Ten

Ana beards the lion

GRAHAM'S SPY CAMERAS HAD told him I was coming, of course. By the time I arrived, he had the champagne buffet photo up on a wall monitor, the image he'd sent me earlier, along with the pieced-together photo Zander must have uploaded. Except Graham shouldn't be able to burrow into my unnetworked laptop. The bastard's invasion of my privacy was the least of my triggers right now.

I picked up a file folder and swatted him upside the head with it. "Gym, now," I commanded.

"We have nothing to fight about," he said stiffly, not bothering to turn and face me. "Your sister is embroiled in a nest of nastiness so huge that even Magda has to investigate. Do you want my help or not?"

"Why now?" I shouted in furious frustration. "You abandoned me the entire weekend when I needed you, and now that Magda is here, you're offering to help? Why don't I just go bake cookies and let the two of you handle everything?" I whacked him with the folder again.

I finally had his attention. He rose and towered intimidatingly over me. I don't intimidate. I marched out of the room and down to the gym. I'd learned to handle my many anger issues by beating up sandbags. I pulled off my Henley, stripping to my tank top and leggings, then yanked on the boxing gloves Graham had bought for me.

I was pounding the stuffing out of the bag when he finally deigned to enter. He crossed his arms and glared.

"I'm entitled to come and go as I please," he said, taking the offensive. "This is still my house."

I walloped the bag some more, then swung and kicked it as hard as I could. My blow was solid enough to swing the heavy bag in his direction. He didn't flinch but kicked it back with an easy side-sweep.

"This isn't about ownership!" Well, it probably was to some extent, but that wasn't what was eating at me. "This is about respect!"

I'd finally produced a brief look of surprise out of him. Then he frowned as if I were a misbehaving child and tugged on his gloves.

"That's ridiculous," he concluded. "You're angry because I wasn't here to listen to you whine about your family. They're not my family. I want no part of them."

It was a good thing the bag was closer than he was or I'd have taken out his nose. My rapid tattoo blows immobilized the heavy bag before I dared reply.

"You are not Magda," I screamed at him as he jabbed the bag back in my direction with a lot more muscle than I possessed. "*You care!* You don't want to. You're doing your best to turn yourself into an automaton in the middle of the Matrix, but you helped Tudor when he needed a male role model. You let EG sneak up here to steal your damned cat! I can't even go in her room anymore without sneezing. Juliana went missing in a powder keg of dead bodies, big egos, and missing money. And you damned well left me stranded because you couldn't bear to watch a disaster in the making."

The things that escape my subconscious when I let it all hang out. . .

Jaw tightening, Graham slammed the bag with a power that should have taken down the ceiling. "I left to look for another place to stay. If I'm signing this place over to your family, I need a new office."

That was a blow to the gut. I'd known it was coming. It was better to have it out there. But it still hurt.

I slammed the bag in his direction again. He punched it back at me. His t-shirt revealed the burn scars up his arms, but his over-long black hair fell over the one searing his forehead. All that rippling muscle distracted me as he seriously got into battering the bag. His anger issues were weightier than mine.

His words hurt more than the punishing blows I swung to keep the bag from taking out my knees. I couldn't wrap my tongue around all the exclamations of horror and dismay that he'd rattled loose. "Did you find one?" was all I could say.

"There are lots of modern offices better wired than this ancient hellhole." He whacked the bag hard enough to send it half way across the room.

I dodged backward, kicked sideways, and drove it back to him. I wasn't angry now, though, I was scared.

"You have this entire floor for your use," I finally had the brains to shout. "The only reason you want to leave is because you're afraid to care about anyone again. That's the reason you stood us up at Thanksgiving, isn't it, the reason you never come to dinner?"

"I'm not your damned family!" he retorted.

Sometimes, pounding the crap out of something opened my head and gave me insight.

Panting hard, I stepped away from the bag and pulled off my gloves. "Max was your family," I said, no longer shouting. "Mallard still is. That's why you took him with you. You *care*, Graham. You may not want to, but you do. And even if you might not want to be part of *us*, we accept *you*. Blood doesn't make family."

Graham smashed the bag so hard, the chain creaked.

I walked out. I needed a shower now that I'd cleaned out my thoughts.

Juliana works overtime

JULIANA READ THE TEXT message from Zander again and wept: I HAVE MET OUR MOTHER.

All her life she'd longed for the woman she remembered as a beautiful golden angel. She knew their mother was no angel, but the little-girl need to know her was still there, eating at her.

And Zander was the one to finally meet their mother. She glared at the burner phone and turned it off. She'd set it to buzz for texts while she worked alone in the office, but this wasn't the message she wanted to hear.

Had they figured out the photo she'd given them? She hoped so, because she had another one.

She'd been offered the position at Jesus World because of the praise she'd received for the video she'd produced for the school in Zimbabwe. When she'd first arrived in DC, the school had given her access to their security cameras so she'd have materials to put together fund-raising videos for the project.

But they'd also talked of an entire film celebrating the creation of the reverend's grand vision once the park was completed. For that, she'd needed far better equipment than JACAD possessed, so she'd bought and installed her own in strategic positions.

But last night, the recordings had been deleted from the school's camera overlooking the back field by the pyramids. No one knew that she'd installed a better camera back there.

The discovery of the missing recordings worried her. After everyone had gone home, Julie used Mrs. Overcamp's computer to access her camera files for the missing time period. She'd uploaded them to her cloud account for safety, as usual, but she hadn't dared take the time to look at them until now. She stared numbly at the results.

There was the bulldozer again. Her own video camera produced less grainy images than the security ones. This time, she could tell the figure being shoveled into the hole with the dirt was a *man*, but it was impossible to recognize his face from that distance.

A man, being shoveled into a pyramid foundation. She wanted to freak out, but last time she'd done that, it had got her nowhere except in trouble. She had to stay calm, stay cool, and plan better this time, no matter how fast her pulse raced and how worried she was.

It was time to bring in the experts, she decided. That was smarter than freaking. Tongue caught between her teeth for concentration, she copied that segment into a separate file and named it. Heart pounding harder, she used her new burner phone, and texted Zander the cloud password and file name. She didn't think her brother would know what to do, but if their mother was here. . . Maybe someone would know what should be done next. She prayed, she prayed hard.

Julie still had to find out if anyone had heard from Esther or the other two second-year girls who had left without completing their courses or their tasks. She wasn't ready to quit on the reverend just yet.

As the message beeped *Sent*, she heard a noise in the back of the empty office.

"Hello, Miss Kruger, we meet again."

The Reverend Arden. And he'd caught her at Mrs. Overcamp's desk. When could she start freaking out? Now?

***

Ana the Annoying Gnat

AFTER MY SHOWER, I trotted down the stairs to admire the inexpertly-wrapped gifts beneath the tree. I needed to wrap the ones I'd bought today, and the ones stored upstairs in my closet. I hadn't bought Magda anything—not because I hadn't anticipated her arrival, but because I didn't know what to buy. Perfume bottles filled with pepper spray weren't easily available at the mall.

Tudor and EG were there, fighting a video battle in the flashing lights from the tree. They fidgeted in glee as I checked out each gift, looking for my name. I shook my packages and made wild guesses aloud like *supersonic missile* and *world peace.*

When EG again demanded popcorn chains, I sent her in search of Magda and Mallard. Then I pointed Tudor toward Graham's office. "He will never admit it, but he can use your help. Offer it. Or ask him what he wants for Christmas. He likes having you around."

I freely acknowledge—I'm an annoying gnat who won't give up. Besides, I was starting to think that Graham really shouldn't be alone all the time. And if he meant to abandon us, then I was free to annoy the heck out of him.

At this rate, Magda, Mallard, and Graham would all come after me with hatchets before the season was over. They might as well kill me now, because I refused to do this all by myself any longer. I wouldn't run away as I had before. I was more mature and confident these days. And I had *money.* I wasn't ever going to be anyone's doormat again.

Zander was still in the library, looking seriously bleary-eyed. At my appearance, he turned the laptop so I could see the screen. "I cannot do this. She has sent me access to video files of every single solitary day she has been there, over three months of daily files from a dozen cameras! It is impossible."

I studied the list of neatly time-dated files. "Any clue what she wants us to find?"

"That's what makes searching the files compelling." He hit the keyboard and opened up a single photo file.

I pulled up a chair and sat down to study the image. It was taken at night, so even though it had probably been filmed in color—which meant it wasn't a normal security camera—the colors were dimmed. All I could see was a puddle of white light, presumably from a security lamp, and the black silhouette of what appeared to be one of the park's phony pyramids. Off to one side, almost out of reach of the camera, was a darker shadow that might have been a bulldozer.

The only real color in the whole image was a red stripe hanging from an object spilling with a load of dirt from the bulldozer. I assumed the load was dirt and not gravel, but the darkness made it too difficult to be certain. Why was a bulldozer operating after dark? There had to be safety regulations about that.

I enlarged the photo and focused on the red stripe. As I zoomed up, the object attached to the stripe became more human-shaped. Swallowing a lump of fear, I zoomed again and a man's face appeared—or a white oval with indents where features should be emerged. It wasn't exactly a close-up, and the dirt or debris all around him added to the muddiness of the image. The red stripe could have been a necktie. He might have been wearing a white shirt and dark coat. Identification was impossible.

But he was pretty definitely dead.

"Is this just another angle of the photo she sent before?" I had to ask, because the similarities were striking.

"I'm no expert. I can't tell, except the angle seems different. This one is dated from two days ago, though. We can see traces of snow still on the ground. The one Julie cut up... had no date and there was no snow. The original image might be somewhere in all these files, but I have no idea how to search." He gestured in resignation at the list of videos.

"She just sent you the password into her cloud account?" I asked. "Without us asking for it?"

He shrugged. "I texted her to say our mother was here. She has always wished to meet her, so I thought it only fair that she know. The link and the password were her reply."

"She wants Magda to look through these files and tell her what to do?" I asked incredulously. "Telling Magda anything is like lighting explosives. One thing you will learn about our mother— Magda may flirt, insinuate, infiltrate and otherwise use subterfuge to get what she wants, but when it comes to our safety, she is much more direct. She will head straight for Reverend Arden and pull his hair out through his nose if his park is endangering your sister."

Zander smiled a little at the image. "That would almost be satisfying." His face sagged again as he gestured at the piles of paper. "But I fear you are right, and Julie is sitting on a dangerous situation. I don't know how her photographs and these documents relate, but all is not right in Jesus World."

"Does your faith recognize that Jesus was a Jew?" I asked out of cynical curiosity as he handed me the first stack of paper. I was too tired to read through lines of what appeared to be expense statements.

"It is Julie's faith, not mine. Our father attended the Episcopalian Church. Julie got caught up in the school-building and loved the idea of evangelizing through good work. She does not have a scientific mind and wouldn't know a dinosaur from an armadillo. She may be a very practical person in many ways, but she still wants to go to Disney World for the fantasy of pink castles and Goofy dogs. That she is sending us photos of dead bodies worries me more than I can say."

And I had yet to tell him about the dead or missing girls. He didn't need that right now. I held up the papers he'd been working on. "And what are these telling me?"

He swiped nervously at his forehead. "That very large sums of money are flowing through JACAD. It may be that the embezzler in the newspaper story was washing his ill-gotten gains through his board position at the park, but the sums are not just coming from the weapons factory. And when they go out, it is to corporations and businesses employed by the park, not to any individual's private account. I cannot imagine how the embezzler benefitted."

"I can." I had more experience than I wanted in how mega-corps and bad guys siphoned funds to offshore accounts—or into Senator Paul Rose's campaign for presidency through powerful PACs. I pulled a bugged table lamp from the closet where I'd shoved it and plugged it in again. "Did you leave Julie's photo on this table when you fixed dinner?" I asked, as much for Zander's education as for the lamp's.

He narrowed his eyes suspiciously and spoke aloud. "I did."

"Don't do that unless you want Graham to see it." I turned to the lamp. "He's all yours. Treat him gently. I have another angle to work."

I got up and pointed at the laptop. "It's not networked to

Graham, although he'll hack it if you let him. If there are files you want him to see, send them to both of us or add them to our cloud account. Our emails and links are in there."

I'd let him figure out what to do if he had files he didn't want to share. Unlike others in this family, I respected the privacy of the adult members.

I was rather enjoying being the annoying voice on the intercom for a change. Let Graham see how it felt to have toxic crap dumped on him in the middle of the night.

Not that it was the middle of the night yet, but it was EG's bedtime since she had school in the morning. That would never occur to Magda. Once more, I'd be the bad guy if I had to go down to the kitchen where mother-worship and popcorn were happening.

To my surprise, as I started down to the basement kitchen, EG was coming up. She carried a plate of decorated sugar cookies complete with neat hanging threads.

"Mallard said we could hang these tomorrow, that adding to the tree each day is part of our tradition." She proudly held them up for my admiration.

A few of them rather looked like purple witches, but I recognized a Santa and a heavily sprinkled star. "We should add one cookie a day?" I asked.

"No, silly, we add the cookies to the tree tomorrow. And the next day, maybe the popcorn. And so on. I'll hang these after school if Tudor doesn't eat them all." She eyed me craftily. "There's still time for buying more presents. Maybe we should add *them* every day too."

There was the Evil Genius I knew and loved. I yanked her ponytail. She had long black hair like mine but usually wore bangs and often colorful streaks. Red was today's color. "Go for it. I'm waiting for Santa. Up to bed with you."

If Mallard was baking cookies for EG, I could almost wager my fortune that Magda had already left the building. As I trotted back to my office, I didn't hear our mother moving around in Max's bedroom or talking to our perspicacious butler.

Now that I had regained access to Graham's sources, I locked myself in my office and sat down with the police files on the missing and/or dead girls.

According to the police report I dug out with Graham's back

door into their system, the body of a park construction worker had been found in a shallow grave in October. He'd apparently been missing since spring and dead of a broken neck about that long. Since Julie hadn't been at the park in the spring, we could assume this was not the body in her photo.

Police had questioned his fellow workers. His family and friends all insisted that he was a good man who didn't drink or belong to any gangs. The cops had reached no conclusions, and the case was cold.

Melissa, the girl who had gone missing from the school in spring according to the newspaper, had been found alive and well in October according to the police report. Interesting. Apparently she had been on the missing construction worker's list of acquaintances, so the cops had tracked her down through his family.

She was currently living the high life as the mistress of one of our prominent citizens, Ed Parker—a name I recognized from JACAD's board. I would have been interested in hearing her good church-going family's reaction, but the police had simply shut their files without that fascinating finale.

The third case, the woman found in the Potomac in November, was the one that raised my suspicion-o'meter. Rebecca Beatty was from a small town in Iowa. She'd been with CAD for eighteen months. She was training as a carpenter, since her family was in the building trade. Her photo in the police file showed a teenage homecoming queen complete with tiara, all long blond curls and big teeth and the usual assets that teenage boys voted for.

Her family didn't have the money for college, and Rebecca was no scholar, but her desire to learn how to build schools in third world countries had been in her essay when she'd applied for scholarships through her church.

Rebecca had lived in the CAD trailer park with the other students until October—about the time Melissa had been found living in sin.

Apparently JACAD's sponsors were in the habit of rewarding the kids with spare concert tickets. Rebecca's roommate had reported that Rebecca had been given a ticket to a boating event on the Potomac—and she'd only returned to collect her clothes and move out.

Some weeks later, Rebecca had given her roommate a new

address that the police report indicated was a condo on the high-priced end of Alexandria—not something the carpenter beauty queen could possibly afford. The condo was owned by a conglomerate related to one of CAD's sponsoring corporations. The police had found no evidence that Rebecca had actually lived there, but they could find no other address for her. If the roommate was to be believed, Rebecca's message arrived one week before her body was found in the river.

Two CAD students ending up in CAD related apartments—now the coincidence was looking a lot less coincidental, but the cases were in different districts and the police hadn't connected them.

Someone had to, though, before the next body arrived on our doorstep—or on Juliana's desk.

Eleven

Ana studies photos

WITH FEAR FOR JULIANA crawling around my gut, I uploaded the champagne buffet image Graham had sent me. I pulled up the police file photos of Rebecca and Melissa and displayed them on a different monitor. The file photos were probably high school senior pictures. They both looked very young, confident, and pretty, but those were headshots.

The screen saver was mostly about beautiful bodies—lots of them. What had Graham's sharp eyes spotted? First off, knowing his background, he probably recognized the less-beautiful fat cats feeding their faces around the table. Even I recognized a few of Top Hat's nasties, although their head nasty, Senator Paul Rose, wasn't present.

I moved on from the tuxes and low-cut evening gowns to study other details. I couldn't determine when or where the photo had been taken, but judging by the designer cake bearing colorful leaves, I'd have to say it was autumn. Graham no doubt had the details.

I finally turned my attention to the smiling female models vying for the attention of rich old men and spotted what Graham wanted me to see. Rebecca the Carpenter's big teeth beamed like a toothpaste ad while she flirted with some hot young exec holding a champagne glass. Her hair had been professionally tinted and styled in a sophisticated up-do, rendering her nearly unrecognizable from her long-haired high school photo. The carpenter from the Midwest had apparently decided to take a different road in some swanky company.

Now that I knew what I was looking for, I spotted Melissa not too far from Rebecca. Melissa's high school photo had shown a pretty girl with brown curls and glasses. Her parents had said she was a good church-going Sunday school teacher. The woman in the photo wore diamond pins holding back luxurious platinum waves and a gown that left very little to the imagination. But the protuberant eyes and lush lips were recognizable.

I checked back to the police files for the name of the prominent citizen who had been keeping the Sunday school teacher in style—one Edward Parker the Third. Old money Harvard alum, graduated 1980, which made him roughly in his fifties. He sat on several corporate boards, including JACAD's, but didn't give evidence of any real job. His name appeared as a major donor for Rose's PACs—unsurprisingly.

The image I was working with could very well be of one of those political dinners where candidates returned favors to their donors with schmoozing—and back door deals. All perfectly legal and American politics at work—we're too sophisticated to use actual bribes.

I dug a recent photo of Eddie the Third from one of the corporate year-end glossies, enlarged it, and compared it to the champagne buffet shot. Receding hair, dyed blond, athletically tall—he was easy to spot on the far end of the table from the girls, conversing with two men in tuxes I didn't recognize.

On a hunch and because these corporate cases always led back to the money, I looked up the police file photo of the gun manufacturer's embezzling accountant. Comparing the police file to the buffet photo—voila, there we were. Whenever this buffet had happened, Eddie the Third was having an earnest conversation with George Paycock the missing embezzler. Paycock had his arm around another unidentified pretty young thing—JACAD's board hard at work.

Out of total disrespect for our government and Paycock's former employer, General Defense Industries, I did a quick image search. I started by searching for gun lobbyists supporting laws protecting American rights to look like third-world assholes and carry AK47s. Gee, whadayaknow, there were Eddie the Third and Paycock again, poster boys for the gun lobbyists.

I noted our civilized, sophisticated, wealthy duo were not outstanding in fields with hunting rifles like their camouflage-wearing companions in the other photos. No sirreebob, Eddie and Georgie were shaking hands with Senator Paul Rose in front of the Capitol. The rifle-toters paid their dues to protect their weapons, and the money went straight into the pockets of the politicians. One had to admire the superiority of this form of bribery where cash needn't to be hidden and no heads got broken over it.

Uncertain what I hoped to reveal, I ran a comparative search on the gun lobby's contributors against a list of CAD's employees and directors—JACAD had very definitely become a *cad* in my mind. Every single CAD employee—including their office manager and general contractor—was a gun lobby supporter.

Juliana talks to the reverend

"AND SO YOU WANT to build schools in Africa?" Reverend Arden asked, stirring fake sugar into his coffee while they sat at a rickety table in the canteen behind the trailer camp market. "I thought most of the southern part of Africa was fairly educated."

"The system is very uneven," Julie insisted. "The school JACAD built in Zimbabwe while I was there is already making a difference. The educational system is bankrupt and cannot reach poor rural villages. These are people who cannot walk the miles to attend government schools. They are needed too much at home. But if there is a school in their village, attending a few hours a day can make all the difference."

"I admire your enthusiasm but don't recommend commandeering Mrs. Overcamp's computer again," he said dryly. "She is entitled to her privacy."

Julie wanted to tell him how Mrs. Overcamp had confiscated her phone, then returned it with a bug inside so crude that even she spotted it because it was sucking up her battery juice. But the good reverend had a habit of wandering the grounds after dark when reprehensible things appeared to happen, so she bit her tongue.

"I will apologize to her," she said, crossing her fingers under the table. "I do not know a lot about computers and hoped I could figure out how to return my internet connection." That wasn't a total lie. The internet had dropped out while she was rummaging through Mrs. Overcamp's files.

She would pray and ask God what one was supposed to do if her lies might protect innocents.

Arden checked his phone and sighed. "The battery is dead again. I can't tell if the Wi-Fi is back. You should probably get some sleep anyway. While I admire your dedication, young people really should have a better balanced life."

"And does that not go for good preachers as well?" she asked.

Late night coffee-drinkers watched them with interest, making Julie uncomfortable. She worked hard at not being noticed, but her height and color were on the conspicuous end of the spectrum in any setting.

"Preachers with dreams deserve what they get. I'll sleep when this park is built and probably not before." He gestured at one of the student workers behind the counter. "Lucas, see that Miss Kruger returns home safely."

She wanted to argue but decided to err on the side of silence. Tall White Boy took off his apron and gestured at a co-worker that he was leaving before falling into step with her.

"So, you and the reverend, what's up with that?" he asked rudely as they stepped into the cold night.

"He either wants me to stay out of the computers or thinks I work too much," she said idly, just because. She waited with interest for his response.

"Their systems are so antiquated, my little brother could hack them. I haven't seen you around. What department are you in?"

Well, so much for worrying over disapproval at her bad habits. She hated not trusting anyone, and she couldn't remember lies if she told them too often. She opted for honesty, or at least bluntness, since that seemed to be what he was doing. "I'm both working and taking classes in marketing. I'll be taking finance classes in town after Christmas. I'm not looking forward to it. How about you?"

"I'm in finance now, but with the feds all over the office, the teacher keeps getting called away. It was pretty lame anyway. Anyone knows that money in non-profits gets spent before it can be invested. Raising funds makes more sense. Does marketing teach that?"

They were almost back to her trailer. A vapor of unease passed over her. Instincts were all she had to rely on, and hers said to keep out strangers, which went against her gregarious nature. "Not really," she admitted. "Not so far. What are the feds and why are they all over the office?"

"Feds, federal government cops. The Rev trusts the wrong people apparently," he said with a shrug. "Word is that all the park's money is gone, so we'll probably be out on our asses next year."

The park wouldn't be built? Because the police had taken over? Julie didn't know whether to panic or be relieved.

"This your place?" Lucas nodded at the fading piece of metal where Julie hoped Maryam was sleeping.

"It is. Thanks for walking me home. I hope you're wrong about the money."

He shrugged. "My parents want me to join the Army anyway. See you 'round."

If the park closed. . . The graves it concealed might never be found. She was beginning to suspect neither would Esther. If Maryam hadn't run the other night, would she have disappeared like the others? Or was she just being silly?

Julie shivered and glanced around before entering the trailer and locking the door. She would have propped a chair beneath the rickety handle, but Maryam wasn't home yet.

It was only later, as she was climbing into bed, that she heard the gunfire and screams.

Ana plays Santa

AROUND MIDNIGHT, I CALLED it quits on my research and carried the gifts I'd hidden to the Christmas tree in the front parlor, although I held back on some of EG's. She'd be smuggling them in for x-rays if she got too excited.

Mallard met me in the foyer and took half the top-heavy stack. "Your mother likes red," he intoned solemnly.

"If you would wear it, I'd buy you a red vest," I said, tongue-in-cheek, as we spread the packages around. "Then she could like you and hang around."

I knew what he was saying. None of the packages under the tree had "Mom" written on them.

"I like a good cabernet," he said stiffly. "That qualifies as red."

I picked up the hint. I'm clever like that. "But Magda won't hang around to share it. As soon as she accomplishes whatever she's after, she'll be gone, even if that's midnight on Christmas Eve." I spoke from harsh experience, not cynicism. I had very good reason for providing the holiday my siblings had never really experienced.

He didn't argue, but if he wanted us to put Magda gifts under the tree, I knew he was hoping to tempt the little girl he'd once known to stay home for a change—or for her own good. Even ex-IRA butlers can be sentimental.

I noticed Nick had hung the picture frame ornament containing Magda and our grandparents on the tree. The crystal frame caught and reflected the blinking lights. I unplugged the display so I couldn't see it. I'd rather not consider the unusual schmaltziness behind my bringing up the ornament and Nick hanging it.

Upstairs, I crawled under the covers of the futon I called my bed. When we'd first moved into the mansion, I had figured our stay would be temporary. So I'd taken my grandfather's old office, where I felt closest to his spirit, and turned it into my bedroom—one of the reasons I'd set up my office in the basement. If we meant to stay, I'd have to consider buying a real bed and maybe a dresser, instead of the filing cabinet, for my undies.

Or maybe. . . I considered the forbidding master chamber next door to this room, the one that had been Max's room before he got sick—and shut out that thought.

Despite the silence, I was aware of Graham working overhead. I had a deep longing to go up and discuss this case with him, but we had too many unresolved issues. Besides, I never knew when or where my mother would put in an appearance. This had been her childhood home. She knew every secret staircase and bolt hole and was as likely to enter Graham's office as she would the kitchen.

I twitched nervously at having Magda under our roof and forcibly tugged my pre-sleep thoughts to Julie and whether or not we should haul her out of that park.

By morning, my lizard brain had presented the whole brilliant plan of how I could find out what was happening at the park without endangering Juliana at all. Having money was amazingly beneficial—which ought to give me qualms but didn't.

Twelve

Ana becomes a philanthropist

ZANDER LOOKED HAGGARD AT the breakfast table the next morning. He'd probably spent the night going through that mess of images in Julie's baffling cloud account. I needed to think about his welfare as well as his sister's. After one of Mallard's bountiful breakfasts, I set Zander down with a computer and one of the smaller mutual funds I'd invested in.

"Turn that into a non-profit foundation," I told him, pointing at the screen with the dollar signs.

He stared at the screen and then at me in confusion. "This is our grandfather's trust? You wish to invest it?"

"This is a *small* part of the trust. I thought this one account might be easily set up as a non-profit. I'll send you the documents we need to file. Our trust can easily afford to make charitable donations."

He continued to stare at the screen. "This is over a million dollars."

"That's not enough?" I asked innocently.

He turned his big brown eyes back to me with a look of utter shock. "Our trust is large enough to donate a *million dollars* to charity?"

"Not all at once, of course. We invest this bit and give away whatever we think is best. We've only just received the funds, and I really haven't had time to think about the best uses. I thought you being a financial analyst and all, you could help out a little."

Now that the initial astonishment was over, he narrowed his eyes, and I could practically see his brain ticking.

"I do not know your laws, but I can learn. How soon did you wish to start making donations?"

"We'll need a bank account," I said airily. "Some fancy financial statements. Call it Giving Back or something equally neutral, and I'll create letterheads and business cards. We can't make contributions just yet since we don't have checks, but we can make a few promises, to get started."

"Will any of these funds actually go to charities?" he asked suspiciously.

I patted his shoulder. The boy was learning quickly. "Yes, very definitely, although we probably need to hold a family meeting to decide which ones. But in the meantime, I need the pretties to flash around."

"If you go to that park, I want to go with you," he said grimly, proving he had a quick mind. "And in case you're interested, this is not one of the best funds to be invested in. I trust the others are in better hands."

"Not yet, but we'll get there." First, I needed to empty an account or two to pay Graham for this house. Then we'd talk about what was left. But I'd given Zander enough to think about for now.

With EG off to school, I had time to run down to my office and send all the necessary information to Zander. Tudor hadn't been at the breakfast table, but teenagers liked to sleep in. After a while, I heard him rummaging upstairs in the dining room. Mallard—in the interest of protecting the kitchen we'd destroyed in the two days he'd stupidly left us on our own—had left cereal and fruit and various other cold items on the buffet.

Magda hadn't been at breakfast either. I didn't even know if she'd come home from whatever she'd been up to, since I didn't hear her stirring in the room above me.

She made me feel out of place in my own house, and that annoyed me. I couldn't go up my secret stairs to Graham's lair without entering her closet. I had to take the public route, where I could be stopped by Mallard or Tudor or anyone else lurking along the way.

I had time to send Zander the documents he needed before one of Graham's urgent missives dropped across my screen. I wished he wouldn't do that. It interrupted the thought flow.

The document looked like an AP wire report out of Alexandria VA. The proximity to Jesus World forced me to keep reading, and my insides were grinding by the time I finished.

To heck with my preferred method of furtively checking out the park. It was time to get Julie out, *now*.

The good Reverend Joshua Arden had been shot by unknown gunmen beneath his own dinosaurs and was hospitalized in critical condition.

My legs weren't long enough to take the stairs two at a time, but I did my best. Tudor looked startled as he emerged from the dining room just as I rushed by. I heard him picking up speed behind me. I didn't need him on this next conversation. I turned and gestured him back.

"Help Zander, if you can. He's going to need someone with him."

I didn't stop to explain or argue. I continued up to Graham's office.

Two of his monitors were flashing scenes of blue uniforms spreading across the muddy park beneath the rusting skeletons of creatures that should never have existed. He'd probably connected to the park's security system. Another of his monitors tracked the hospital entrance where reporters and their cameramen were gathering. Graham's ability to take it all in was beyond obsessive and well into autistic territory, but he was functional, most of the time.

"I'm going in to bring Julie home." I didn't usually bother telling him what I was doing, but I had a purpose, one he wouldn't like.

Graham snorted and didn't turn around. "You ought to fit right in over there, looking like that."

I glanced down at my denim overalls. "I'm not wearing stockings to go out there in the cold! And I'm not planning on joining the church."

"You were planning to go out as a contributor," he pointed out what I hadn't told him. He must have been eavesdropping, per usual. "In denim?"

Of course not. I had my socialite disguise, although now that I thought about it, it didn't include good warm pants. I made a note to make a thrift store run later. "That's irrelevant now. Something bad is going down out there and I mean to find Julie. We haven't heard from her since Saturday."

"And the cops won't let you past the park gates," he insisted. "You can't even pass yourself off as one of the students looking like that."

"Looking like what?" I cried, wanting to smack him upside the head but forcing my temper down. "My sister is there and *she* must fit in! Where's the difference?"

The only reason I didn't box his ears was that he didn't argue with my desperate need to break into a park swarming with cops and possible murderers. Graham *understood*, as few others could.

He changed one of the monitors to pan over a gathering crowd of young people. I could see the dilapidated Ferris wheel structure in the background, so I assumed we were still looking at the park. "You're not exotic enough."

I really wanted to kick him then. I can be pretty danged exotic if I want. I studied the crowd. The students were wrapped in bulky coats and hats—far from *exotic*. Judging by their exposed faces, the kids came in a wide variety of colors, mostly on the lighter side, but I certainly wouldn't call them *exotic*. "It's not PC to call people of color exotic anymore," I informed him.

Graham made a rude snort. "So, what do we call them?"

"By their names?" I suggested. "Your Bigoted Rudeness might prefer foreign or strange or non-American."

"Your mother is definitely strange but not exotic. You're strange but more neurotic. The word *exotic* has its purpose, and I'm not bigoted, just rude. *Look* at those kids!"

Neurotic. I rolled my eyes but I'd finally realized what he was talking about—and it wasn't just color. It wasn't easy to tell beneath the bulky coats, but their height hinted at what Graham had already grasped. Almost all the kids were of above average height. I *so* wouldn't fit in.

They were also all good looking, and there didn't appear to be a single overweight one in the group. If any were skinny, the coats disguised the fact, but after seeing the images of buxom Melissa and Rebecca, I was putting my money on perfection. CAD had chosen perfect-looking young models to represent their campus. I was actually a bit amazed they weren't all white. There must have been some federal funding involved—call that cynicism or reverse bigotry, but I didn't hold high opinions of Arden's followers.

I didn't see anyone who might be Julie in the crowd.

"So, I won't go in as a student. I need to go out there alone. I don't want Zander and Tudor involved."

Graham opened a monitor on the library where my brothers had their heads bent over their respective computers. "I'll block news reports. I doubt if they ever look at anything that isn't on social media, but this isn't big enough to trend."

Understanding went both ways. He wasn't arguing about my need to find my sister, which was alarming in itself. It meant he didn't have any connections and therefore, no control of the situation. He had nothing except that wire report, and he needed someone in there. That would be me. That's where the sticking point came in. I needed an adult in place at home.

"If I go in, I need someone to look after EG. She'll be expecting me here when she comes home, and I don't know how long it will take me to reach Julie."

Graham finally turned around and gave me the evil eye. "You're not saying what I think you're saying? The brat is up here every night trying to break into my equipment as it is. You have money now, hire someone."

It said something of his knowledge of my family that he didn't suggest that Magda or my brothers look after a nine-year-old.

"She's after your cat," I said, glaring him down. "Her room is so full of cat hair now, I have to take allergy pills to enter it." I needed allergy pills to come in *here*, but I was hoping to escape before I started sneezing.

Graham snorted and returned to his monitors. "Huh, that's probably her goal, keeping you out of her room. Have Patra come over to look after her."

Really, I needed to shake him. And possibly EG if she really was using the cat to keep me out of her room. "Patra forgets to eat. Patra is so wound up in her career and Sean that she forgets to come home at night. EG is a kid and needs attention."

"Then send Patra to Jesus World. It will be good for her career."

Actually, that was a good idea, but not for my current purpose. "She'd be after the story and forget to look for Julie! It's not as if I'm asking you to bake cookies. I'll just leave a note to tell EG that you need her help and send her up here when she comes home. Have her look for code in some document, and she'll be happy for hours."

"No, Ana," he said firmly and decisively. "I am not you. I will not become caretaker for your siblings. You have enough money, hire a nanny. And if you're afraid Magda will take off with the kids, hire an armed guard."

And there it was, the fear hidden in my subconscious. I'd left EG in Tudor's care before. The difference now was that Magda was in town, and I trusted Graham more than my own mother.

And this wasn't just about EG. The fact that Magda had been gone all night and that a man had almost ended up dead clamored warnings. That the man had been overseeing a suspicious organization which harbored dead bodies, embezzlers, and had connections to weapon manufacturers fell into a pattern I'd recognized long ago. The only thing saving her from total condemnation was that the preacher was still alive. Magda's enemies seldom survived.

"You are truly evil," I told him, before stomping out.

I met Zander on his way up. He held out his phone to me.

HELP was all Julie's text message said.

Damn.

JULIE HUDDLED OVER A cold cup of coffee in the even colder market coffee shop. Around her, big men in blue uniforms conferred. One of them had the architectural schematics for the park. She wanted to point out where they ought to be looking, but Mr. Gregory, the contractor, was there, explaining the blueprints. She wondered if he knew his bulldozers were burying bodies. Saying anything in front of him might be hazardous to her health.

Now that the police had made it plain that she might be a witness—or worse—she felt as if a big red target had been painted on her back.

"You were seen with Reverend Arden last," the beefy policeman in a plain suit repeated for the forty-ninth time. "Tell us again what you saw."

"I was with Lucas last," she said for the fiftieth time.

"A Lucas we conveniently can't find," the man who had introduced himself as a detective insisted. "There were reports of a woman screaming when the shots were fired."

"I was in my pajamas and climbing into bed," she said *again.* She was not a scatterbrain and could repeat herself obsessively if that's what he required. "I heard screams. I did not recognize the voice of the person I heard screaming. I called 911. The call is right there, on my phone. Why do you not believe me?"

"Anyone could use your phone, and a call means nothing except you were awake when it happened and no one else was."

"There were people here in the shop when I left." She gestured at the clerks behind the counter, supposedly filling coffee cups but mostly whispering and staring.

"The shop closed at eleven, right after you left. The shots weren't fired until almost midnight. What did you do when you heard someone screaming?" He paced in the narrow space between the tiny tables.

"I have told you. I called 911. There are security guards and cameras all over the grounds. There is nothing someone like me could do except keep the door barred and wait for help. What was I supposed to have done?" she cried in anguish, because she wished she *had* done something.

And because Maryam had not come home.

Was it dangerous to tell the police about Maryam's absence? About her own cameras? If calling 911 had her interrogated like this, how much worse would it be if they knew about the cameras? And Maryam would hate having her family know she was out all night.

"You have a right to remain silent, Juliana," an authoritative female voice stated clearly over the noise of the crowd. "You have a right to have your attorney present while they question you. And if you're not under arrest, you have the right to walk away."

Frantically Julie searched past the bulk of the detective and his people until she located a small woman surging through the mob of men far larger than she. The newcomer strode confidently and with a striking presence that invaded people's space until they edged away without even noticing why. She was wearing a warm leopard-print coat with matching hat and boots. Despite her lack of height, the newcomer's long green eyes narrowed and her full lips tightened into an expression as fierce as a jungle cat's, making her seem twice her size. A thick black braid hung over her shoulder. . . .

Julie would remember that braid and ferocity anywhere, and her heart soared. She leapt up, prepared to shout *Ana* in joy and relief, but something in Ana's expression warned her to stay silent. How amazingly familiar that look seemed! She must have dreamed of it a thousand times, seen it in the images of their mother. That fierceness filled her with a warmth that made her feel *safe*.

"I am Jessica James, Miss Kruger's attorney, Detective. . .?" Ana introduced herself and lifted eloquent black eyebrows in question. Her heavily lashed eyes, sharp cheekbones, and slash of dark lipstick gave her the appearance of wealth and sophistication.

Jessica James? Was she wrong about this being Ana? But who else would Zander have sent? This wasn't their mother by any means.

"Detective Hobbs," the policeman answered grudgingly. "How did you know where to find your client?"

"Through the magic of cell phonery, Detective. Now that you have harassed Miss Kruger enough to have her story at least a dozen times over, do you have any more relevant questions or is she free to go?"

Julie thought she might faint in relief. Had their mother sent this woman? And if Ana really was an attorney, why did she use another name? There were so many things she needed to say. . . .

The attorney squeezed her arm warningly while the detective spoke.

"I'll need an address and phone where she can be reached," he said gruffly, eyeing the lawyer with suspicion.

She promptly pulled out a business card and handed it over. "Her family won't allow her to stay in this park any longer. They thought this a safe, respectable religious community. To have a young, naïve girl threatened in this manner does not speak well of our country. We give you good day, Detective."

The imperious attorney turned to Julie. "Where is your coat? We'll go pack your bags."

Julie hurried for the nearest exit, clearing a path for her smaller sister. This had to be Ana. She had once dreamed of Ana as a ferocious panther, baring her teeth and growling to keep away evil. She could see now that that had been a child's fantasy. But this petite person had intimidated a burly policeman with just her *attitude.* Only Ana could do that.

Thirteen

Ana officially meets Juliana

I FOLLOWED MY YOUNGER sister as she easily loped through a crowd of people taller than I was. I had purposely worn comfortable boots without heels but regretted it now. Julie was tall and willowy and beautiful—just like every other student I'd seen on Graham's monitor. I wondered if the kids had noticed they'd been chosen on the basis of looks.

But there were more important matters on my mind. As Julie grabbed a bulky cheap pink coat from a hook by the door and stepped outside the dumpy cafe, I caught her arm. "We need to direct the cops to those trenches where the bodies are buried."

She followed me outside and whispered, "You have to be Ana! Why do you call yourself by this other name?

I grinned at her quickness. "You remember me! I hoped you would. You'll understand about the name later. Right now, I need to know what to tell the cops. I want those bodies dug up."

She glanced worriedly toward the dinosaur skeletons. "Do I tell them about the cameras I posted? I was afraid I would be in trouble. The park's cameras were very poor quality and often went out. I wanted to do a good job on my video so I bought better ones."

Which was presumably why her cameras had caught the bodies and the park ones hadn't. Nasty, and I didn't want to turn the cops loose on that piece of information. Once the cops knew that Julie had photos of the bodies, the bad guys would know too, and they'd want to make certain she didn't have photos showing their faces.

I thought about it as we hurried toward the ugly group of dilapidated mobile homes. "I know someone with a security company who can feed them the information. Maybe they'll believe your cameras belong to his company."

"That would be most excellent," she said in relief. "Can he search for Esther and Maryam too?"

"Esther and *who*?" I didn't need any more lost girls on my list. I just wanted Julie home for Christmas and to enjoy a nice simple holiday for a change. If our political kingpins wanted to embezzle and use each other for target practice, it was no concern of mine as long as my family was out of the way.

"Maryam is my roommate. She didn't come home last night. Esther shared the trailer with us when I first arrived. She was always angry, although she never really said why. And then one day she packed up and said she was going home." Julie yanked open the door of a faded blue trailer. The park had evidently not spent money on the students. These tin cans looked older than me.

Girls who didn't come home overnight weren't high on my radar, but one missing for months fell into a pattern.

"But Esther never got home?" I guessed. "How do you know?"

"The office would bring us messages from people trying to reach Esther. The office thought she was still living with us. It seemed strange. And I'd asked Esther to call us when she returned home, and she said she would, but she never did."

I *knew* I hadn't wanted to hear about any more lost girls. I needed to yank Juliana out of this hovel and take her somewhere safe. "Pack everything you own. It won't be healthy to come back here, especially if the gunmen realize you were the one to call the cops. They'll be afraid you were a witness. There are some really bad men using this place for their own purposes."

I hated to scare her, but I knew my family. Julie would dig in her heels for her friends otherwise. She had probably already hung around too long looking for her friends—and *to uncover the mystery*. I sighed in exasperation as I realized this. I should have known.

She threw me a worried look over her shoulder as we entered, but then she shouted for Maryam. Even I could tell the trailer was empty.

"Staying out all night is not enough for panic. Leave her a note with your phone number," I suggested. "Tell her you're going home, and she should do the same. I doubt JACAD will survive much longer, so she might as well leave now."

"I don't like it that she's disappeared. It's not like her," Julie said, pulling items out of cupboards and from inside the bench seats.

I put my panic alert button on hold. Julie came first. "Is your phone completely disabled? You can call her and arrange to meet her in town." I found a box and started adding the items she retrieved into it.

"My phone is *bugged*," she said with surprising vehemence. "I have quit using it."

Argghhh, panic alert flashing. What on earth had she got herself into? I needed her out of here yesterday. "Keep it turned off. We can unbug it. Leave your number. Save the burner for emergencies. Zander will be out here looking for us if we don't return soon. I practically had to tie him to a chair."

I began throwing things into her boxes as fast as I could.

"Zander is really here?" she asked, finally showing excitement. "He came for me?"

Relieved to have a less stressful subject, I started on the suitcase. "What did you think he would do when you didn't answer his messages? I think you took years off his life. I'm just glad he had the sense to come to us. I wish I'd known you were here sooner."

She turned and hugged me. It was awkward. She was over half a foot taller and I didn't do hugs. But I patted her shoulder and appreciated the gesture.

I had my toddlers back, and my heart felt whole for the first time in forever—although in this family, that might last all of ten minutes. I glanced out the window to be certain no one was watching.

"I didn't know you were here!" Julie cried. "I had hoped to look for our grandfather. My father left us his address. But then so much started happening. . ." She gestured helplessly and returned to shoving clothes in a suitcase. "It is amazing to see you again! I didn't think you would remember us."

"I doubt a day went by that I didn't think of you," I said gruffly, hiding my reaction. I quit crying long, long ago, but having my family together again. . . cracked the bomb shelter I'd built around my heart.

"My family still speaks of you with awe," she said with a laugh. "You must come home with me sometime and meet them. I cannot believe you came for me! Are you really a lawyer?"

I didn't even have a high school diploma, since we never stayed in one place for me to graduate. I had my GED and my online courses, but a lawyer? In another lifetime. "'Fraid not," I admitted. "I lie for a living."

She looked up from her packing to stare. "That can't be true. You are an honest person."

I checked cabinets for anything that looked as if it didn't belong.

"What on earth makes you say that? I'm unfortunately like our mother. I am whatever I need to be at the moment."

"I don't know our mother, but it's not you." She shook her head. She wore her tight curls a little longer than Zander's, but not by much. Her head and cheekbones were so elegantly sculpted that they didn't require the disguise of hair. "Perhaps you lie to others, but not to family."

I considered that. "It's okay to lie to others if I don't lie to family?"

"And friends," she added firmly. "With those close to us, we must be honest, or we cannot trust each other."

That set a standard I couldn't promise to keep, but I appreciated the thought.

"Where are we going?" she asked as she zipped her suitcase.

"To our grandfather's house. He died last spring and left it to all of us." Already, I was lying. Or half-lying by insinuating the house actually belonged to us. It was so much more convenient than long, involved explanations.

A variety of expressions crossed her face. Unlike Zander, she couldn't conceal an emotion if she tried.

"I am sorry to hear about our grandfather, but I am very surprised that he left Zander and me anything. He did not know us. We live half a world away. He had no reason to even acknowledge our existence since our parents did not marry. Are you sure he meant us?"

I hefted the box and let her haul the suitcases. "His *grandchildren* covers all of us. He knew what he was doing. There are many complications still, but we'll work our way through them. I just want you to recognize the house as yours as much as it is any of ours."

A single home for all our family had been a goal of mine since Patra was born, and I was old enough to change her diapers as we escaped still another war-torn town on a train in the dark of night. I doubted anyone understood my degree of determination.

Juliana stopped to scribble a note to her friend and laid it in the middle of the table, firmly held down by salt and pepper shakers. "I do not know what I will do with myself if the school closes. My degree in art does me little good."

"A degree in anything shows that you have a well-rounded

education and the ability to work hard for what you want. It's worth a great deal," I argued as we left the trailer and locked it behind us.

I checked my watch—just after noon. If we could make it out of here without interruption, the car should have us home before EG.

I scanned the muddy field between us and the gate. Police cars everywhere, yellow crime scene tape tied to winter-bare trees in the distance, a few uniforms blocking the road. I'd called the limo in light of Julie's urgent message but ordered it to park out of sight. I texted the driver to pull up now.

Graham's luxuries were corrupting me beyond redemption. I punched in a call to Patra as we trudged toward the gate. Now that Juliana was safe, I was free to wreak havoc.

"News flash," I said to her voice mail. "Talk to Zander, then start checking into JACAD and Reverend Arden. I've got Juliana. See you at dinner."

"How is the reverend, do you know?" Julie asked anxiously when I stored the phone in my pocket.

"I'd only just heard about him when we received your message. If anyone can find out, we can, but I want you safe under our roof before we start making inquiries. If you want honesty, you'll have more than you can handle once we're there. You're not going to like it."

"Everyone treats me as if I'm a fragile fairy," she said with a hint of hurt. "I am not. I set up those cameras on my own. I knew when my phone wasn't right. I wanted to find out what was going on by myself."

"And we respected that," I reminded her as a policeman blocked our way. I flashed my fake lawyer business card. "Detective Hobbs said we could leave," I said in my best voice of authority.

He made a call, then opened the gate to let us pass. People had begun to gather outside. I figured some might even be reporters, but the limo rolled through, nudging them from the road. Sam, Graham's driver, leapt out to load our box and suitcases, and I shoved Juliana inside before most of the lookie-loos thought to whip out cameras or snap phones.

As the limo rolled back to the highway, I pulled out my phone, connected with my cloud account, and produced the screensaver photo Graham had sent. "I don't know if you can recognize anyone on this small screen, but do you see your friend Esther in this image?"

She enlarged the image and steadily worked her way around the buffet table. She punched some buttons and handed back a cropped image of a chestnut-colored chignon. The head was slightly turned so I could see a rather emphatic chin and tan complexion. What I noticed most was that this was the pretty young thing George Paycock, the Embezzler, had his arm wrapped around.

"That could be Esther," Julie said. "She wore her hair like that once when she went to a concert. The coloring looks right. Why?"

I fought a nervous shiver, saved the image, and opened it back to the larger one. "Because two of the women we've identified in this photo were JACAD students. One of them died. The other is living with an older, wealthy man, one of the development's supporters. And you're telling me Esther and maybe your roommate are missing. As far as I can determine, a large number of the men around this table are contributors to Jesus World."

She took the phone back and studied the image some more. "I did not accept the one invitation I was offered to the theater, but the other students sought them eagerly. They would tell of the concerts, but no one mentioned parties." She zoomed in again. "But I think I recognize three, maybe four of these women as students I have seen. This is a small school, but our classrooms are scattered, and the second year students are in different offices around town. I've probably talked to them in the canteen."

"What about the men? Did you ever meet any of the development's sponsors?"

She shook her head and handed the phone back. "No, never. I do not like parties. I am most surprised that these students in the photo owned gowns and jewels."

"I suspect that the men bought them what they wanted," I said cynically, returning the phone to my bag. "I think it's a good thing you don't like parties."

She made an inelegant noise. "I am not white enough for parties like that. I cannot pass for European. Even Maryam, who is half English, half Pakistani, was not invited, even to a concert, until recently. I thought at first I was being ignored because I had not worked hard enough. Now I see the truth."

I frowned, trying to work that out. "The students here come from all around the world. They are of every color, and from what I have seen, they are all beautiful. You are saying only the white ones were invited to concerts and parties?"

"Only the whiter *women*. There are no male students at that table." She leaned wearily against the headrest. "I made videos to promote the park which I've been told are very successful—possibly because everyone here is photogenic. I had not given that much thought until now. I just thought I'd been lucky in my choice of shots, but you're right. In all my classes, there is probably not one person who would not look good on camera. It probably helps in fundraising."

As did showing off the students at concerts and dinners, I thought cynically. And girls willing to be used in that way . . . were either naïve or looking for a sugar daddy.

"So whoever chose students to study or work at Jesus World did not choose by color but looks, and one hopes, by education and inclination?"

She nodded agreement. "Their applications were very rigorous, which is why I did not think so much about how we looked. All of us are college graduates, many of us at the top of our classes, all recommended by our churches and communities. This is a very small but prestigious program."

"How long has the program been in place?"

She wrinkled her nose—Magda's patrician nose—in thought. "Reverend Arden's church was building schools in our village when I was very young, so at least for fifteen years, probably longer, well before Jesus World existed. I know the workers who built the school in Zimbabwe that I worked on weren't beautiful. What would be the purpose?"

"I think the *park* makes the difference. Whoever is sponsoring it hopes beautiful people will help raise funds and work at the park after it opens," I suggested. "They want good-looking representatives for marketing purposes."

"All good Christians are handsome?" she asked in disbelief. "Is such blatant discrimination not illegal in this country?"

"Discriminating by religion is illegal, so they'll have a tough time working around that law when it comes time to hire—another good reason to have all of you on board already. Hiring based on looks. . . that's not illegal, unless it's obviously race, which it isn't. I'd like to talk to whoever did the student screening, but that's only because I'm nosy. I can't see how it affects anything else."

"I should have found work in the administration department

instead of marketing and learned more about their acceptance policies," she said with a sigh.

"Then you wouldn't have had those camera images. And you had no way of knowing the reverend would be shot and that you'd have to leave so precipitously. One thing at a time. Once you tell me as much as you know about Esther, we'll dig around and find out more."

"Do you think I am the only one on the entire campus who did not understand that rich old men might gift us with gowns and jewels if we smiled on them?" she asked.

"Did Rebecca and Melissa and Esther and the others you recognized in the photo know each other?" I asked, guessing the answer just from her frown.

"They were second year students. This is not a university. There is a limited number of classes for learning how to build schools, depending on which direction one takes, so yes, they would have shared a class or two and known each other."

She closed her eyes and shook her head in disbelief. "I cannot accept that Reverend Arden knew we were being used in this way. He kept telling me that hard workers ought to be rewarded with occasional time off. The office never offered me tickets, as they did the others. *He* was the one who offered me tickets."

Fourteen

Ana introduces Julie to their mother

FORTUNATELY, WE ARRIVED HOME before EG. Magda was front and center when I entered with Juliana. Rather than confront her with my suspicions, I left the twins happily hugging each other and chattering with their new-found mother while, duty done, I trudged upstairs to Graham's lair.

"If the cops are any good, they'll find Juliana's cameras," I told Graham as I entered. "We need to send them the clips so they can locate the bodies."

"Done," he said curtly. "I've moved her video cloud account and disconnected any trace of the old one. All the cameras feed into CAD's storage now."

I'd stripped off my hat and coat as I climbed the stairs, but I hadn't returned to my room to deposit them yet. Now that I'd done all I knew to do, I felt as if the entire weight of the world was on my shoulders as I turned to leave. I had my family under my roof, but that didn't make the cruel world outside go away.

"Joshua Arden's father is a decent man," Graham said. He still hadn't turned away from his monitors.

He did not feed me information without reason. I dropped the heavy coat on the floor and sank down on it, resting my forehead against my knees. "Do I really want to hear this?"

He actually swung his desk chair around to look at me. Graham is everything in a man that I want. The electricity between us is lightning bolt shocking. That he actually dragged his OCD self away from his monitors should have straightened my spine and made me preen.

But I was having heavy-duty flashbacks to my Magda-dominated youth, and it was all I could do to resist the urge to find a cave somewhere and pull the mountain down around my introverted self. The downside of one of my Magda-like performances is total energy drainage. I needed to rest and regroup.

"I grudgingly admit that our working together has proved beneficial," he said.

That shocked me out of my foul mood. My head shot up, and I narrowed my eyes at him. "Are you looking for a fight? Because I could kick you six ways from Sunday right now."

I swear, his eyes crinkled with what might have been laughter. Maybe. Possibly. But he hid it quickly and returned to growling.

"Magda has a long-standing feud with General Defense Industries."

I reeled that name through my encyclopedic brain and recalled it as the company Georgie the Embezzler had hoodwinked. It also resonated with some deeper memory I couldn't pull up. They probably had a CEO in Paul Rose's cabal of powerful lunatics.

"Gun makers," I dutifully replied. "She hates them all."

"They killed our fathers. She has reason. Once upon a time, Reverend William Arden—Josh's father—advocated gun control. From the power of his pulpit, he condemned weapons manufacturers for creating a culture of world violence. He started a movement that actually put gun control laws on the desks of Congress."

"Before my time," I suggested.

I'd have to look up William Arden. My isolated childhood hadn't contained computers or even televisions most of the time. I missed a lot of pop culture references. I only knew Brody Devlin, my father, from microfiche newspaper articles I hunted when I had the chance.

"Ancient history," he agreed. "Our fathers laughed at him."

"Negotiating peace was not a concept most angry young men, can relate to." I'd been in war zones. I'd seen the fury of frustration fueled by testosterone and fed by politicians with agendas. My father's generation wasn't the first or the last to believe violence would cure the ills of the world.

I had only a vague understanding of my father's history. I hadn't fully realized Graham's father was a part of his cadre of angry young men. I knew Graham had been my grandfather's protégé, so it made sense that his father and my father had been in cahoots in some manner. And presumably, Sean O'Herlihy, Patra's lover and a man almighty curious about our family, had a father who had been in the same gang—the name was a dead giveaway.

"Our fathers related to peace well enough," Graham corrected. "They simply thought it had to come at the point of a gun since the ballot box was loaded. But by that time, everyone in Ireland was tired of the fighting, and our fathers were willing to negotiate—from a position of strength."

"While this is all very interesting, why are we discussing it now?" I crossed my legs on my faux fur coat and studied Graham's scarred face. He'd been through hell. I was inclined to believe he was on the side of the good guys, but in our world, good was a lighter shade of gray.

"Because William Arden was a brilliant, determined man who threatened GenDef's bottom line in every way he could. Your father was a famous, fiery orator. He raised sympathy for the plight of the Irish Catholics while he was raising funds to secretly import weapons for a terrorist organization. Money, weapons, and international sympathy for his cause would give Brody the strength to return to Ireland and make demands."

I waved away this deluge of words. "History of the World 101. I take it you're telling me that Arden used my father as a tool in his political arsenal and talked him out of buying GenDef's weapons?"

"Your mother did. She convinced Brody to listen to Arden."

My mother? *Magda* talked my father out of blowing up half Ireland? I tried to process this but my mind wouldn't compute and Graham kept talking.

"You'll have to ask Magda what the discussion was. I don't even know for fact that the purchase was cancelled. The world was told that our fathers died in a disagreement over weapons, and everyone assumed it was over type of gun or price or just a deal gone sour. But the rest I learned from your grandfather. At that time, you were a toddler, your father wanted peace, and his only enemies were presumably across the pond. Nothing short of a deal gone bad could have justified blowing up three promising young men."

Oh crap. My mother had told me flat out that she blamed herself for my father's death. She'd spent her life avenging him— undoubtedly fighting the weapons dealers she thought had killed him. In my own sick way, I had to admire her determination. Guns were the tools of the devil—or so she'd taught me.

She'd also been so furious with my grandfather that she'd turned her back on all his wealth and never returned. At one point, she'd told me they'd argued and she'd called him an Oracle of Mammon. My tired brain kicked that over and I winced.

My grandfather had been an extremely wealthy man who had

been hand in glove with the kind of corporate sharks behind Senator Paul Rose's current campaign. That meant his investments had undoubtedly included weapons manufacturers. In a way, we were now living off blood money. I could see where Magda might refuse to take it.

Magda and William Arden had talked my father out of buying guns. I got it, sort of.

"You want me to talk to Joshua's father," I said, rubbing my forehead and trying to rearrange my thoughts. "You think GenDef is involved in the park, at the very least. Weapons and Jesus do not compute."

"They do if Joshua Arden needed funds for the park, and Paul Rose needed the support of Josh's large fan base. Desperate people make strange bedfellows. I sent a file to your box." He wheeled back to his bank of monitors and scrolled through visuals of the park gates—where reporters were gathering. He brought up shots of the hospital—where a vigil of Arden fans held candles.

So, GenDef had probably had a lot of people killed over the years, including my father and Graham's. I let that knowledge sink in. What were a few assassinations measured against the hundreds of thousands of innocent people their *guns* had killed? GenDef and their lobbyists were responsible for corrupting a lot of silly people into believing prophets and George Washington carried AK-47s, fine.

I didn't like any of it. But right now, right this minute, all the people who mattered to me were safe and almost all under one roof. I determinedly ignored Juliana's concern for her roommates.

"Make me care," I muttered obstinately. "I do not want to be part of Magda's vendetta."

He gave a frustrated sigh but didn't turn around. "I don't *want* you involved. I want you and your siblings scattered across the country, teaching school and petting ponies. I want Magda and her cohorts to all go to a hell of their own making. And I want peace on earth and goodwill toward mankind."

He zoomed up two monitors to show videos of Patra and Nick. Patra was looking rather posh in a fitted red cashmere blazer and matching beret she'd no doubt bought at a thrift store since her paycheck wouldn't cover it. Her red lip-sticked smile dazzled a security guard—outside the hospital? I'd told her to check on the park story.

Nick—my lovely golden Nick—was looking harassed. The Windsor knot in his pink and blue tie was loose, and he ran his hand through his thick hair as he engaged in argument—discussion—with his British embassy employers. Nick never argued exactly. He talked people to death. I'd comment on Graham's spying on an ally embassy but I was too busy trying to figure out what Nick was doing.

Graham zoomed closer, shutting out people and focusing on a desk covered in glossy photos—photos of my father, me, Magda, and *Juliana*. In the photo, Julie was talking to Joshua Arden in a ratty-looking coffee shop.

Patra was already investigating GenDef. Nick was being asked about us. My family was already involved in this rubbish. My opting out wouldn't help.

"Filthy bad word." I dragged myself and my coat up. "This all has to be Magda's fault somehow." I lied, but it made me feel better to blame her.

"This"—he gestured at the screens—"is why I want you out of here."

"That"—I leaned over his broad shoulder, hit the keyboard, scrambling his monitors, then bit his ear lobe—"is why I cannot leave."

This time, instead of letting me go, he reacted. He grabbed my waist, yanked me down on his lap, and kissed me until I thought my head had lifted from my body and my mind had entered an altered state. One thing to say about quiet men, they could be explosive kissers.

"I know," he growled against my ear when he'd put me in my place. "And that is what is making me crazy."

"Crazier." I stood and straightened out my sadly wrinkled lawyer suit. "There is no sane place for intelligent people in this world."

With that pithy, if somewhat ambiguous, remark, I gathered my coat and hat and departed.

Juliana meets her mother

"MY, LOOK AT THE two of you! You were adorable as toddlers but now—you're nothing less than impressive. I can see your father so clearly. . . ." Their mother sniffed tearfully and patted Julie's cheek.

Strangely, Magda was not the vision Julie recalled from her oldest memories. She'd no doubt embroidered reality with the fairy tales Ana had read to her. Magda was merely a statuesque middle-aged woman with dyed blond hair, impressive cheekbones, and a domineering personality. Julie had lots of experience with domineering personalities. Her *antie* and *gogo* had out-domineered Magda. Nothing beat having your own family war party.

"It is good to finally meet you as an adult," Julie said, hugging Magda again and feeling her mother resist the gesture. Then turning to Zander, she gave him another enthusiastic hug. He was more receptive. "Thank you for looking for me. I really was fine, you know."

"Not if you couldn't communicate with me," he said stiffly, leading the way into a formal parlor adorned with an eccentrically tilted Christmas tree. Julie pulled out her phone, wanting to take a photo, then remembered the bug just in time.

She held out the phone to Zander. "Ana says the bug can be removed. Do you know how?"

Magda exclaimed in annoyance, grabbed the phone, and marched off with it. "I'll be right back. I just had my fingernails done and don't want to break them."

They both watched her go. Zander shook his head in bewilderment. "I have imagined meeting our mother in many ways, but I have never thought of her as. . ."

"A one-woman army?" Julie suggested. "Really, our father tried to tell us. It is our own fault if we did not believe."

"She is very beautiful," Zander said with a hint of uncertainty.

"But we are looking for a mother, someone human. I am sure she is a very good person, but we were probably better off being raised by our *anties*." Julie wandered over to examine the tree. She found the hanging photo ornament immediately. "Is this our grandparents?"

"Yes, and Magda as a child. Our brother Nicholas hung that. I want to think of something personal I can hang, so they remember us when we are home again." Zander leaned over to examine the packages under the tree. "I have ordered a few gifts. Do you think we might stay until after the holiday?"

"What about your employer?" she asked, crouching down to read the tags.

"Work is slow this time of year. I have emailed them to say I am meeting with a very important client. Ana has asked me to look after one of our grandfather's funds. There may be more, so I am being honest."

"There is a package for me!" She rattled the oddly decorated box.

"I think the package you are holding is from Elizabeth Georgiana, our youngest sister. Her wrappings are. . . interesting."

The paper was purple with super-hero characters and a big black bow. Julie smiled and allowed herself to relax, just a little. She had been worried about her friends and Reverend Arden and what she would do next, but right now, right this moment, she was safe with her twin and the mysterious family she'd always wondered about.

"I should go shopping for gifts too. I have been afraid to do anything online for fear that I was being watched." She sat cross-legged beneath the tree, found the tree light switch, and turned them on against the dull gray day outside.

The lights flashed like a little piece of heaven against the cheap plastic ornaments and the colorful packages.

"Do you have any idea why you were being watched? Or if everyone was?" Ana asked, striding into the room.

Julie glanced up and blinked in surprise. The assured, sophisticated lawyer had morphed into a short woman in an ugly denim maxi dress over a knit Henley. Without any of her earlier toughness, Ana curled her legs up in an old chair and simply waited for an answer. She was wearing what appeared to be sandals with heavy socks. Only the shiny black braid remained the same.

"You are a chameleon," Julie exclaimed. "But you choose not to blend into these elegant surroundings. Why is that?"

Ana's long dark lashes blinked in surprise, then she tilted her head in consideration. "A chameleon changes colors when it feels threatened. Here, I'm at home and can be myself. I am an introvert by nature, a basement-residing spider who prefers to watch the world through my computers."

"Agoraphobia is the danger of introversion," the lamp beside the chair intoned.

Julie thought her eyes might pop out. She stared as Ana patted the lamp shade fondly.

"That's Amadeus Graham, the pot calling the kettle black," Ana explained. "Except he's not a natural introvert, just a tarantula hiding in the dark, waiting for his next victim. Never expect privacy in this house. Back to the bug in your phone. . . ." She waited expectantly.

Magda sailed in, holding said phone out in triumph. "All better now. I'll see if anyone can trace that fairly crude mechanism."

Ana snatched the phone from her mother's hand before Julie could stand up. She pulled a tool out of her dress pocket, pried the back off, and removed a tiny card. "There, now you can turn on the GPS when you want, and Magda doesn't have to know if you're meeting your boyfriends."

Zander took the phone and handed it over to Julie so she didn't need to stand up. "I see I have much to learn if I'm to know our family," he said warily.

Magda glared at Ana, who didn't even bother turning to look at their mother.

"Understand that you are loved," Ana said. "But accept that our love comes in the form of protection, which means we all lack privacy. I try to respect boundaries. Magda doesn't know boundaries exist. And Graham. . . I won't even try to explain. But we need to know who was watching you and why, because it wasn't us doing it, so it was most likely someone who didn't have your best interests at heart."

Julie bit her bottom lip, studied her newly-freed phone, and reluctantly responded. "I told my supervisor I thought the security cameras had caught a man being murdered, and I stupidly showed her the image on my phone."

Fifteen

Ana ponders family

I WATCHED AS MAGDA pretended to study the Christmas tree while Julie spoke. The whole setting felt exceedingly strange, yet strangely familiar. I had barely shared the same space with our mother in a decade. It had been nearly twenty years since we'd jointly shared a home with the twins. I felt the presence of the twins' formidable father. Before he died, he had been that strong a character.

If I felt him, how did Magda feel?

But Magda was an adult who could take care of herself. The twins weren't quite there yet, so I focused on Juliana's horrifying revelation.

"Mrs. Overcamp treated me as if I were a criminal after I showed her that photo," Julie explained in bafflement. "I wanted to call the police. She said the administration would handle it. It looked as if a body had been dumped into one of the construction holes, and she didn't immediately call someone to look? I was appalled and confused. Shortly after that, I couldn't find my phone. I retraced my steps, hunted all over, and it turned up in my desk the next day. I *never* kept it there. So I was suspicious. And then I noticed the battery ran down too quickly. I got very nervous after that."

"I assume that was the end of October, early November? The same time you drew out all your cash and stopped using your bank account?" I probed deeper, hoping this was the only incident that had panicked her.

"I didn't like knowing my phone was bugged. I assumed my computer was also not private," she said with a shrug. "I was taught to keep a stash of money for emergencies, so I went to town and withdrew everything. As odd events continued, I didn't return to the bank. I feared I might be followed. I tried to stay to myself and monitor my cameras in hopes of finding definitive evidence of what was happening."

"You should have notified us at once!" Magda exclaimed.

Julie looked mulish. I tried not to roll my eyes.

"She doesn't know us any better than she knows Mrs. Overcamp," I pointed out. "Even less so, actually. Julie did exactly what she should have done under the circumstances—look for evidence to give to the authorities. But now it's time to combine our knowledge and try to figure out what is happening."

Magda hadn't sat down since she'd returned to the room. She was like a trapped bird. She flitted to the foyer doorway again, and I could feel her tension. I knew what came next and didn't even bother to turn to see her scowl.

"It's rather obvious what is happening. I'll handle this. Tell Elizabeth I'll see her tomorrow. I may be late this evening." She took flight down the hall.

"Mallard will be disappointed you won't be home for dinner," I said to the empty doorway.

So would EG, but she's a tough little kid and was used to our vanishing mother. The twins. . . looked a little shell-shocked.

"This is why your father let your family take you away," I explained as gently as I could. "But you're adults now. You make your own decisions. As I've told you, this house belongs to you as much as any of us, so you're welcome to stay. For now, the expenses for food and Mallard and so forth come out of our family account, but you'll have to pay for personal items yourself until everything is sorted out."

"But what of Reverend Arden?" Julie cried. "I cannot go home until I know what is happening."

I hid my smile of satisfaction. "Then we work together to find out. Zander is helping by digging through the foundation's accounts. Do you think you could start contacting all the students you know to ask about your missing friends? And possibly find out more about the parties the second year students attended?"

Julie nodded. "Is there a computer I can use?"

Zander and I exchanged grins. He'd learned quickly that computers were our bread and butter.

GRAHAM HAD ARRANGED A meeting between me and Reverend William Arden. I was already heading for the Metro when Nick called me.

"Is Juliana okay?" he asked first.

"She's with us. Graham is spying on the embassy," I informed him as I hurried down the wintry street. "You don't have to get involved if it's a problem for your career."

"I'm not certain I'm cut out to be a flunky," he said unhappily. "General Defense is an international industry with offices in the UK. The ambassador wants to know what Graham knows about them, and they're encouraging me to stay in the mansion for Christmas, which means they've bugged my phone or my suitcase or something because they know Graham is bugging them. I think I'll go back to cheating at cards. It's less stressful."

"I'll have Zander send you his analysis of the GenDef embezzlement and how the funds were being shunted through Jesus World. That ought to give them a bone to gnaw on while Magda struts her stuff. Best not to discuss more on the phone. Come home and Graham will find the bugs and send your Brits whatever makes him happy. Keep remembering that once we have our finances straightened out, you won't have to work for them if you don't want to. That might throw them into a bit of a tizzy."

I could almost *hear* him smile. "I like that, a gentleman of leisure condescending to give them the time of day out of loyalty to the Crown. It's flunkydom to which I object. Power, I can handle."

I snorted inelegantly. That was *so* Nick—Queen of the World. "I'm heading into the Metro. See you at dinner?"

He agreed and signed off. I checked my watch. I'd left EG happily working with Julie on video footage, so she should be well occupied for the moment. If Nick went to the house for dinner, I could take as long as I needed. Rush hour to Alexandria was not a good commute by rail or car.

I caught my Uber lift from the Metro station to the Reverend William Arden's spacious home and grounds outside Alexandria. An electronic gate blocked the drive. A reporter hanging out on the corner noted the Uber car's license plate—one of the many reasons I didn't like limos; their tags can be traced back to the owner. The driver announced my name into the intercom and the gate swung open.

I gave the Uber driver a tip and told him that, if anyone asked him, I was the good reverend's substitute nurse. The driver grinned and pocketed the extra cash. Since the Uber website specified that customers needn't tip, he probably didn't see a lot of cash coming his way. I expected he'd be happy to oblige.

Normally, I'd wear full-dress business camouflage at an interview with a stranger, but I was a little shocked by Julie's observation of my chameleon habits. I had decided to stay truer to myself while still being respectful of an elder and a friend of Graham's. I wore comfortable leggings, a long sweater, and my leopard boots. I could pass as a home nurse.

A slight, gray-haired woman in tailored tweed and sturdy shoes answered the door. I introduced myself, and she led the way to a dark, paneled den. I admired the overflowing wall-to-wall bookshelves, but the light was too dim to discern titles.

Arden rose from behind his desk. I'd done my research and knew he was in his eighties and had been physically frail these past years. But he retained a full head of silver hair, a craggy jaw cut much like his son's, and a towering height that even now, reduced to skeletal, seemed powerful.

"Magda's daughter," he said in amazement as he studied me. "As I live and breathe, this I never expected. Have a seat. I've called for tea and coffee. When Amadeus phoned, I thought he was pulling one over on an old man, but you look just like your parents."

"Graham respects you too much to lie to you," I said. "And I'm thrilled to meet someone who knew my father. That doesn't happen often."

He nodded sadly and sitting down again, folded his gnarled and spotted hands over his royal blue sweater. "Brody Devlin was a brilliant man with a promising future. He could have accomplished so much had he lived. It takes all my faith in God to accept that the good die young for a greater purpose."

"Well, religion likes its martyrs, I suppose. I can't say his death and the others with him improved the world in any great way, not if they were about to end the violence." I didn't have much patience for making nicey-nice, and I didn't want to take a lot of his time, so I directed the conversation to my purpose in coming here. "How is your son?" I asked as the housekeeper returned and filled our cups.

"He's in ICU and they're keeping him sedated. One bullet grazed his head and caused swelling in his brain. We're praying for a full recovery." His sadness was so palpable, the housekeeper patted his shoulder and shot me a nasty look.

He waited until she left before continuing. "You are not here to ask about Josh. Magda told you the true story about your father, did she? It's not what the world believes."

"No, Graham told me what little he knows. Magda has been on a vendetta ever since they died. She blamed my grandfather, I believe, and she's not happy with me for returning to his house. But that's not why I'm here. I'm here because I'm afraid General Defense may be involved in your son's shooting. I'm hoping you will trust Graham and me to track down the shooter."

He looked even sadder as he sipped his coffee. "I warned Josh multiple times that he was in over his head, but he wanted to make a name for himself. He didn't want to ride on my coat tails, as he put it. He's a good man, but he's never had to raise money the way I did. I fear he's financially naïve. Jesus World was all his own idea, a means to finance his school building projects."

"Just buying the park land would have cost heaven and earth. He needed wealthy supporters," I said without inflection, sipping my tea—an excellent Darjeeling.

"His mother left him much of that property. He has ardent supporters who helped with the planning and fundraising. Joshua is dedicated to his cause, to both the school program and the park." The wily fox waited to see how much I knew.

"Your son publicly supports Paul Rose's candidacy for president, and Paul Rose's confederates financially support your son's projects in return. I am not my parents' daughter for nothing—I understand what happens behind the scenes. From the looks of it, the embezzler at General Defense ran his ill-gotten gains through your son's foundation. I would like to believe your son knew nothing of this. Perhaps he found out and is in a position to testify?" I suggested.

The old man's face collapsed in a waterfall of wrinkles as he rested his chin on his chest. "He swore to me that he knew nothing of the embezzlement from GenDef, but he admitted he left the financials to others. His interest was in fundraising and overseeing the park. I believe him. He isn't a political creature. He accepts people at face value. I wouldn't trust GenDef's management, but Josh has no reason to question them. They don't hate him as they do me."

"I want to believe that for my sister's sake. Juliana admires your son and is devoted to the school program. She's been taking classes and helping out at the park, but there are activities there that even caused her to doubt. Like your son, she takes people at face value, so if she dared to question those activities. . ."

"Perhaps Josh did too, you're asking? It's possible. He wouldn't have confided in me, if he did. Father-son rivalry is never pretty, and he would hate to admit that he had been wrong. So if you're hoping I can lead you in the right direction, you'll have to return to Amadeus empty-handed."

I rubbed my brow and sought a new direction—missing students. "Did he ever mention anything of the concert tickets and parties his students attended? I believe the tickets were provided by some of the park's sponsors."

The good reverend frowned. "He mentioned that the foundation was often given concert tickets, and the students enjoyed rubbing elbows with the sponsors. Part of the school training is about fundraising, so I assume learning to visit with the wealthy was part of his program. But I would be wary of anything voluntarily given by some of his corporate sponsors. They are wicked men of Mammon, not of God."

Well, now I knew where Magda had come up with the reference to Mammon.

"Anyone you specifically consider wicked? Embezzlement and shooting cover a lot of territory."

He narrowed his eyes, presumably in thought. "I am not close to the park project and don't know all the names involved. But some of Rose's close friends have been mentioned, and I wouldn't trust most of them. George Paycock from GenDef, of course, was on the board. He's been known as a womanizer for years and now he's been accused of embezzling. Tony Jeffery, George's boss, actually seems to be a decent fellow, though. I believe I heard Tony's daughter Laura might take George's place. Ed Parker is still on the board, I believe, but I've never heard anything untoward of him. He fancies himself an intellectual, but that doesn't make him wicked. I wouldn't suspect him of hurting anyone and certainly not Josh."

I wished I dared record this, but I didn't want to interrupt his ruminations.

"The others, well—Archie Broderick was on the park board. I would be suspicious of anything he did, but since his media corporation collapsed, I haven't heard any scandal about him. Goldrich, from the mortgage company, has always been slime. I wouldn't trust him with my piggy bank. Neil Hammond, from Hammond oil, has been going through a messy divorce. I wouldn't trust him with my daughter, if I had one, but he doesn't need money. If it helps, I'll try to think of others involved in the project."

I nodded, not giving away that I'd had anything to do with the demise of several of those greedmeister careers. "Please, if you would. I think I know most of the names, but it wouldn't hurt to compare. Did Josh ever mention drop-outs from his program?" I asked, digging desperately to the bottom of my list of questions.

"Not that I'm aware of, but drop-outs are hardly unusual. Most of the students are young and don't know what they wish to make of their lives yet. Dedicating their lives to helping others is not always a gratifying path, as Amadeus learned the hard way. What is he doing now? I was told he was dead until he called and reassured me otherwise."

Fair was fair. I gave him a carefully edited version of Graham's successful security business without explaining that he was hiding in our attic using a dead man's name.

"And your mother?" he asked when I finished. "You said she was on a vendetta. Does she still believe in her conspiracy theory about your father's death?"

"As far as I'm aware, evil finds evil, so there will always be connections that invite conspiracy theories. Whether there is any actual purpose or intelligent thought behind those connections is a matter of opinion. Magda doesn't confide in me. You might be interested to know that another of her daughters is currently dating Sean O'Herlihy, son of another of my father's friends. It's a small world."

He almost smiled. "It's good to know the world goes on despite the devastation we inflict upon it. Shall I give your name to the hospital as someone allowed to visit Josh when he awakens?"

Do boll weevils love cotton? I tried not to display my eagerness when I nodded. "Graham would appreciate that." I had saved my warning for last, hoping not to alarm a frail old man, but he seemed to still be a tough buzzard, so I added, "He also told me to tell you that it would be best to station guards at your son's door. If Joshua knows something worth being killed for, there's likely to be another attempt. Graham can provide the guards, if you like."

I threw in that last on my own. I hated to worry the old man who had been so kind, if not helpful. Graham could suck it up.

Reverend Arden closed his eyes as if in prayer, then nodded

reluctantly. "Yes, I think that would be best. I know police are stationed there now, but one never knows. . . ."

"Exactly. One never knows. I'll tell Graham to increase the security. Please, let us know if you hear anything, and I mean *anything*, that might help us get to the bottom of this. I believe my grandfather would have wanted us to help."

An old-fashioned gentleman, he rose when I did, holding out his hand to take the card I offered. "Max would have had his hand in the pie, one way or another. He was a man of Mammon, also, craving riches, so we did not always agree. Still, after Magda's departure, I believe he learned wealth was not everything. He told me shortly before his death that he was shedding his investments in the weapon industry."

Pow, socked in the jaw with still another reason why Max might have died, but the reverend didn't need to know that, and I didn't want to invite Magda's conspiracy theories. We made our farewells, and I called for my Uber car as the housekeeper led me to the door. As we waited, I impulsively handed the woman my card. "If the reverend needs anything, let us know. His family and mine are old friends, and we need to look out for each other in these desperate times."

I gave her one of my real cards, with my real name. She glanced down and smiled when she read it. "Brody's daughter? Your parents were frequent visitors long, long ago. I think Josh may have had a crush on your mother at one time."

I almost sank through the floor and simply nodded dumbly as the same car that had brought me here blew its horn in the drive. Learning the past had a twisted way of affecting the present.

The football hero reverend and my cynical, devious mother? The mind boggled.

Sixteen

Ana gathers her family

"NICK BROUGHT MORE PRESENTS!" EG exclaimed, dancing through the hall when I returned home. "And Zander is upstairs wrapping his. This will be the best Christmas ever!"

No matter how world-weary I became, I'd always have this moment of pure joy. The cynical, purple-haired gremlin who had showed up at my door last spring was now an almost-normal nine-year-old bouncing with perfectly ordinary holiday excitement.

"We're all buying you toads," I told her, hanging onto the tote bag on my shoulder which held a few stocking stuffers I'd picked up on the way home from my visit with Josh Arden's father. "Purple toads, sparkly toads, horned toads. How many are we for dinner?"

Being a fan of bats and not toads, she grimaced and attempted to peek in my bag.

"The gang's all here," Nick announced, emerging from the library across the hall. "Patra is upstairs with Juliana, primping and exchanging dirty family secrets."

"The whole gang?" I asked, lifting a knowing eyebrow as EG gave up on spying and danced off to examine presents again.

"Well, except the head cuckoo," he said, understanding. "Mallard is crushed but keeping a stiff upper lip."

Our tough butler idolized Magda, doting on the memory of her as a little girl. He tolerated us because we'd brought her home after all these years. Magda thrived on adrenalin these days and would never settle down, but like so many, Mallard liked to dream of the good old days that never really were.

"Now, if we could drag Graham from the attic, we could have a true three-ring circus," I said in mixed satisfaction and frustration. I wanted family around me. Graham was becoming part of my family, but he refused to acknowledge it. Smart boy.

Zander trailed out of the library bearing his tablet computer. He solemnly showed us the screen.

Body-sniffing dogs had led the police to the grave in Julie's photos. They'd uncovered one corpse and the dog indicated there were others. The headlines screamed about the good reverend being a suspect. Dang. I'd been afraid of that.

Pragmatically, I hoped it drew attention away from Julie, because I knew she wouldn't let up about her missing friends. I wanted her under the radar while we searched.

"The truth will out," I said. "We just need to see that it's the whole truth. We'll talk about it after dinner."

Mallard, as usual, had produced a feast fit for the varied diets of an eccentric family. I noted with interest that the twins dived into my favorite dish—a Persian frittata made with spinach and goat cheese. Nick, Tudor, and EG preferred the meatloaf and potatoes— although Mallard's wizardry had added cheese and nearly-invisible vegetables for the nutrition-avoiders. Model-thin Patra took minuscule shares of everything, particularly the vegetable side dishes, preferring to taste but not to actually *eat* a full meal.

Copper-haired adolescent Tudor was an introvert like me, but even he relaxed at a table full of people capable of understanding his formidable mind. I'm not a Pollyanna by any means. If we'd all been raised to sit at the table together every night of our lives, we'd probably have abraded each other's weak spots until our patience wore out. The fights would have been the stuff of legend.

But we were still in that happy getting-to-know-each-other stage, and it was Christmas. This was as close to peace on earth, goodwill toward men that could be expected, and I lapped up every minute of it. I needed to store the joy for the bleak days to come, when they all left again.

"I brought home an ornament-painting kit," I announced after dessert—a Black Forest Cake to die for, given the level of cholesterol ingested. "EG, I thought you could use some of the paints for finishing that camel for the Christmas play at school. Tudor, I thought you could use Graham's 3-D printer to make your own ornaments for EG to paint."

Tudor gaped. "A 3-D printer? *Really?* May I go upstairs now?"

The candelabra centerpiece—Graham's window on our world— didn't object, bless his pea-pickin' heart. Our attic spider liked encouraging Tudor's dangerous technical skills.

"The kit with the paint is on my upstairs desk. Take a look at what real ornaments look like so we don't end up with all Star Wars figures, please. EG?" I lifted an eyebrow in her direction.

She wasn't enthusiastic about the camel, but at the mention of Star Wars figures, I could see her contemplating what evil ornaments she could persuade Tudor to make. She nodded and trotted off after him. I knew my siblings. They might want to know everything that was going on, but they were still kids. They liked their toys. And they were smart enough to know they could fish out interesting information later, after the boring talk.

"You are wickedly manipulative," Nick admonished as he produced the brandy from the sideboard.

"I learned from the best." I poured hot water over a ginger-infusion tea.

"You have a creative mind that took what you learned to the outer limits," Patra corrected, not necessarily with approval, as I poured her tea.

Zander sampled Nick's brandy. Juliana went for the tea. Both intelligently sat back and waited.

The Council of War had begun.

"Have you heard from your friend yet?" I asked Juliana.

She frowned and shook her head. "I heard a woman's scream before the gunshots. Maryam wasn't home. I am very worried. It is not like her to not respond to my calls."

I hadn't put together a timeline yet, but I doubted there would be time to bury a body in this scenario, and the police would have found any other bodies by now. There was hope for Maryam.

"But the police only found Arden at the scene, and the security tapes don't show anyone else present. No women," Zander said. "Mr. Graham has the most amazing contacts. We know everything the police know."

I wouldn't tell our goody-two-shoe siblings that Graham had probably hacked police computers. There was some possibility he came by the information legitimately. He occasionally surprised me—not often, but sometimes.

"How much of the area where the shooting took place was covered by the cameras?" Nick asked, sprawling his long legs under the table and tilting his chair back. "And why do we care what happens to a pompous airhead?"

Since that had been my question earlier, I had to point out the less-than-obvious. "Because Magda cares. And because Julie—and her friend—may be in danger. And because Reverend William Arden, Josh's father, is Graham's friend."

"Really?" Patra suddenly looked interested. "Could he get me in to talk to the son when he wakes up? I've already taken the information about the park's money problems and built up background, but if I could have Josh Arden's story. . ."

We had Patra hooked and on the case. I lifted my eyebrows at Nick. We'd been through enough together that he understood without words. He tossed back a swallow of his brandy.

"The Brits pretty much know everything we know about Rose and his partners. Presidential elections are hot topics over there. My boss would owe me if I provide whatever we find out about the embezzlement at GenDef and its connection to the park, since GenDef is an international weapons dealer suspected of selling to terrorists," he admitted. "Not exactly altruistic reasons, but I'll help where I can."

"World peace is a reason," the candelabra intoned. "Which might happen if you'll remove your mother from the premises. She is currently dragging an ex-CIA agent through the mud at the park, along with the police chief. She will undoubtedly be parked at the hospital next, and has an appointment in GenDef's office at noon tomorrow."

Eyes widening, Zander and Julie stared at the ornate Victorian silver centerpiece. Nick whacked his fork against the base, probably hoping to ring Graham's ears. Since we needed our spider's cooperation, I didn't shove the microphone into the sideboard as had been our wont when we first arrived.

"Josh once had a crush on Magda," I threw into the teapot for flavor.

Silence reigned. It was lovely.

Before Graham could steal the show again, I brought the discussion back into focus. "Have they dug up any more bodies? We need to start identifying missing people, tracing their whereabouts before they disappeared, and following the money. Where did the embezzled funds end up? They'll come down hard on the reverend if the park really is in financial trouble."

"He didn't shoot himself," Julie protested.

"There is no honor among thieves," Nick said cynically. "That's how cops think. We have to prove he didn't know about the embezzlement or any bodies. That's a lot of naiveté."

"And you said he offered you concert tickets," I reminded her. "If it turns out that these tickets lead to parties where rich men pick up young girls for immoral purposes, then he's in way deep."

"I think he is a kind man and people are using him," she said stubbornly, crossing her arms.

"I'm inclined to agree," Patra said. "I've done the research. Josh Arden turned in a high school coach who wanted him to throw a game in return for a free ride to college. In the pro's, he reported team members to the gaming commission for using under-inflated balls. The guy is a walking target."

"He's a hero," Julie protested.

"Which makes him a target," Nick explained. "There is nothing criminal minds like better than to prove that good is a weakness and nice guys finish last. It justifies their existence."

Impressed, I raised my teacup in salute. "Wisdom is, Master."

Zander held up the tablet he'd been typing on. "The police dogs have been working on the incomplete foundation for one of the pyramids. Apparently concrete was to have been poured a month ago, but work has slowed to a crawl, so they're still able to dig. Speculation is that the male body they have sniffed out is that of the missing embezzler, George Paycock, but the coroner has not confirmed it. It has not been there long. There is a female corpse as well, but it has been there a while, and there is no identification yet."

Julie frowned worriedly. That might be the first body she'd filmed.

"I suppose they found them with Magda looking on," Patra said. "What are the chances that her cohorts were the ones who revealed Paycock's embezzlement, and she bears responsibility for his death?"

"He disappeared weeks before Magda arrived. That's a pretty large leap, grasshopper," I said, trying to puzzle through her logic.

"Not when you know Magda has spies in every defense industry organization on the planet," the candelabra reported. "She's playing a larger game. Stick to the small fry and leave the planet out."

I stuck my tongue out at the ornament, not caring if Graham was monitoring us visually. If he was, I knew I was raising his temperature in lewd ways.

"Back to Joshua Arden. Was he near this grave site when he was shot?" I asked. "We have way too many crimes and loose ends and I want connections."

"No, he was not near any of the interesting structures where I aimed my cameras," Julie said. "That is why the videos of the shooting are bad. The school's security camera caught him walking toward a maintenance shed. There are several gunshots. He crumples, holding his middle, as if the bullets come from the shed or the shrubbery nearby. We see no women screaming. No one runs to him. If I had not heard. . ." She let the sentence drop.

We could all imagine where it would have ended. Josh would have bled out and died before anyone found him—unless there were witnesses, which the screams seemed to indicate there were. "Did anyone else call 911 at the same time you did?"

"The police reports confirm the shooter was in the shrubbery near the shed," Zander reported, zipping through his tablet. "Dispatch reported two calls to 911, one of them untraceable, the other Julie's. They are trying to follow an unknown call to the reverend's phone placed ten minutes before the shooting, but they suspect a burner phone."

"Julie, you still have yours?" I asked.

She reddened and shook her head. "I had hidden it in my drawer. I couldn't find it when I returned last night, that is why I used the bugged phone to text Zander and make the 911 call. But Reverend Arden couldn't have received *any* call. His phone battery was dead."

"Might Maryam have your burner phone?" I suggested gently.

Julie opened her mouth, closed it, then looked at her newly cleaned-out phone. She flipped through her contacts and pushed one, presumably to Maryam. She got no reply but left a message. Then she looked at Zander. "I do not have my burner number in here."

He pulled out his phone and showed it to her. She added to her contact list and hit it. I held my breath as it rang through the speaker.

"Hello?" a faintly accented female voice answered warily.

"Maryam," Julie said in relief. "It is me. I am with family. Where are you? Can we help?"

"Julie." The voice sounded weepy. "Are you all right? We were so worried. Lucas said you were with the reverend last night."

"Lucas is with you?" Julie asked.

I didn't have a clue who Lucas was, but she obviously did. We all waited, although not patiently. Nick poured another brandy. Patra picked at some chocolate peppermint candies on the sideboard. Zander looked as if he might hyperventilate.

"We're witnesses," Maryam whispered through the speaker. "I need to go home to my papa before my brother finds out. Lucas wants to go to the police, but I told him it's dangerous."

I was fairly certain the candelabra groaned in exasperation. Or maybe that was me.

"Introduce me to your friend, please," I said, holding out my hand for the phone.

"My sister wishes to talk to you," Julie said hurriedly. "She knows important people. You can trust her." She handed over the phone.

I turned up the phone speaker.

"Reverend Arden may die if we do not catch the shooter," I said. "Julie is in hiding for fear the shooter will think *she* was the witness. The police are digging more bodies out of graves on the campus as we speak. You and Lucas need to tell us everything you know. It's probably not good to return to your homes yet, so we'll arrange a safe hiding place."

I could hear whispering on the other end of the line. I would have liked to reach through the phone and drag her into the twenty-first century, but Julie had said her friend was from Pakistan. Her fear of authority probably came from her family and demonstrated strong survival instincts. I knew nothing of Lucas, which worried me, but at least he wanted to talk to the police.

A man's voice came to the phone. "Maryam still wants to go home. Can you arrange to send her there after we've talked?"

I grimaced and glanced around the table. No one looked happy with that alternative, but Nick reluctantly nodded. The others followed his lead.

"If the police don't object, we can get her out. You will be doing the world, and Reverend Arden, a favor by telling us what happened."

"We don't know much at all," he warned. "We just don't want to be on anyone's radar. Find us a safe place, and we'll talk." He gave us the address of their hotel.

"Give us half an hour," I suggested, crossing my fingers and hoping we could come up with something. "For safety, we'll call you back on another burner phone. The one you have shouldn't be tapped, but it's best to avoid using anything else the school might have had access to."

Julie grabbed her phone. "Maryam, these are good people. They will help, I promise."

"I'm sorry I ran," the female voice said, obviously crying. "I was so very afraid."

The phone clicked off. I had to hope that at least Lucas understood my warning, and that they wouldn't throw away the phone that was our only means of reaching them again.

"Can we bring them here?" Julie asked anxiously.

"No," thundered the candelabra.

Since that was my reaction as well, I didn't argue. "If you're still a suspect, it's best not to bring them near you," I said more politely. My more personal reaction was that I didn't want dangerous strangers inside my family fortress.

Zander's tablet beeped. He glanced down at it in surprise and read off an address that I instantly looked up on my phone—a secure neighborhood on the edge of the Adams-Morgan district north of here and near Nick. Our attic spider was quick. All we had to do was wish for a safe house and he produced one. Knowing Graham, though, he probably had access to secure houses all over the city, maybe a few states.

I showed the location to Nick, who nodded approval.

"How?" Zander asked in confusion, staring at his screen.

I pointed at the silver centerpiece, and his eyes widened. Graham had that effect. I should quit calling him a spider in the attic and refer to him as our Evil Genie.

The discussion broke down into the hows and whys of transporting them from the too-public hotel where they were hiding to the safe house. It was too late to go over to the park and retrieve Maryam's clothing. That would have to wait until morning. I left Nick with Julie and Zander to work out details of rescuing our witnesses.

Patra donned her coat and swung her heavy purse over her shoulder. "This has been enlightening, folks, but I have to go. Let me know if we can get in to see Arden and keep me up to date on our paranoids."

I followed her out of the dining room. She didn't immediately leave but stopped in the parlor to examine our distorted tree.

"Give Sean my regards," I said dryly, since she had a perfectly good room upstairs.

Ignoring my goad, she produced an ornament from her bag and looked around for an empty place on the branches. "I intend to pick Sean's brains on what he knows about your father and his and GenDef. He had access to his father's papers, but he's not communicative on the subject."

"Will he help if he knows GenDef is a suspect in this case? They're high on my list for assassin hiring." Not that I saw a point in hiring professionals to kill an embezzler, if that really was Georgie's body, but that was the way my mind worked. A lover's spat didn't seem likely to end in concrete.

"Sean knows Rose's cohorts had *my* father killed, but he's still not sharing, so I can't say. He's probably trying to protect us." She hung a shiny gold wreath on the branch. "But it's time Sean and I had a little heart-to-heart. I'll let you know what I find out, if you'll do the same."

Her father had died years ago, but Patra had only recently discovered he'd been killed by our own side in a middle-Eastern war zone—while investigating some of the warmongers currently behind Jesus World.

"Knowledge may be dangerous, but ignorance is deadly," I said, giving her my promise in words we both understood.

Patra pulled on her beret, gave me a peace sign, and slipped into the early evening winter gloom.

I checked the ornament she'd hung. She'd had it engraved to say *In memory, Patrick Llewellyn, beloved father, RIP.*

Seventeen

Juliana runs into trouble

JULIE ANXIOUSLY TWISTED HER fingers as the limo pulled up in front of the small hotel set back from a busy street where Lucas had said they were hiding. "This does not look like a cheap hotel."

On the seat facing her, Nicholas checked his watch. "There is no such thing as a *cheap* hotel in DC, but they may have found the only two-star on this side of town. It's safe enough, as these things go. Come on, we need to keep moving." He climbed out of the limo and opened the front passenger door to talk to the driver. "Sam, drive around the block. Let's not attract more notice than necessary."

"Ana prefers Uber," Zander said tentatively, stepping out and holding out his hand for Julie. "Is that not more private?"

"Nothing is private in this town. But we have no reason to believe anyone is watching us, yet. It's best not to be noticed, but a limo isn't completely out of place here." In his rather expensive-looking cashmere coat over a tailored business suit, Nicholas strode toward the hotel entrance.

Julie had a hard time believing she was part of a clan sophisticated enough to include Nicholas and private limousines. She glanced down at her own bright-pink nylon jacket and wondered if she could ever manage to look as elegant as her older siblings—or if she wanted to. Zander didn't look much better than she did in an ill-fitting coat he'd borrowed from Nicholas.

The old hotel had only one small elevator. They rode up silently. Heating was evidently not a priority. Julie clenched and unclenched her chilly fingers as the mechanism lurched upward. The elevator smelled of cleaning fluid, although there was an even less appealing odor underlying it.

She was already nervous and feeling antsy when the elevator doors opened.

Loud pinging noises rang out, shattering what was left of her composure.

"*Skort!*" she cried, tugging Zander's coat and dropping to the floor the way she'd been taught to do when bullets flew. "Watch out!" she translated uselessly for Nicholas, who now had his back to the elevator wall. Zander crouched in front of her on the opposite side.

The advertising poster on the elevator wall shattered in a cascade of broken glass. Julie bit her lip to keep from screaming.

The elevator doors automatically creaked to close. Julie's teeth chattered. The door took eternity. Crouching low, Nicholas rolled into the hallway before the doors shut.

"*Bladdy hell*," Zander whispered, then jammed the open-door button.

Julie muffled a shriek of protest as the door opened again. To her relief, no more shots rang out. Instead, heavy feet pounded against the thin carpet in the opposite direction. *What had happened to Maryam?*

Nicholas uttered a curse worse than Zander's, stood up, and loped off down the hall.

Wanting to see if Maryam was safe, terrified to find out what lurked in shadows, Julie peered around the door. A dark figure fled toward an erratically blinking exit sign on the far end of the corridor with Nick hot on his trail. He could be shot that way!

Zander started to run after Nick, but Julie grabbed his hand and forced him to pull her up from the floor, delaying him. "We must see if Maryam is all right, *nè*? You have no weapon to fight a gunman." Did Nick?

Zander scowled but grabbed her arm and tugged her down the corridor, checking door numbers for the one they sought.

At the far end, Nick smacked a fire alarm on the wall, causing glass to tinkle, and a siren to wail. Julie clapped her hands over her ears to block the shriek and glanced around in panic.

Doors popped open all along the corridor and heads peered out, but no one seemed too concerned. With the alarm howling, Julie winced, uncovered her ears, and rapped on the door of Maryam's room.

At the other end of the hall, Nick misdirected the people spilling into the hall by pointing at the exit near him and shouting, "*Fire*! We have to go this way!"

Confused, Julie didn't know if she was supposed to follow his instructions or wait for Maryam. Zander pounded the door louder.

"He's putting people between us and providing cover so he can run after the gunman. They were shooting at the lock." He pointed at the shattered key slot and slammed his shoulder against the door to jar it loose. "It's okay, it's us," he shouted as he did so. The door opened—as it would have done for the shooters had they not interrupted.

Inside, Maryam cowered behind a couch. The Tall White Boy—Lucas—to whom Reverend Arden had introduced her, stood with a chair upraised, prepared to bash heads—or a gunman.

"*Eish!*" Julie cried, dodging out of his reach.

He dropped the chair in relief, apparently recognizing her.

"Lucas is hurt!" Maryam exclaimed, jumping up from her safe place. "We must take him to a hospital."

"It's just a flesh wound." He winced and grabbed his left arm now that the chair was lowered. "Let's beat it."

"Don't be *dof*." Julie winced. Her American English apparently escaped her in emergencies, but *dumb* sounded like dumb in any language. "Zander, find some towels so he does not bleed all over. I'll take a look at his arm when we are in the car." Alarmed by the blood seeping through his fingers, Julie looked around for baggage, backpacks, anything.

"We ran without taking anything," Lucas explained. "Did you see the shooter? Is it safe to leave?"

"Our brother Nicholas set off the alarm," Julie explained, taking the towels Zander returned with.

"He's leading the other hotel guests down the far stairs, away from us. There are more stairs closer, beside the elevator. It's probably not safe to take the elevator if the fire department or alarm might shut it down. Let's go." Zander took Maryam's arm and tugged her toward the door.

Julie tied one of the thin cotton towels around Lucas's large bicep. "We have a car, if we can reach it."

"How do we know we're safe with you?" Lucas asked, sensibly enough, stopping to check the hall before leaving the room. "The shooter arrived after we talked to you."

"We'll have to figure out how that happened later." Julie tried to sound urgent. "Did one of you use your normal phone, for instance?" she asked as he finally followed her out.

"Just to call for pizza," Maryam said, hurrying with Zander in the direction of the elevator.

Lucas whistled in disgust. "You didn't use the burner?"

Julie kept looking over her shoulder as they ran, but the other guests must have followed Nick down the far stairs. The hall was empty. Their feet pounding against the cheap carpet couldn't be heard over the wailing alarm.

"It was just pizza," Maryam said, a trifle breathlessly as they hit the stairs.

"Your phone may have had a bug in it like mine," Julie told her. "You couldn't know. This is all so very *vrot*. Bad, wrong," she corrected.

They didn't waste time arguing once they reached the bottom of the stairwell. Zander peered cautiously into the lobby. "People aren't going outside. They're just standing around looking puzzled."

"Staff should escort them out," Lucas said in disapproval.

Sirens screamed in the distance. The fire alarm still clamored. Peering from her side of the stairs, Julie didn't see anyone looking particularly concerned. Surely gunmen wouldn't open fire in a crowded lobby.

"*Bakgat*, I see Nick."

"Awesome," Julie translated for him, relieved to know she wasn't the only one who reverted to slang when shaken.

Zander held the door for Maryam and Julie. Lucas checked behind them and in front of them and stayed between Julie, Maryam, and the crowd, guarding them with his greater height. Julie couldn't decide if this was charming or sexist.

"This way." Nick arrived to block all of them from the lobby view. He pointed toward the rear of the hotel. "There's always a rear exit. I couldn't find the shooter in this mob, but he's probably lurking out front, waiting for you to come out."

"Or he ran like the rat he was," Lucas said. "There are too many people for him to strike again."

"I like the way you think." Nick led the way down a dark corridor to a door that opened onto an alley. "This isn't exactly the Plaza. I told Sam to meet us down the block. This alley is a trap otherwise."

Lucas had struggled into his bulky coat so his towel bandage wasn't visible. Julie hoped they looked like tourists fleeing a fire alarm as they ran down the alley past office buildings and hit the sidewalk half a block from the hotel entrance. The limo was already waiting for them.

No one said a word until they were all inside and the car was rolling again. Julie glanced down the street in front of the hotel as the limo cruised by. Fire engines and police cars blocked traffic. Very few people from the hotel had bothered going into the cold. They didn't seem too concerned by the threat of fire. "Do fire alarms usually go off in the middle of the night here?"

"All the time. Drunks, smokers, kids, people like us with ulterior motives—be glad we only had three flights," Nick said from the front seat. "Jules, you might want to introduce all of us before our guests panic and leap out the doors."

"Juliana," she told him, "Or Julie. Jules is rude."

He flashed her a provocative grin. "There's the Magda in you. Julie it is."

"I'm Alexander Kruger, Juliana's brother," Zander said stiffly, preventing Julie from responding to the taunt about their mother. "We are still learning about our new family, but the annoyance in the front seat is our half brother, Nicholas Maximillian, a British diplomat."

Nick performed a rolling salute as if greeting a pasha.

"And this is Maryam Rathore, my roommate." Julie continued the introductions as best as she could. "Lucas, I don't know your last name."

"Lucas Schmidt, criminal justice drop-out, second-year at JACAD, aiming for a degree as a professional student." He held his arm as if in pain.

"Just like Julie," Zander said with brotherly disrespect.

Julie punched her brother's arm before gesturing at Lucas. "Take off the jacket and let me see your wound. Nicholas, may we stop somewhere to buy bandages and antiseptic? One of the many studies my brother scorns included first aid."

"The bullet just ricocheted through the shoddy door. It's nothing," Lucas protested.

A police siren blasted behind them, and they all jumped.

Ana chooses an ornament

I SHOOED EG OFF to bed after admiring her interestingly painted camel, complete with tattoos of bats and crowns. My phone rang as I made my way up to the attic to kick Tudor out of Graham's lair.

"I have them," Nick reported. "We had a minor incident. They called in a pizza order from a bugged phone, and we interrupted a gunman shooting down their door. I thought it best to pull them out rather than call the cops."

Graham had already sent me the dispatch call of a fire at the hotel. I'd been holding my breath for the past half hour. "I take it you used the fire alarm ploy to escape."

"Exactly. It seems rather evident the bad guys are after our pair. There are cops as well as the fire department, so someone may have called in the gunshots. Lucas's name is Schmidt, if you want to look him up. Maryam is a Rathore. I'll give you more after we've all finished sizing each other up. Jules and Zander are hoots, and by the way, don't call her Jules."

I laughed as he hung up. I ought to be more worried, but my babes were in good hands. Nick knew all the tricks I did, and Graham's safe house should be just exactly that—safe.

I continued up the stairs to find Tudor glaring in disgust at a blob of plastic that might have been a tortured Jedi warrior. Or a pig.

"I want that one," I told him. "The first piece of art by world-renowned Leonardo de Bullfinch. But it needs glittery gold stars."

"It's rubbish."

He started to throw it at a trash can but I caught it. "Mine, I told you. You can work on a better sketch in your room. Superhuman over there has a planet to save or worlds to blow up, and he can't do it with you watching. No phone booth."

He shot me a teenage look of disgust and stalked off.

"You have a way with words," Graham said from his Star Trek console where he manipulated keyboards and monitors better than any spaceship.

"If that means I lie well, thank you. Julie told me I must be honest with family and friends, but honesty isn't easily defined. Nick has our witnesses and is on the way to your Bat Cave. Someone shot at them." I came over to stand beside him and watch the flickering screens. I easily identified the hotel with fire engines. "Did you see anyone?"

He brought up the interior lobby view in real time. It was pretty grainy.

He zoomed in on two men in leather jackets slouching in a corner, studying the crowd. "They were some of the first to come down the stairs."

"Two? That can't be good. Assassins aren't cheap. They must be on the clock to hang around this long." I studied their pale complexions and shaved heads, committing them to memory. "Can we run facial recognition software?"

"I can run it against police files, if they have priors. The software is only as good as the database." He already had one monitor flipping through a motley collection of mugshots.

"What about against Julie's videos? Would it help to know if either of these two have been lurking in the good reverend's park?"

"It won't identify them, but we can check." He scrambled a few more screens while I studied the hotel situation.

As the lobby continued to fill with men in uniform, the skinheads displayed increasing nervousness, shifting from foot to foot and edging further into a shadowy corner. DC no longer banned handguns, but concealed carry was still pretty much a no-no. I'd lay wagers they had no permits at all, if these were our shooters.

They muttered to each other, then one drifted toward the front door.

"No way of getting the cops to stop them?" I asked.

"Working on it." He had blue tooth earphones plugged in as he punched at his keyboards.

I adored watching a geek at work, but I kept my eyes on the clowns in the lobby. "I'm taking a wild guess here to say they're not pros."

He was murmuring into his microphone and didn't answer.

On the screen, the hotel night clerk stopped one of the police officers and pointed out our leather-clad pair. Graham called the night clerk? Enterprising.

The thug edging for the front door increased his speed. The other began to move as well—in the opposite direction.

The cop intercepted Thug Number One, who reached in his jacket, probably for a gun. Always an extremely bad move. He was lucky he only got Tasered in the groin for his efforts. Ow. That would teach him to wear a longer jacket.

Panicking, thug Number Two shoved through the milling crowd. Another man in blue pushed after him.

"Gonna be hard to hold them when there are no witnesses to the shooting," I commented as a blue-haired lady in a bathrobe screamed in outrage when Thug Two shoved her into a wall.

"Weapon violations, possible probation violation." He nodded at one of the screens that now showed mugshots for our skinheads. Score! That would take them off the streets for a few days.

A balding old man with a dashing goatee stuck his cane between Two's legs. Down he went—grabbing at the plastic Christmas tree to catch himself. I winced as silver and gold balls scattered across the tile floor. Cop boots smashed the ornaments into pretty pieces of glass while Thug Two got cuffed.

"The hotel should charge an entertainment fee," I said as the old man with the cane handed his handkerchief to the weeping blue-haired lady.

Our witnesses were safe for now.

Graham turned off his microphone and removed his headset. "If they don't, I will." He yanked me down on his lap, and I went more than willingly.

Finally, we had the place to ourselves and no interruptions anticipated.

Thrilled, I reached for his belt. "Entertainment, am I?"

"The price I have to pay," he muttered, shoving my skirt higher.

Eighteen

Juliana plays nurse

IN THE SAFE HOUSE living room, Julie finished wrapping a bandage around Lucas's rather. . . muscular. . . bicep. "You probably should take some acetaminophen. This isn't likely to feel better soon."

"I've jabbed nails into my foot and had concussions worse than this. I'm good." He shifted on the black leather chair and leaned into the cushion. "Thank you."

Nicholas was studying his phone, but he looked up once she started putting away the first aid supplies. "The cops may have the shooters. Let's have some answers so maybe we can keep them in custody."

Maryam sat huddled on the matching leather sofa, her hands curled around a cup of tea Zander had made for her. Since we'd not had time to fetch their clothes, she was still wearing the pretty white Punjabi gown she'd worn when they'd fled. "We really know nothing," she protested. "We were just in the wrong place at the wrong time."

"Why were you out at that hour anyway?" Julie asked in exasperation.

"You weren't home to talk to. I was lonely. I went out to look at the stars and think of home. I don't think I belong here." She said this last defiantly, glaring at her.

Julie thought she understood. Maryam had been quiet since that humiliating episode at the concert hall. She sat beside her and squeezed her hand. "I think there are bad things happening at the park that have nothing to do with the reasons why we are here or with us personally."

"If there are bad things happening, then we should try to stop them." Zander paced behind the couch. "Tell us what you saw."

"I saw Lucas," Maryam said. "He was walking toward the back of the park. We are working on a project together, and I thought we could talk a little until Julie came home."

"I'd just walked Julie home," Lucas explained when Nick raised a questioning eyebrow. "Reverend Arden had asked me to do so. I've talked to him a few times about security concerns, and he'd asked me to start a student security committee. I knew he often walked the park after hours, and after I left Julie, I followed his usual path hoping to catch up with him."

Julie sipped her own tea to fight a sudden chill. Lucas and Maryam describing a perfectly normal evening seemed out of synch with the aftermath. She sent up a prayer for the reverend's health as Maryam took up the tale.

"I was on that big hill by the Ferris wheel, where there are no trees, looking up at the sky when I heard Reverend Arden coming down the gravel path. His head was bowed, as if in prayer. I didn't disturb his peace. But then I saw Lucas and he saw me."

Lucas rubbed the shoulder above his bandage. "She looked like a ghost in that white wispy thing she has on. It was too cold to be out there like that."

"I wore a shawl," Maryam protested.

"And she wears long underwear under those wispy gowns," Julie added with a smirk. "She's too vain to mar her pretty gowns with ugly overcoats."

Maryam glared at her.

Nick and Lucas looked amused. Zander colored and stared at his hands. *Domkop.* He'd spent all of university studying and not enough time partying if a discussion of underwear embarrassed him.

"Continue the tale, please," Nick ordered.

"I told Maryam I would walk her home," Lucas explained. "She said she didn't want to go. So I gave her my jacket, and we followed Arden. He always heads for the maintenance shed to pick up one of those big construction flashlights so he can examine what's been done during the day. I thought we'd catch up with him when he returned to the main path, and then I'd take Maryam back to the trailer."

"Only if I was ready to go," Maryam said mutinously. "You are not the boss of me."

"He is that kind of man, Maryam," Julie pointed out. "He can't help himself. Let it go." She rather liked the way Lucas narrowed his eyes at her when she sized him up as a bossy, over-protective leader, but she *didn't* like what had brought them here. She needed to be out of this cold place and back where she felt safe so she could puzzle all this out. The world was much simpler through the lens of a camera. "What did you see?"

Maryam's shoulders slumped, and she didn't respond.

Lucas ran his hand over his shaggy brown curls. "Arden had gone past the bushes around the shed where we couldn't see him from the road. We heard shots. Maryam screamed, and I pushed her down to the ground. I watched as two men ran out of the bushes in our direction. There was a lot of noise, so there may have been others, but I only saw this pair."

"Lucas knocked me down and rolled me under the bushes!" Maryam said indignantly, shaking the silver-threaded fabric to show the dirt smears.

It said something about Julie's state of mind that she hadn't even noticed the mud stains on Maryam's delicate skirt. Appalled at how close they had come to being shot, she merely hugged her friend.

Lucas ignored them and completed his report. "They were cursing each other. One wanted to run back to be certain the 'job got finished right.' The other was intent on looking for witnesses—they must have heard Maryam. But they didn't look hard. One of the motion detector security lights kicked on, and they ran in the direction of the rear construction gate. I heard a car engine not long after."

Julie thought he might have made a good policeman. She wondered why he hadn't finished the college course.

"Did you see their faces when the light came on?" Nick asked. "Can you describe them?"

Lucas rubbed his hair harder. "That's the problem. They both had shaved heads, but I'm pretty sure one of them was a bodyguard for Mr. Jeffrey, one of the park's sponsors."

Nicholas uttered a profane expletive, and Julie hugged Maryam tighter.

They would have to call the police.

Ana gets involved

"I NEEDED THAT," I murmured into the musky scent of Graham's bare shoulder. I'd opened his shirt at some point. I licked his sweaty skin, and he tightened his grip.

We'd not made it out of his chair. My skirt was hiked to my

waist. His jeans were unfastened. We were hot and messy, and his powerful arms still held me in place, even though we'd just blown our minds on desperately insane sex.

Like any drug, sex wore off eventually, but the temporary high was worth it.

"Don't make anything more of it than that," he warned, while he caressed my buttocks. Or groped them—fine line there.

Since I was doing my best to avoid any thought at all, I nibbled his ear in retaliation, then ran my hand over his massive chest, and tweaked his nipple. "You're such a predictable clod." I was in too much of a blissful haze to argue in this rare moment of time out of the hectic pace of our lives.

One of his gadgets buzzed urgently. His very clever hands stopped their seductive massage. I understood his hesitation. With a reluctant sigh, I swung off his lap, pulling down my skirt. "Answer it. Maybe it's the president offering you a medal for saving Outer Turkistan."

"It would more likely be a warning that Outer Turkistan has just been blown to smithereens," he muttered, reaching for one of his phones.

"You are the company you keep," I admonished, hunting around on the floor for my panties and shoes. That he didn't deny the president could be calling proved nothing. Graham was as tightlipped as any good robot.

"It's your brother." He held up the text for me to see. "The company I keep seems to be deteriorating."

I swatted his kneecap and took the phone. KIDS IDENTIFIED ARDEN'S SHOOTERS IN YOUR HOTEL PHOTO. JEFFREY'S BODYGUARD ONE OF THEM.

"Jeffrey, as in CEO of GenDef?" I asked in despair. "This will not turn out well. Couldn't I just put all these Top Asshat one-percenters in a room and blow them up?"

He took back the phone and returned the text. "Get some sleep. Jeffrey will still be around in the morning."

I glanced up at the mugshots still on the screen. "If one of those creeps is the bodyguard, and we apply the company-you-keep rule, the CEO of GenDef has some serious social problems."

"Go to bed, Ana," he said in that stern voice he'd probably learned from my grandfather. It had once irritated me.

These days, his voice shivered my spine with pleasure. Yeah, I'm perverse. Defying authority is what I do best. I stood up, panties and shoes in hand, and bent over to plant a kiss right on his smackers. He responded with amazing speed, giving me what I wanted, then pushed me away.

I hit his thick head of hair with my sandal and marched off. It gave me a gut-deep thrill knowing I had my own super-human watching me. So, call me shallow.

The next morning, after a shower and a good night's sleep, I was ready for whatever the world flung at me. I might even have floated on air a little bit. I didn't have a romantic bone in my body, thank goodness, but Graham had done my ego, and my hormones, a lot of good.

Juliana's and Zander's doors were closed. They'd come home, at least.

EG was the only one at the breakfast table. I handed her Tudor's warped hunk of plastic. "Paint this for me, will you? With red and gold stars and not black and purple?"

She squinted at the misshapen object, then up at me. "Why?"

"Because I asked you to? Because that's my special ornament for the tree. Because it makes me happy. Take your pick." I poured my tea and grabbed a wheat bagel.

"You want to hang this?" she asked in incredulity. "It's ugly!"

"To me, it's real. It's not glimmer and flash and make-believe. Trust me." I left her contemplating the lump and wandered toward the stairs to my office. I had work to do.

Magda intercepted me in the hall. "Keep Julie out of that dreadful park!"

"And good morning to you, too." I sipped from my mug and admired her early morning attire of tailored black slacks and silk sweater topped by a dashing red and gold scarf. She wore her not-completely-natural blond hair in an elegant chignon. I was in my usual denim maxi and Henley. I'm short. Slacks never fit and look awful on me. "You don't admire dinosaurs and pyramids?" I asked when she simply scowled at my greeting.

"I don't admire dead girls. Stay out of this one, Ana, and keep Julie out as well. The Ardens and I are old friends. I'll handle it."

"Ummm hmmm." I sipped my tea and ignored her curtness, as I would her orders. I didn't do the screaming arguments of my adolescence any longer, and I was feeling mellow today. "Did you have a chance to talk to Josh yesterday or is he still in a coma? And when you stop by GenDef this morning, get photos of Jeffrey's bodyguards, if you would. He has his own personal army."

So, my version of mellow was to reveal I knew she was sniffing around my case. I made up that last part about an army just to annoy. It could be true, for all I knew. I'll have to admit, honesty isn't as much fun as making stuff up.

"Stop spying on me," she shouted at Graham's bugged chandelier, knowing where I'd got my information. She stormed off to the breakfast room.

Good, she and EG needed a little personal time. EG would be thrilled.

As I settled into my basement desk, the intercom interrupted. "You and Magda fight as if you were sisters."

I finished my tea before answering. "If you think about it, the difference in age between me and Magda is about the same as between me and EG. I'm the middle child."

Graham snorted. "Then let your older sister deal with GenDef and Jeffrey. She's right. You need to stay out of it, Ana."

"Let me know when you need another attitude adjustment." I flipped off the switch. There was nothing I liked better than a little opposition. I had no intention of leaving Julie and her friends as walking targets.

I had connections to find between a weapons manufacturer CEO, his bodyguards, an embezzler, and the park. If I could throw in two skinheads and a champagne-guzzling party crowd, I'd do that too. It would be a gift to myself.

Nineteen

Juliana talks to the police

JULIE ADMIRED THE TILTED Christmas tree in the weak morning sun through the open draperies. She found Zander's ornament among the greenery—a surfing Santa. He'd spent a summer at the beach with friends learning to surf and had vowed to go back one day. But life had never given him the opportunity.

Now that she had a safe computer and could use her bank account again, she had ordered gifts online, but she couldn't think of what ornament she wanted to hang. Her future in building schools seemed to be in jeopardy. She wondered if the school was still having classes, but she was afraid to call anyone and ask. At least being out of work didn't leave her homeless.

Her phone rang. *Maryam.* She answered immediately.

"Nicholas says he has made an appointment to talk to the detective at the police station at ten," Maryam said worriedly. "I do not wish to go. I saw *nothing*. Can you and Lucas not do it?"

"Lucas needs your corroboration. All you're doing is giving them information. You've done nothing wrong," Julie reminded her. "They will take statements and it will all be over."

Nicholas had tried to reassure her that once the police had statements, Julie would no longer be a suspect, but she was as terrified as Maryam. The detective had been mean and intimidating, and she really didn't want him asking questions over and over again. She didn't do well under pressure.

But she believed in honesty and wanted to help Reverend Arden, so she must face the task.

"My papa will hate this," Maryam said miserably. "He didn't want me to come here. I will have to go home and marry our horrible neighbor."

"We will figure out our futures another day. Today, we talk to the police," Julie said firmly. "Is Nicholas there yet?" He'd left with the limo last night after dropping off her and Zander at Ana's mansion.

Her mansion. She and Zander owned a share of a mansion. It was hard to comprehend. They'd never been poor, but they'd always lived modestly.

"Lucas is talking to him now in the front room. I have spent two nights with him! This is all wrong. Your sister said I could go home if I told you what I know."

"Only after you give the police a statement, and they say you may go. Those men could come back and try to kill the reverend! We must stop them. Lucas has behaved himself, has he not?" Julie paced the room, wondering if she should let Maryam talk to Ana. But she didn't like to be a nuisance or behave like an incompetent child.

"He's bossy, like my brother," Maryam said petulantly. "They're telling me to hurry up. I will see you shortly."

Holding her tacky nylon coat and watching out the window for the limo, Julie startled when Mrs. Hostetter—Magda—her *mallie* entered. She had a mother who looked like a movie star. That was almost harder to believe than the mansion.

"There you are! Don't you look lovely this morning." Magda glanced disapprovingly at the nylon coat. "We need to take you shopping. And then I've arranged for you to meet with someone who is very interested in building schools in underprivileged countries. Come along, and we'll have time to hit the stores before the meeting."

She threw on a fur coat and marched on high heels for the foyer.

Julie stared after her.

Magda turned around impatiently. "Well, come on. What are you waiting for?"

"Nicholas," Julie said politely. "And Maryam. They are to pick me up shortly. Could we not have this meeting another day?"

"I don't know that I can stay another day. Whatever Nick is doing, it can wait. We have important people expecting us."

Julie was torn. She'd been taught to respect her elders, and she'd idolized her mother from a distance all her life. Magda was offering her the opportunity she'd been working toward, the reward for all her hard efforts without the inconvenience of training with JACAD. How could she say no?

She had nothing to offer that the detective didn't already know— but *Maryam needed her*. Maryam wasn't accustomed to being around men like Lucas and Nicholas. She would freeze and say nothing or run away. Maryam always ran away.

Julie's shoulders slumped. "I cannot. I made a promise, and I cannot renege on it. I am sorry to disappoint."

Magda opened her phone and hit a number. Without speaking to Julie, she said curtly into the phone, "Ana, you will come up here and talk with your sister. She is throwing away her career for nothing. Make her understand."

Julie thought she heard a crash emanate from the phone and hid a smile. She did not know Ana well, but she knew enough to know her sister would not like that tone of voice or an order like that. Perhaps she should take lessons from Ana.

Julie's phone rang. To her amusement, the call was from Ana. "Yes?"

"I can do anything Magda can do, only better," Ana said distinctly. "Our mother is accustomed to doing whatever she wants, without consideration of any principles but her own. You are under no obligation to obey unless it's what *you* want. You are a grown woman, and there's no reason she should walk into your life now and pretend she knows what's best for you."

"She is telling me what I want to hear," Julie admitted. "I don't want to go with Nicholas to the police station. I would much rather go shopping and speak to someone about schools."

Ignoring Julie's conversation, Magda was on her own phone, typing out texts with long red fingernails.

"That's your choice to make," Ana said, although Julie heard disapproval in her voice. "Just don't let Magda make it for you."

Julie's eyes widened slightly as she realized Ana was right. Adults could make their own choices—and opportunities. As much as she would have liked to have had Magda helping her when she'd been a child... or maybe not. Growing up thinking for herself, instead of being controlled as Maryam had been, had made her a stronger person.

She watched the limo pull up out front. She could explain to Nick....

"Thank you, Ana. I wish to be fierce, like you. I want to do what is best for all and not just myself. Wish me luck." With decision, she shut the phone, donned her coat, and proceeded to the front door.

"I made a promise," she told Magda as she opened the door. "I must keep it. I would be ashamed of myself if I did not. I hope you will understand."

Her mother tilted her sleek blond head, narrowed her eyes, then nodded. "I was younger than you when I made my own choices. I may not approve, but I understand. I would prefer to keep you from making my mistakes."

Daringly, Julie leaned over and kissed her mother's powdery cheek. "Thank you." She dashed out in the cold before she could change her mind.

Ana beats Magda

I WILL NOT GET involved. *I will not get involved.*

I set down my phone and forced my attention back to the screen. Julie was an intelligent woman, not a toddler. I could give guidance only when asked.

I could not call my mother and tell her to take a flying leap off the Washington Monument. She loved us, but her obsessions prevented her from understanding that a real mother would want what was best for her children—not what was convenient for her. When one's view is global, it's hard to see the ants you're walking on.

"They've charged last night's gunmen on a battery of misdemeanors and working on more." The intercom interrupted my musings.

Sometimes, the interfering box said what I wanted to hear, so turning it back on had been too much temptation. "Score one for the good guys," I muttered, appreciating that Graham had known I needed the reassurance that the bad guys wouldn't be trying to knock off Julie on the way to the station.

"Arden is awake," the intercom continued. "Want to go over to the hospital before your mother does?"

I was out of my chair before he finished speaking. "You know the way to my heart. Keep an eye on the kids," I yelled at him, grabbing my army jacket—the faux fur was upstairs. Mallard would see that EG got off to school. Tudor was still asleep. I wasn't asking Graham to do much, and he certainly had the resources.

I ran down the hall to the rear exit. I didn't want to waste time arguing with Magda if she was still upstairs.

I had several bolt holes to choose from but took the easiest—through Mallard's kitchen. He looked up without surprise as I scampered through. I would have to buy him a really expensive bottle of red for Christmas. Or better yet, the corner bar.

EG needed the limo to get to school, so I caught the Metro to Alexandria and had my favorite Uber driver waiting when I emerged from the station.

"I wasn't sure it was you," he said when I climbed in looking like a homeless person in my battered army jacket and Birkenstocks.

"I come in many flavors." I texted Graham to let him know where I was—one of the rules I tried to teach my siblings. Always let others know where you are, just in case.

The driver laughed and left me to my work. For that alone, he'd earned another tip. Graham sent me the name of the person I was to hunt down at the hospital who would slide me past security and into Arden's room. One of these days, I'd really have to ask myself why I did this kind of thing, but it would probably boil down to—because I could.

Once upon a time, I had done it for the money. This time, my bank account would be poorer unless I started billing Graham for expenses. Only this particular adventure was for me and mine as much as for Graham. Life was becoming increasingly complicated. I handed over a nice wad of cash to the happy driver and went inside to the hospital information desk and asked for Graham's contact.

The stiff-rumped, shaved-head, ex-military security officer I was directed to looked at shrimpy me with suspicion, but I pulled out my passport and proved I was the minion he'd been expecting. I had no idea what story Graham had given, so I didn't offer any explanations. I just waited until he confirmed my access and led me upstairs, where he passed me off to another guard outside a hospital room door. These weren't everyday cops, so I was guessing they belonged to Graham's team.

The last time I'd visited a hospital, I'd tortured a crook. Today, I had to go in assuming Arden was a good guy—not nearly as much fun.

The room was filled with bouquets and cards and balloons. A nurse frowned as I entered, but the guard indicated it was okay. She finished taking blood pressure, noted a chart, and left, still scowling. Did I really look that bad?

The man in the bed did. Far from the powerful golden giant portrayed in his promo shots, Joshua Arden looked pale and waxen.

A bandage wrapped his head, and I was guessing another wrapped his torso from the way he was holding his side as he pumped the bed into a sitting position.

"Security said you needed to talk to me?" he asked weakly, coughing a little.

"Your father, my mother, my sister, and a whole host of people want to talk to you," I said, sitting on the edge of a chair where he could see me. "I'm just the one they let in. I'm Ana Devlin. Magda is my mother. Juliana Kruger is my sister." I waited for his brain on drugs to register all that.

His eyes almost lit up. "Brody's daughter? You're little Anastasia?"

"I'd rather be called Ana, please. Executed Russian princesses are not my style. Are you up to talking a little?" I could be nice when required.

"Brody always called you his *petit* princess. I'm still trying to see you as old enough to be sitting there! Is Magda doing well?" He straightened his shoulders a little, as if just the mention of my mother made him remember his masculinity.

Up until he was proven guilty, I had to assume this man was innocent, so I was blunt. "My mother is more than doing well, right up until the moment I have to strangle her. She'll be over here to see you, I'm sure. Don't let her bully you. All I want to do is find out who shot you so Julie can sleep at night."

Well, that was partly the truth. The rest was conspiracy theory.

"I've already told the police I don't remember anything, I'm sorry. I have no idea why anyone would shoot me. I assume a thief was breaking into the shed, and I caught him by surprise. We must pray that we will win the war on drugs so good men are not tempted by the evil of the devil's habits."

And he looked as if he honestly believed that. God save me from the virtuous. Or perhaps he'd suffered one too many concussions before he retired the field. He really seemed naïve enough to believe all of mankind could be saved from their bad habits if he could just have a word or two with God.

I opened my phone and showed him the mugshots of our culprits from the hotel. "Do you recognize either of these men?"

He frowned a little. "The second one looks a little familiar, but it could just be the ring in his nose. Everyone has them these days, it seems."

"He's a bodyguard for Tony Jeffrey of General Defense." Graham had verified that earlier. "Has Jeffrey visited the park or have you visited with him at some point that you may have seen him?"

He frowned. "Tony always has security. He's in a dangerous business. He's been out to the park a few times, so I may have seen this man then. My father doesn't like his trade, but Tony is a decent man, following in his father's footsteps as I followed mine."

Ah yes, the family business. I was familiar with that line of reasoning, much to my chagrin. "Would Mr. Jeffrey be upset with you for any reason?"

"Of course not." He sounded genuinely shocked. "He's a good Christian who donates time and money to the church and to the park. We've never so much as disagreed on any topic. You think *Tony* would have had me shot?"

I almost wanted to whack him on the head again. Tony was an *arms* dealer. What part of "peace on earth, goodwill toward man," did that fall under?

"Has he ever asked you to do anything for him or his company?"

"Besides pray?" Arden shook his head in utter bewilderment, so obviously not understanding my implications that I had to consider his reply genuine. "No, I don't think so. His wife has multiple sclerosis, so she's always on our prayer list. Oh, wait, now that I think about it, he's asked me if I'd support Senator Rose. They're good friends."

Duh. "Did you agree?" I asked impassively.

"Not exactly," he said a little warily. "The senator has given generously to the church and park, but I'm not a believer in mixing church and state."

The first smart thing I'd heard him say. He looked as if his painkillers were wearing off, and this line of questioning was going nowhere, so I tried a different tack. "Did you authorize the use of bulldozers after hours?"

He flipped his hand dismissively. "The contractors handle all that." But he finally looked worried—here was something he was smart enough to know wasn't quite right.

"Did the police tell you about the bodies they found in the back lot?"

"They said they found George," he said, definitely fading out. "And a woman. I told them about Esther being missing."

I tried not to let my eyebrows hit the sky. "Esther went missing at the end of September. George was around until recently, wasn't he?"

He closed his eyes, and finally, I saw world weariness. He *knew* George.

"I'm sorry to say it, but George was a womanizer. I prayed for them both."

This wasn't about the embezzlement? I hated badgering an ill man, but I needed to know all he could tell me. "George and Esther were in a relationship?"

"I didn't approve. I told Esther she'd have to leave the program, that the school owes families the right to believe even their adult children are in a moral environment. She was a strong-willed young woman, and George was a wealthy man. Once she left the school, I had no right to interfere, although I asked Tony to talk to his employee. But Esther was an ambitious young lady and knew what she was doing."

Julie had said the school hadn't known that Esther had left. I didn't want to press him on this possibly irrelevant issue—although he was looking too weak to press the bigger ones as well. I grimaced and tried one anyway. "Will the park be in financial trouble after the embezzled funds are untangled?"

He didn't answer. That was answer enough. I patted his hand. "I'll tell Magda you're doing as well as possible."

"Give her my regards," he said with a trace of a faint smile.

Cynical Magda and gullible Arden—a match made in hell. He had no idea how lucky he'd been to escape that fate.

On my way out, I pondered my next move. Summoning the audacity to do what I had in mind, I skirted an empty gurney to reach the elevator. While I waited for the door to open, some tall clod invaded my space. I was about to step into the elevator when a hard object shoved at the back of my army jacket. He had to push pretty hard for me to notice through all the layers, but he had my attention.

"We need to have a talk with you. Stay cool and nothing will happen."

Famous last words.

Twenty

Ana fights for gun control

GUNS TRULY ARE USELESS unless one shoots them immediately and unexpectedly. Anything else, and you give your victim time to think, so the guy holding his metallic penis to my coat was not only a *cowardly* criminal, but a stupid one.

If I were half a foot higher, I could have smacked my head backwards and taken out his nose, but I make up for lack of height with meanness.

"A gun? In a hospital? Really?" I asked with incredulity, staggering sideways as if caught off-guard.

My staggering was deliberate. Before he could reposition his gun, I bumped the gurney into his thigh with my hip, throwing him off balance. At the same time, I screamed for help, stomped the arch of his foot as hard as I could, grabbed his elbow in a freeze lock, and shoved his gun arm upward. I expected him to blast the ceiling but heard only a click.

He hadn't removed the safety. Score one for the ceiling.

My shriek of fury paralyzed the nurses at the desk, but it alerted the security on Arden's door. They dashed to grab Stupid's gun arm before he could bring it back down and blast me off the planet. Not that that would be a smart move, but it was the one I'd expected and prepared for.

Since I didn't need to break his arm, I dropped and rolled out of the way to let men bigger than me grapple with the gun and goon. "Call 911," I shouted at the frozen nurses. One already had the phone in her hand, and I gave her points for responding quickly.

"It could be a diversion. Don't leave Arden's door unguarded," I barked at the body builders once they had the goon's arms behind his back. They looked down at bossy me in startlement, but one ran back to man the door.

The other manacled the goon and commandeered the gun while I scrambled to stand up again. "Boss said you were a brat," was his only comment.

"That's a term of affection in comparison to what he usually calls me." I dusted myself off and studied Stupid. He narrowed his eyes, set his thin lips, and showed all sign of refusing to speak. I didn't want to talk to him anyway. I reached for the bulge in his back pocket and removed his wallet.

"They make them dumber by the day," I said with a sigh as I found his license, a credit card in a different name, and photos of half-naked women, along with a crisp hundred-dollar down payment. You get what you pay for.

I used my phone to snap pics of the license and credit card and one of the more stacked women and sent them off to Graham.

"Problem is, there's more of them than us," the muscle said with a straight face.

"I like you," I said with a genuine smile of approval before punching the elevator button to open the door again. "So I'll let you make him scream before the cops get here. Tell Graham if he says anything at all interesting, but that C-note speaks for itself. This isn't a pro job."

"You need someone to go down with you," he protested when he saw I was leaving. "There could be more of them down there."

"You would deny me my fun? Just wait until my mother shows up, and you'll understand." I had utterly no doubt that her spies had told her Arden was awake. I didn't want to hang around and watch the drama.

Wearing my camouflage army coat and a bored expression, I stepped into a crowded elevator and left goon and guard staring after me in disbelief. I'm used to that.

When I'd fled my non-traditional life of Magda's war zones in third world countries, I'd had a vague idea of living a normal life, one without terrorists and assassins on every corner. But even then, on my own, I'd ended up in a slum, fighting muggers and ultimately, hunting for my grandfather's killer.

Like it or not, I am my mother's—and possibly my father's— daughter. In another life, I could have been the assassin or terrorist, but I'd been gifted with brains and a choice. I didn't have to earn hundred dollar bills by threatening unarmed citizens.

Avoiding the lobby where more hired thugs, or their boss, might be waiting, I exited the elevator on the second floor in a pack of people wearing scrubs. I needed a better cover than my army jacket, but it was loaded with the tools of my trade, and I didn't want to ditch it. Visiting hours had just started, so I wandered through antiseptic-smelling halls with people wearing outdoor gear until I found a group of aides going off shift. I grabbed a trash can and drifted along with them down the service elevator.

I left through the back door into the parking lot under the cover of departing workers. I didn't see any more Stupids lurking.

I hid in the crowd at the bus stop and pinged my favorite Uber driver.

The only question was where I wanted to go. My phone provided so many interesting temptations. . . . Or I could go home and harass from my desk.

I was trying to think why that goon would want to talk to me and how much trouble I could be in when the Uber car pulled up.

"I can make my day's quota off your tips," the driver said happily. "Where would m'lady like to go now?"

I checked my phone for messages. Graham wasn't screaming at me yet. Julie and Zander hadn't hollered for my assistance from the police station, and they hadn't told me they were on the way home yet. It was before noon, so EG was still in school. Graham could keep Tudor occupied. Decision made.

I dug through my on-line files and produced the address the police last had for Melissa Winters, former JACAD student and mistress of Edward Parker III. It was time someone talked to her.

I flashed the address at the driver, and he took me to a high-rise condo. We drove right up to the building, and I hopped out, offering a tip if he'd wait to see if I could get in. I loved having money to spread around—it would be like Christmas all year long if I could keep doing it.

The vestibule gave me intercoms with names. Winters/Parker sounded like a good bet. I wasn't looking much like a lawyer in my army coat, but I was still on an adrenalin high after the hospital encounter and didn't intend to turn back now. I never used my real name if it could be avoided—I didn't want to be traced back to my family. I had to come up with something quickly.

So when a voice actually responded, I just pulled rabbits out of a hat. "Hi, I'm Linda Lane. I'm a student at Arden's school. Esther gave me your name. I wondered if you could help me?"

She buzzed me in. I leaned out to give the driver a thumbs up, and he waved and sped off. Really, I knew better than to enter a stranger's home without research, but I was dealing with way too many loose ends. If I meant to have a peaceful holiday, I had to put this puzzle together now. I texted Graham my location as I took the elevator up to her top-floor unit.

Melissa opened the door to greet me in the hall. Like most of the CAD students, she was model skinny and tall. The good Sunday school teacher had ditched her glasses for either Lasik or contacts. Her brown curls were now platinum, luxuriously long, and salon-styled with enough product to give them wave and not frizz. She wasn't glamorous by a long shot—button nose and eyes too small—but she had a friendly smile. Money might not buy happiness, but it could buy decent looks.

"You've heard from Esther?" she asked anxiously as she ushered me into a professionally designed studio unit. Underneath the clutter of books, colorful scarves and purses, and a corner filled with easel and art equipment, I could see the neutral taupe and brown of the original design. The black quartz kitchen counter was buried under brochures, catalogs, and probably unanswered mail, along with a few carry-out boxes and menus.

"It's been a while, which worries me," I said, removing two scarves and a sweater from the chair she indicated and taking a seat.

If she noticed that I was half a foot smaller than most of the students, she didn't seem concerned. She curled up on a corner of the plush sofa, clutched her hands, and seemed to disappear into the cushions. "I heard they found Mr. Paycock's body at the park, and I've been so worried."

"We all are. Esther was so angry when she left. . . . Well, I hoped someone who knew her could tell us she was okay." So everyone knew Esther was George Paycock's girl? That led to a lot of speculation. . . and possibly the identity of the other body. Except, why would Esther have been buried long before Paycock disappeared?

Melissa shook her head. "She and Mr. Paycock had a horrible fight over the school. What year are you, may I ask?"

"I had to drop out last year, so this is my first year back. Esther was rooming with us until she said she was going home." I stuck to the truth as Julie knew it, sort of.

"But you know about the parties, right? That's how Esther and I met. She and Rebecca were learning school construction, but I wanted to do fundraising and marketing. The construction department wasn't very supportive of its interns. The lack of funds caused a lot of argument." She gestured at the easel. "Without Ed, I'd still be starving in those awful trailers and selling my work on street corners. He's the sweetest man. Have you met him?"

Support? Was that what they called whoring these days? Or was I missing something? "I haven't had the opportunity. I'm still dealing with the home situation. Esther doesn't attend the parties either?"

"Not since the fight with Mr. Paycock. And now I hear he may have been embezzling from the school as well as his job! That's just doesn't seem right. Everyone who works for the school supports Reverend Arden's cause. Why would anyone steal from the park?"

Was she really the airhead that she sounded? Probably—brains and talent didn't guarantee common sense. I tested her knowledge a little more. "Maybe Rebecca knows where Esther is? I can't find her either. Do you know how to reach her?"

She sank further into the cushions. "I thought Rebecca had gone back to the school! Like I said, construction didn't pay their interns well, and she had some kind of quarrel with the guy she'd been dating about the apartment he'd set up for her. Ed said she was a whack job, but I liked her."

She didn't know Rebecca was dead? Wow, she lived in her own little world, which apparently didn't include newspapers. I didn't think I wanted to be the messenger who got shot for telling her, so I played dumb too. "Do you know who she'd been dating? Was he in construction? Maybe I can ask him."

She shrugged. "Big guy, surly attitude. He seldom came to the parties so she must have met him on the job. I don't know what she saw in him except his fancy truck and boat. But they talked contracting together and went fishing. They would sometimes come here for drinks and to complain about how slow progress was on the park. They said we needed money coming in faster, and they'd talk about things I didn't understand. They called him Bill, if that helps."

I rubbed my nose in irritation. I knew this space cadet had the answers to my questions buried somewhere in her oblivious skull. I just didn't know how to drag them out without a police interrogation. And "Ed" would have her lawyered up if that happened.

I had a sneaking suspicion I didn't want Edward Parker III to know anything until we had our culprits in hand—because with this many loose connections and one dead embezzler, there could easily be more than one villain.

I pulled another name out of my memory file. "Mrs. Overcamp will be unhappy to hear we've lost another student. I'm afraid the school will close soon."

Melissa's eyes widened. "Mrs. Overcamp helped us all find supporters. Surely she knows where to find Rebecca and Esther! I thought maybe you didn't want to ask her."

She started looking suspicious. I didn't even know who Overcamp was except Julie had said she might have bugged her phone.

"Since Reverend Arden was shot, she's been inconsolable. I just didn't want to bother her," I improvised.

"Reverend Arden was shot!" She jumped up and flung her long arms around in a kind of a gazelle-like panic. "That's just *wrong*." She paced up and down through the clutter. "No wonder Ed hasn't called. . . . Oh, I just don't understand any of this!"

She swung around quickly. "The reverend is okay, though, isn't he? He's not like. . . not like Mr. Paycock?"

I barely kept myself from rolling my eyes. "He's in serious condition and not being allowed visitors." Maybe scaring her was the way to go.

"I need to talk to Ed. I don't think I can help you anymore. I was going to do the concept artwork for the park, but this all sounds. . . I don't *know*!" she wailed. "My friends have disappeared. People are getting shot! I don't like it. You probably ought to go back to school and just keep your head down."

"But Mrs. Overcamp wants me and my roommate to go to a Christmas party on Friday. Are you saying we shouldn't go?" I stood up, more than ready to leave, or I'd have to kill her out of frustration.

"I don't know *anything*! Give me your number, and if Ed says you shouldn't go, I'll let you know."

I handed her one of my old Linda Lane, teacher, business cards. "Please, keep in touch. We all need to stick together at times like this."

She almost looked grateful—and I suspected she needed friends.

I also suspected she'd lose the card in the clutter the instant I walked out the door. I noticed a magnetic whiteboard on her stainless steel refrigerator and walked over and penned in the phone number there, underlining *Linda* several times.

"Maybe I'll see you Friday," I said, heading for the door.

She nodded and didn't even look up from her phone as I let myself out.

As I walked toward the Metro station, Graham texted me a mug shot of the gun guy from the hospital. A small time thug off the street, he had priors including assault and battery.

Then Graham sent a second image showing the thug's employment ID card from Gregory construction, the company building the park.

My stomach started to roil as a few connections popped in place. I needed to whack myself upside the head for not seeing the obvious earlier.

Twenty-one

Juliana learns to sneak

"THANK YOU FOR ESCORTING US," Julie said to the two uniformed policeman standing at the trailer door as Maryam hurried in to pack her bags. "It is very disturbing to think a place of godliness is polluted by a murderer."

One shrugged and turned his steely-eyed gaze to the park. The other just nodded impatiently.

Lucas pushed her toward the steps. "Pack and hurry it up. Maryam's brother is waiting for her."

Maryam had finally broken down and given Julie her brother's number. Ana's magic genie in the attic had somehow summoned him to do his duty to his sister.

"I packed my things already." Julie squeezed past Lucas's big body to address the policeman again. "May I run over to the classroom to collect my laptop?" She pointed at the two-story block building just down the road.

"We can't be in two places at once, miss," the taller officer said disapprovingly.

"You can see me walk over." Unlike Zander, she didn't have a little tablet with all her life inside it. The laptop was all she had.

Lucas jumped down from the trailer steps and gestured at the officers. "If you'll look after Maryam, I'll go with Juliana. It shouldn't take a minute. I have a key to the classroom."

The uniformed men looked relieved. Juliana wanted to have a tantrum but, accustomed to the attitude that she was a frail helpless female, she merely hurried down the road. Tantrums were wasted if she was getting her way.

As they approached the concrete block building where classes were held, she could see the door was already open. She hesitated. "Did they not say the school was closed?"

"Yes. Everyone was dismissed early for the holidays," Lucas confirmed, halting with her.

"I hear voices." She glanced over her shoulder. One of the

policemen was looking in their direction. She aimed for the side of the building, as if that had been her goal all along.

Amazingly, Lucas didn't argue. They walked past a ragged hedge where they couldn't be seen and ducked down beneath a window.

"That jackass has left us bankrupt!" A man's low roar nearly rattled the thin pane over their heads. "We need their bankrolls. Surely there has to be some of those girls still around. They didn't all fly off to Never-Never Land."

A woman's angry reply didn't carry as well. Julie strained to hear but could only catch the tone and inflection. "Mrs. Overcamp?" she whispered to Lucas.

He shrugged and fiddled with his phone.

Annoyed, she returned to listening as the man shouted again. "Look, Ed has a party coming up. There's no better way of getting these guys to open their checkbooks than getting them drunk, and they'll do that with pretty women around. You got a better way?"

Again, the low murmur. The man cursed and stormed out. Julie ducked into the hedge and only saw his heavy construction boots stomp by.

"She's leaving," Lucas murmured, listening to his phone. "Give her a minute and we'll get your laptop."

She widened her eyes and stared at his phone but kept her mouth shut as she heard a key scrape in a door. A moment later, Mrs. Overcamp's Uggs stamped by.

"*Eish*, you have the classroom bugged?" she asked in horror, staring at his phone as he put it away.

"Do you want to know what she was saying or not?" he asked smugly, leading her around to a rear door and unlocking it.

"Who *are* you?"

"Security, like I said. Don't ask questions. Just grab the laptop and let's beat it before someone comes to check on us."

She ran down the rear hall to her classroom, snagged her laptop, and emptied her desk drawer. Finding an unused USB drive, she flung it at Lucas, who was examining Mrs. Overcamp's computer with interest. He caught the gadget, raised his eyebrows, and without a word, plugged it in and began copying the hard drive. Mrs. Overcamp always used the school password that everyone could access.

"The machine's too slow," he griped as Julie packed all her

things into her briefcase and came over to watch him. "And the computer is filled to capacity."

"We'd be doing her a favor to take it with us and clean it out," she suggested mischievously.

"Theft of information and grand larceny, nice." He unplugged the USB when it hit capacity and shoved it in his coat pocket. "Let's go."

They left by the rear door, locking it after them. One of the policemen was already walking down the lane in their direction when they emerged from behind the hedge. He looked relieved and motioned them to hurry up.

And there, watching them gather in front of the trailer, was Mr. Gregory, the contractor she'd seen with Mrs. Overcamp before. His scowl was threatening as he took in their faces. Without a word, he walked back toward the construction area.

He was wearing heavy-duty construction boots.

"Not good," Lucas muttered as they hurried toward the waiting police car outside the gate.

"Could you take us to the police station instead of home?" Julie requested as they climbed in.

"You've already given your report," the taller policeman said. "We were told to see you safely delivered to your residence."

"Then you had best make certain we aren't followed." She glanced nervously out the back window and opened her phone when it buzzed.

WHERE ARE YOU? Ana texted.

LEAVING PARK. WITH POLICE.

Julie could almost hear the urgency in the instant flash of an image on her screen. She studied the photo, didn't recognize the face, and then realized what she was looking at—an ID badge from the general contractor working on the park—the contractor who had just glared at them.

Looking at the screen over her shoulder, both Maryam and Lucas made inappropriate noises.

"Who would follow a police car?" the policeman driving the squad car asked scornfully, although she noticed he checked his mirror.

She held her phone out to the policeman in the passenger seat. "This man has just been arrested for assaulting my sister." The cop took it, examined it, and frowned.

"That was his boss scowling at us when we left," Lucas said, taking the phone back and using it to text Ana back.

"*Yoh!*" Julie protested. "What are you doing?"

"We can't even take you to the safe house if we're followed. I'm telling your family we need to get you out of here."

Julie snatched the phone back. "I am not hiding. No *skebanga* will drive me from my family at Christmas."

She smiled at Ana's text and held it up to Lucas. JULIE STAYS WITH US. YOU STAY WITH MARYAM.

"She knew it wasn't you texting?" Lucas scowled at the phone, took it back, and started copying her contact list.

"You are such a. . ." The only English word she could think of was one Zander had once used—*dick*. She thought that might be inappropriate. She snatched her phone back again and texted to Ana that she would go with Maryam to meet her brother, then return home.

Ana texted back that she would send a limo to pick her up when she was ready.

"Construction truck on our tail," the policeman driving the car said as Maryam huddled in the corner with her carry-on and Julie fought with Lucas over the phone. "Prepare yourselves." He hit the siren and the gas pedal and left the truck in his dust.

Ana takes over

"SHOW ME THE TRAIL of the embezzled money," I ordered, standing over Zander's shoulder as he pulled up a spreadsheet on the computer screen. He'd returned from the police station by Metro, leaving Julie and Maryam with Lucas and the police. I admired his dedication to his task.

"The FBI has already done most of the work," he said, almost apologetically. "They have traced the funds leaving GenDef and being deposited into an account that the board of Jesus World controls."

"But they've not found any wrongdoing at the park?" I asked in disbelief.

"They've only begun looking. I have downloaded the park's financials from Mr. Graham's files. The park is spending buckets of money; much of it appears to be for legitimate expenses. Reverend Arden signs off on most of them, although several board members and employees can apparently approve invoices and control money transfers. I have a list of the largest contractors and businesses receiving payments. Will those help?"

I studied the list of expenditures he brought up. Trusts, LLCs, corporations, no individual names. These guys knew how to make it difficult. "There, that one." I pointed at an account named WGCI. "That's a Virginia bank and the park contractor's name is William Gregory."

"Then it should be perfectly legitimate," Zander complained. "They are constructing the park, and they *should* be paid large sums."

"We'll need the construction contracts, see how much they were supposed to be paid. I can't see how that park can have spent this much on rusting skeletons and used tin cans."

He frowned at the screen. "I will need the contracts and the construction company's books. I only have the park's."

I sat down, took the computer away from him, found the bank account where WGCI's payments were being deposited, called up Tudor's hacker program, and rolled my eyes as I broke in easily with User ID: WCGI and password: 123456. Office grunts liked things simple. But all I wanted was the address to which the statements were sent, and if I was really lucky, to find out if the bank downloaded into WCGI's bookkeeping system. They did.

I turned the computer back to Zander. "Here's the contracting office's computer. One can hope both contracts and bookkeeping are in it. Merry Christmas."

I ran down to my office to line up my thoughts. Julie texted that they were taking Maryam to her brother at the embassy. Graham IM'd that Magda was *not* on her way to the airport. Magda was the X factor in any equation, and I wanted her out of our hair as much as he did.

I made my own spread sheet. The police had been busy. We had three known bodies at the park: (1) an unknown construction worker last spring who died of a broken neck, (2) George Paycock—police records had confirmed that the dumped body Julie had videoed was his, and (3) and they'd uncovered the remains of an unidentified woman. Since Julie's friend, Esther, was the only student unaccounted for, I feared the worst.

Rebecca had worked at the park but hadn't been buried there. She had been strangled and her body had been found in the river. Thanks to Melissa, I now knew her park construction boyfriend had a boat, so I counted her as a fourth park victim.

It was too early for a full post mortem on George Paycock and maybe-Esther, but police reports indicated they'd suffered gunshot wounds before being bulldozed into one of the park's unfinished foundations. Broken neck, strangulation, and bullets—just the varying manner of deaths said we might have multiple killers using the barren wasteland of the park as a burying ground, which made the river case an outlier.

I needed motives.

I went back to my spreadsheet. CAD received large sums from many donors, most equal to or exceeding the ones from GenDef. Paycock had been *accused* of embezzling from his employer, GenDef, and hiding the theft by depositing the funds into CAD. He'd not been convicted in court, however.

What would be the point of killing someone who would be going to jail—unless he knew more than the feds did and was about to spill the beans.

Tony Jeffrey, CEO of GenDef, also had access to the company accounts. His name was on the park board, too, although he didn't seem to be an active participant and wasn't authorized to sign off on invoices or bank accounts. That made him a little less suspect than George. Besides, I couldn't see any reason why a well-heeled, lawyered-up CEO had any reason to kill a man accused of embezzling. He would just want his money back.

Or maybe this wasn't even about the embezzlement. If Paycock was a womanizer. . . one of those construction guys could have taken objection to his attentions to the wrong woman.

Then we had William Gregory, construction contractor. Money from the park was pouring into the WGCI bank account, which was presumably his company. Julie's summary of her encounter at the school raised him high on my suspicion-o-meter. How could WGCI possibly be almost bankrupt with a money flow like this?

Melissa had said someone called *Bill* in the construction department had argued with Rebecca. I needed to find out if William Gregory might be that Bill. If so, it would enhance his standing as killer material, but why would he dump her in the

Potomac if he was using his bulldozers to bury Georgie and others in the park?

I needed to speak with Mrs. Overcamp and Ed Parker III, trust fund baby, as well as William Gregory. But first I needed to know more about them. I fired up my Cobalt Whiz and began digging.

It didn't take long to discover that Mrs. Dorothy Overcamp had previously been married to Bryson Gregory, a construction contractor. They had a son and a daughter. Surprise, surprise, *William* was the son and had taken on daddy's business. Mrs. Overcamp held part ownership of her son's construction company.

That smacked of collusion, but the son could have just arranged a job for his mother. Overseeing the marketing department wasn't exactly a highway to wealth.

EG came home just as I was trying to match Ed Parker's income with some of the expenses in the park's books. She usually went straight to her gothic tower, but today she favored me with a visit.

She set Tudor's plastic blob ornament on my desk. It was now painted a lovely red with eccentrically wobbly gold stars and a few white stripes I thought might represent starlight. My sister is a genius. That does not mean she's an artist.

"I haven't hung my own ornament," she declared, flinging herself into my wing chair. "Tudor is working on something top secret and won't make what I asked."

"He hasn't made his own," I pointed out. "You can't expect him to make one for you first. Google *origami*. I'm betting you can make something special with just construction paper and glitter."

"Glitter?" Her eyes lit. Her eyes were green like mine and dangerous when narrowed, but they were wide with interest now. "I have lots of glitter and some plastic jewels."

"And glue?" At her excited nod, I knew I would regret this. "Then go for it." I handed her a silver Sharpie. "This would look good on purple."

"Yeahhh," she breathed happily, snatching the pen. "Can I make more than one?"

"Knock yourself out." It felt good to steer her creativity down constructive paths for a change.

"Lock her up with the cat," the intercom said after EG happily ran off to pester Mallard for cookies. "Magda is breaking into Arden's hospital room, and Patra is over at GenDef's weapons warehouse pretending she's working for Jeffrey's office. Lock them all up with cats."

"You don't think I haven't tried that over all these years?" I asked with annoyance.

"Your other sister and her FBI informant boyfriend just told Sam to return the limo to the park."

This is one of the many reasons I try not to use Graham's limo service. He spies on us. In this case, that was a good thing, I thought, maybe.

"*What*? You mean Juliana?" I was on my feet and two steps from taking the ladder stairs up when I realized Magda's suitcase sat on my trap door. "FBI informant?" I asked weakly, dropping back in my chair.

"Lucas isn't a college drop-out. He's Rebecca's brother, a trained officer who left his job to spy on CAD. He's a free-range ticking bomb. And he and Julie have just uploaded Overcamp's computer contents into Julie's laptop."

I didn't know whether to boggle more over the company Julie was keeping or the fact that Graham was actually *talking* to me instead of burying me in documents. Well—I glanced at my computer—he was doing both. He had hacked Julie's laptop and was downloading file copies as fast as she uploaded the originals.

I skimmed through the documents and opened one at random. It appeared to be a B-list of DC political lobbyists. My eyebrows rose at the sums attached to their names.

"Convoluted," I told the intercom as I opened a few more of the files Julie had apparently stolen from Mrs. O. Julie had texted that the police had delivered her and Lucas to the safe house after their hair-raising police ride.

"Party lists," he suggested, presumably scrolling through the same files.

I ran a search on the name *Rebecca*, and found her on a list of other female students with cryptic letters and numbers after their names. Esther and Melissa were there, too. Was Overcamp the one responsible for choosing photogenic students—so she could send them to *parties*?

"Overcamp hooks up political sleaze balls with eager students in exchange for what?" I demanded.

"PACs raise billions," he said with an audible shrug. "A choice of available young women might be a reward to fundraisers who meet quotas."

"Cynic." But he was probably close to right. Julie had said it sounded as if someone was using the women as lures to open checkbooks. "Rich Ed, Jeffrey the CEO, and Georgie the Embezzler are all on this list for an October party. Gregory isn't, so how did he hook up with Rebecca?"

"He's a blue-collar contractor without money or political ambitions. But he does have control of the bulldozer. Keep Julia out of the park."

My stomach dropped. The intercom clicked off.

I didn't think too highly of an FBI informant or unemployed cop who would let my little sister walk straight into trouble.

I called Julie. "Gregory could be a killer. Don't be Magda. Come home and let's work out the evidence."

"The evidence is likely to be in the construction office at the park," she responded. "Gregory has gone home for the day."

"He just tried to follow you a few hours ago! He probably has mutant goons working for him. Tell Lucas I know who he is, and I'll call his handlers if he doesn't bring you back here."

"Who he is?" she asked dubiously, quoting me.

"Come home, and I'll tell you."

"You told me to make my own decisions. Unless you tell me Lucas is a killer, I must trust him."

Argh, save me from my own advice! "Fine. Then tell him Magda will hoist more than a petard if she finds out where you are. And look up petard."

I hung up. There wasn't much point in arguing. I could order the limo home, but I had to respect Julia's choices. Although I was pretty sure Lucas would be in Julie's hot seat shortly.

Lucas was Rebecca's brother. He was looking for the killer who strangled his sister. Would he still protect Julie? I thought a litany of curse words while I did a quick search through Mrs. O's files. I found no smoking guns. Antsy, I checked what Zander was doing. He had begun an insane spreadsheet showing large sums of money feeding into the park as donations from numerous sponsors and out again to companies that didn't exactly say "Mechanical dinosaur creator."

"Going snipe hunting," I told the intercom. "Zander and Tudor can help you mind the cat."

I thought my spider may have thrown the intercom across the room. I heard a crash, a crackle, and dead silence. Worked for me.

Twenty-two

Juliana breaks and enters

"I THINK YOU'D BETTER tell me who you are," Julie said stiffly as Lucas sorted through a ring of keys and opened the construction office trailer.

He shot her a look of irritation. "Arden hired me for security. In my muddled career, I have accumulated some experience."

"Ana would not refer to Arden as your *handler*." She turned on her phone's flashlight and studied the office's disorderly interior. Papers cluttered an aging desk and worktables. Smelly take-out containers and open beer cans littered the kitchen area. File cabinets hung half open, with files half-sticking out in haphazard disarray.

This was not the office of an organized person. "Do they not have a secretary to handle documents in some quiet office elsewhere?" she asked in dismay.

"This ought to be the construction site office. He should only have blueprints and work orders here," Lucas said. "But with all these filing cabinets, it looks like his company's main office."

"No computers." She opened the desk drawers. "No checkbook. And you haven't answered me."

"I don't see why I should. You're here because you want to be." He flipped on a flashlight to examine the file folders sticking from the cabinet drawers, presumably the most recent ones accessed.

"Fine, then I'm under no obligation to tell you anything I find or explain anything I learn elsewhere." She unfolded a long sheet of accounting paper on the desk. It contained an old-fashioned spreadsheet containing an incomprehensible list of names of people she didn't know. Each name had what appeared to be large dollar amounts next to it. She took a picture and sent it to Zander.

She discovered a trove of professional photos of gatherings of beautiful people, similar to the one Ana had shown her with students mixing with sponsors. She didn't think the phone could do the images justice, but she disliked stealing. She snapped copies and hoped for the best.

Lucas was still rifling the file cabinets. "Computers would be easier," he grumbled.

"I gave you Mrs. Overcamp's computer," she reminded him. "The best you can hope to find in here is the gun used on Reverend Arden."

"Not likely. The cops caught the skinheads I saw at the hotel. They're still testing the guns, but they probably had nothing to do with Rebecca. She was strangled, so there was no weapon involved."

"Rebecca?" Julie glanced up in puzzlement.

"My sister. One of these construction bastards killed my sister. She didn't know anyone else in this town, and she didn't go out with strangers."

Julie widened her eyes. "I am very sorry for your loss, and I can understand your anger, but this is bigger than your sister. You're missing the elephant for seeing only its toes."

"If the toes did the smashing, then I have to examine them. I'll get to the rest of the elephant later. The big guys can cover it better than I can, and they don't have any interest in Rebecca. But Becka was a smart girl. She knew construction. She told the family there was something peculiar happening here—and she was probably killed for it."

"You still won't find evidence of it here. You need to talk to people, work with the architects, study the whole situation. That's bigger than both of us. We need a specific goal in here, something to give the police reason for a warrant. I don't watch TV, and even I know that."

He glared at her, and she gulped.

Ana gets restless

PATRA WAS DOING WHAT I wanted to do—investigate Tony Jeffrey and GenDef from the inside. Men with arsenals were seldom pussycats, and I had to resist fretting.

That didn't mean I couldn't text her to see how she was doing.

She called right back. "I'm outside the warehouse. I need security clearance to get in."

"Surprise, surprise. Why are you at the warehouse and not headquarters?" I ran a search on GenDef's location while I talked.

"Rumor has it that the embezzlement wasn't just cash. I wanted to talk to some employees."

Translation: Patra meant to use her stunning looks and reporter's guile to chat up a few unsuspecting young guys, charming them into complaining about their jobs and going from there.

I pulled up a Google map of the area. "There's a bar called Guns 'N Bolts one block to the east of the warehouse. Put on a Redskins cap and wait there at shift change. Who needs security badges when beer will do?"

"That was my next step, but I really wanted to see inside."

I could hear her heels clicking down the sidewalk. I glanced at the time. Almost four. "Graham can probably get that, if you don't mind grainy video. Find out what you can about Jeffrey while you're at it. I need to talk with him."

"He's at a private PAC event at 701 tonight. Sean's trying to sneak me in as the gossip reporter."

"I was hoping for an office meeting, but a crowded event might just do it. Maybe I'll see you there." I hung up and started working my contact list. As a virtual assistant, I'd developed an extensive list, but most of my previous work hadn't been in DC, so that list was shorter.

Graham, on the other hand, was a DC insider from way back. Out of curiosity, to see how cooperative he was feeling, I messaged him and asked for an invite. He'd done it before, so I wasn't stretching my imagination too far.

Five minutes later, I had what looked like images of two gold-embossed cards and a description of the messenger I should meet at the door where I could pick them up. I never knew whether he stole these things or if people just sent him whatever he asked, and I didn't intend to inquire.

"Want to go with me?" I asked the intercom.

His snort was all the answer I'd receive. Graham preferred his privacy. If and when he went anywhere, it was in the guise of Thomas Alexander, a lesser-known security consultant who just happened to be dead. Graham had taken over the company, and people just made strange assumptions. The late Alexander's face wasn't easily recognizable, but Graham's was. It was an iffy proposition for him to mingle with DC insiders. He'd been recognized just from a video of him entering a building the last time he'd left the attic. Like Clark Gable or George Clooney, he has that kind of timeless star quality, even with the scars.

So I called Nick. Just the club's name had him hooked. It was one of DC's more elegant venues with a menu and staff to match.

The limo returned Julie safely as I was on my way upstairs to examine my limited party wardrobe, and I breathed a sigh of relief. She had her arms full of boxes, and the driver was helping her carry them, leaving the car illegally parked on the curb.

"May I help Zander in his research?" she asked, gesturing at the driver to leave her boxes on the floor. "Something is *bosbefok* at the park."

Personally, I thought the whole concept of Jesus World was *bosbefok*–crazy mad—but my opinion didn't matter. "Did you find anything relevant at the park?"

"Only that Lucas is as *dwankie* as I first thought. I will help Zander go through the information we found."

I bit back a smile at the epithet. It seemed our very proper sister thought it was okay to insult people if she did it in a language she thought they couldn't understand. That she called Lucas lame and uncool said he'd not followed her orders.

"You're good at photography, aren't you? Why don't you sit down with those months of videos and see if you can find anything that does not compute?"

Her eyes narrowed as she thought about it. "I never had much time to study them for anything other than good shots for marketing. I can do that."

"Excellent." I lifted some of her boxes and started for the stairs. "I need to go out this evening. I'd appreciate it if you and Zander would keep EG out of trouble. She's making more ornaments for the tree."

"Elizabeth is such a pretty name. Why do you not use it?" She followed me up with the rest of the boxes.

"Once you know her better, you'll understand," I promised. "Although of all of us, she's the one most likely to live up to her royal namesake."

Julie smiled at that. "I doubt I shall ever resemble Queen Juliana. Mother must have been feeling very fatalistic when she chose Anastasia for you."

"At the time, she believed Princess Anastasia was still alive and living in secrecy. She has a strong subversive streak." I left her to arrange the boxes in her room while I contemplated my lack of glamorous attire.

I already knew I had only one choice. It just depended on how I wished to accessorize it—with killer boots and attitude, or polite heels and invisibility.

I opted for nerdy harmlessness. Patra could sashay in screaming glamor if she liked. There was a very good chance Magda would also be there. She had an affinity for wealth and power, and any party at the 701 would be packed with both. As usual, I chose not to compete.

Nick scowled as if he'd bite my head off and spit me out when I came down the stairs later.

"Glasses, Ana? Really?" He glared at the offending black frames I'd picked up on one of my thrift-store sorties. "And why didn't you just wear loafers and bobby socks while you were at it?"

He was turned out in tailored tux complete with white tie and blue cummerbund, his blond hair precisely styled to whatever the latest male fashion was. He looked very James Bondish.

"Kitten heels are better for running than spike," I informed him, donning my faux fur without his help. "I'm not wearing a braid. I thought that would please you."

He glared at the smooth chignon I'd accomplished after half an hour of pins and stabbing myself in the head. My hair is long, thick, and tediously black. It doesn't lend itself to stylish hairdos.

"Stick a fascinator on it and wear a blinking sign that says *nerd*, why don't you?"

I glared at him, then checked on Julie and Zander working hard in the library. I waved to indicate we were leaving. They barely looked up from their computers to wave back.

"What's a fascinator and where can I get one?" I asked as he opened the door.

"The driver will have one waiting," the chandelier overhead intoned. "It's wired for sound and video."

I almost rolled on the floor laughing at Nick's expression. I was in serious danger of falling in love with the Evil Genie in the attic who understood me too well.

Twenty-three

"NOT QUITE THE TAJ Mahal," I said, trying not to gape at the modernistic decor as we handed over our invitations at the hired venue.

"I swear, I can't take you anywhere," Nick muttered.

He was obviously trying not to glare at the black feathers adorning my hair and dangling down my nape. Fascinators were quite fascinating, I'd decided. "Then toddle off, keeping your eyes open for any of that list of suspects I gave you. I promise, I will not feel abandoned."

He eyed the formal buffet table draped in purple and white linen. The china and silver were illuminated by glass globes above, and crystalline torches in the all-white centerpieces below. They probably had chocolate fountains and shrimp mountains behind the purple drapery along the edges of the open room. The lounge area was occupied by a small orchestra playing soporific Bach. Always happy to oblige, Nick deserted me for the food.

I'd swear there was a cat in the room just from the way my eyes watered, but I suspected I was overloading on bouquets of lilies and French perfume. Nick was right—he really shouldn't take me anywhere like this.

I focused on the tuxedo crowd. Reality was hugely different from studying a fixed image on a computer screen. I needed a facial recognition program to run behind my glasses. I'd ask Tudor about that later.

I found Edward Parker III first because he was standing next to Melissa. He was tall, slim, had a receding hairline, and dyed his probably graying hair blond. Definite sag along the jawline that he'd probably have tightened soon, if his artificial tan was any indication of his vanity. He wore a diamond and gold ring on the hand he draped over Melissa's shoulders.

Looked like I'd be Linda Lane, schoolteacher and student, this evening. I texted Nick to let him know. He was already chatting with an elegantly-attired older gentleman. He looked down at his phone but didn't even glance in my direction as he tucked it back in his pocket.

I scanned the room again, hunting for anyone who might resemble the company photo of Tony Jeffery, the man I'd come to see, but I came up blank. Tony might be the reason I was here, but Parker made a good substitute. I grabbed a passing champagne glass—I hate champagne but loved the look of the crystal in my hand—and worked my way through the mob.

I doubted that the bug in my fascinator could pick up more than soft violin music, loud crowd noise, and blurry images, but I figured if I screamed, Graham would notice. It was probably his security on duty, or at least one of his men would be embedded in whatever company was here. That would explain the easy invites. He was sneaky that way.

"Melissa," I cried as I approached. "It's good to see you here!"

She looked momentarily blank. I understood. My long braid and army coat had registered one impression. Super nerd elegance was quite another. "Linda Lane," I reminded her. "We spoke this morning about the school."

She brightened. "It's nice to know someone at these parties. Ed, I'd like you to meet a friend of mine. Linda, this is Ed Parker. I may have mentioned him."

As her *supporter*, yeah, right. "Good meeting a supporter of the arts, Mr. Parker. Melissa was trying to help me decide what to do if Reverend Arden's school closes. I'd really hoped to be a part of the program. It's a good cause."

Ed looked bored. He frowned at my eccentric hairpiece, dismissed the rest of my bland attire, and returned to studying the crowd over my shoulder. "There's always another good cause on the horizon, although I haven't heard that JACAD will close. I thought it was simply out for the holidays."

"Well, no one knows if Reverend Arden will recover, and this business with Mr. Paycock has everyone suspecting the funds are gone. In this tough economy, we're all up a creek if JACAD can't provide jobs."

He snorted derisively. "As if building shacks in the jungle is a job. You'd be better off working at Walmart."

That was a fine attitude for someone on CAD's board of directors. And he wasn't confirming anything about the funds. Since

I wasn't accomplishing much with this topic, I switched it up. "My brother told me I should apply at General Defense since they're a big supporter of the program. I was supposed to talk to Mr. Jeffrey this evening."

"Oh, Mr. Jeffrey is a real sweetie," Melissa exclaimed. "His wife is ill and can never attend these functions, but he's always so polite to all of us! I thought I saw him at the buffet a few minutes ago."

Parker frowned haughtily. "One does not talk business at affairs like this. If you wish to see him at his office, I'll mention your name. Call his secretary in the morning."

That was a load of crap if I ever heard it. I gave him my best fawning smile. "That's very generous of you, Mr. Parker! I see why Melissa is so fond of you." I pulled a card out of my purse and handed it over. "Thank you so much."

"It's nothing. Perhaps you'll be able to help us out sometime," he said in a decidedly bored and distant voice as he tucked the card in his pocket.

I had no idea who "us" would be and doubted I wanted to help a wealthy trust fund baby who dangled Sunday school teachers on his string, but I tried to sound enthusiastic as I turned to Melissa.

She surprised me by taking my arm and breaking away from Ed's. "Let's check out the buffet," she suggested, "I heard the chef outdid himself tonight."

I hoped she actually had something to say and wasn't just looking for escape. "It's been a pleasure, Mr. Parker." And I started across the room, dragging an anxious Melissa with me.

"Rebecca is dead!" she whispered. "I just heard she was found in the river! Why did no one tell me?"

"Dead?" I looked at her in blank surprise, more interested in how she'd found out than in old news.

"I can't believe it." She was almost crying and her hand dug into my arm. "She loved boating. She could swim. How could she die? Do you think Esther may have been with her, and they just haven't found her body yet?"

Huh, sounds like she didn't have *all* the information yet, if she didn't know Rebecca had been strangled before she'd been left to sink. "I have no idea," I said in what I hoped sounded like horror. "I heard about the body. How do you know it was Rebecca?"

"Ed told me," she whispered, glancing over her shoulder. "He thought I knew."

Ed wasn't telling her that Rebecca had been *murdered.* I debated and came down on the side of knowledge being better than ignorance and hoping Melissa would pack her bags and go home if she learned the truth.

I pretended to admire the artistic stack of unidentifiable appetizers and whispered, "If we're talking about the same story, I heard the woman in the Potomac was strangled. And that a woman's body was found in a grave with Mr. Paycock's. I'm thinking we all need to go home."

She was so silent, that I had to glance over. Her chin was quivering, and she was fighting back tears. "That can't be right," she murmured. "After Owen died, Esther said. . ." She glanced back across the room. I tried to follow her gaze, but the room was too crowded. She seemed to set her mouth in decision and removed her phone from her designer bag. "I need to talk with someone. This just isn't right."

She left me to admire the sushi. I'm not a real detective and can't go bugging private phones, no matter how much I longed to find out who Melissa was calling. I just hoped whoever it was would tell her to go home. When she mentioned Esther and Owen, had she been referring to the construction guy who'd died last spring?

Melissa seemed headed for an anteroom off the foyer. Instead of following her, I returned to my real purpose here and searched for GenDef's elusive CEO.

A murmur and undulation of the predominantly male crowd caused me to study the entrance. Patra had arrived. She handed a fur wrap to a tuxedoed greeter, revealing her form-fitting, Christmas-red evening gown. She wore her thick chestnut hair in a fancy 'do pinned with zirconia that flashed just like diamonds. Tongues were probably hanging out, but I'd seen this reaction to my sister often enough not to bother watching her work the room.

Melissa had disappeared from view. I picked up a plate from the buffet and glanced back over my shoulder. Ed Parker was talking to a vaguely familiar face—perhaps one of CAD's other board members. I tried to place the stranger's round, cherubic visage on the roster and thought he might be one of the oil company sponsors, possibly the one involved in the AGA, the gun lobby that Ed belonged to.

I had a brief mental image of all the execs producing their concealed carries and having an old-fashioned gunfight, but I suppressed my eccentric humor and continued to search for Jeffrey. I found Nick first.

My genial, extroverted half-brother was holding court and expounding on the lack of good tailors in this country for an audience of half a dozen sartorially-impressive gentlemen in tuxes. My guess was that they all had tailors in Thailand, and Nick was trying to find out their names. The embassy didn't pay enough to keep him in bespoke suits.

I was about to skirt him and look for Tony Jeffrey at the dessert buffet when I noticed a gentleman leaning against a column almost hidden behind a half-wall, listening to Nick's discussion group.

Gray-haired, medium height, with a slight stoop to his shoulders, he looked familiar. He wasn't wearing a fitted tux, just a decent business suit and tie, as if he'd come over from the office. Then I spotted Patra zooming in on him, and comprehension sank in—this was Tony Jeffrey, looking far older than his stockholder image on the firm's brochure.

Dang, why did so many of the people involved with CAD look like decent guys? Shouldn't they look shifty and mean? The man standing there in the shadows owned a large part of a corporation that provided handguns to every gang in this country and around the world. He was responsible for the deaths of innocents by the thousands, maybe millions. And that was before we got into the big guns for the military and police forces.

He looked like somebody's aging accountant father.

A bodyguard stopped Patra before she came too close. While I filled my plate with cheese and olives, I watched Senator Paul Rose and his entourage approach the gun manufacturer. No wonder Jeffrey hid in shadows. Everyone wanted a piece of his time.

I texted Patra and asked if she could hear anything. She looked up, found me, and shook her head.

I had too many deaths and not enough suspects. I stood in the shadows, nibbling my dinner, and watched the crowd. Lots of men glad-handing, exchanging cards—politicians and lobbyists would be my surmise. A few of CAD's corporate sponsors schmoozed at the bar, but not many. This was evidently not their kind of affair. The people here were into serious political arm-twisting.

I assumed the older women in this crowd were mostly wives, although several of the whitened-teeth flashing group were probably lobbyists. A few nubile young things like Melissa were attached to older men. A few others worked the crowd.

I thought I caught a glimpse of the back of Magda's head as she steered a gray-haired tall dude into an alcove. I would avoid going in that direction.

In the shadows along the walls lurked security with Bluetooth earphones and weapons beneath their coats. Senator Paul Rose, as a leading presidential candidate, would be heavily guarded. Men with billions, like Jeffrey, might have their own parade, except some of his uglies were in lock-up tonight, I hoped.

The lack of women was so evident that I decided to follow their movements while Nick and Patra tried to close in on Jeffrey. A polished, business-suited female about Magda's age whispered to Jeffrey, then swung her slender hips in the direction of the back of the bar.

Guessing that was where the restrooms were hidden, I moseyed along after her. I didn't think I could take a photo in this crowd, but maybe I could fake it in closer quarters. Anyone who got close to Jeffrey was worth investigating.

I checked the angle of my fascinator in the mirror and refreshed my lipstick while the unknown female used the facilities. When she emerged to wash her hands, I was shoving pins into my hair. "I hate my hair," I said, because most women hated their hair and it made a great conversation starter. "If Frankie would just let me cut it all off, I would."

"It's lovely hair," she said graciously but stiffly, reaching for a towel. "But if you want it cut, then you should. Men shouldn't dictate how we use our bodies."

I raised my eyebrows in surprise at her reflection. "You're not part of this crowd, are you?"

She smiled faintly. "I accompany my father because my mother can't. That doesn't mean I have to agree with his politics or old-fashioned attitude."

Ah, that meant she was probably Jeffrey's daughter, not his plaything. Dang, I wanted a good reason to hate him.

"Smart lady," I said approvingly. "And when my career takes off, and I'm rolling in my own money, I'll whack my hair." Liar, liar, pants on fire, but I was just making conversation. "I'm Linda Lane, friend of Melissa Winters." I stuck out my hand.

She shook with her fingertips, as if I might have a communicable disease. Her nails were manicured with nearly indiscernible polish, her hair was a brownish-blond, and her gown was beige—as if she worked at invisibility. "Melissa. . . Ed Parker's date?"

Date, yup. "Yes, an interesting couple, aren't they?"

She shrugged and picked up her beige clutch. "I figure she's his beard, but maybe she really does have talent. Good meeting you, Miss Lane."

Beard? Ed Parker was gay? And in the closet in this day and age? Weird. Wouldn't the macho guys in the AGA love to hear that?

Travel had taught me to always be prepared. Now that the place was empty, I figured I'd avail myself of the opportunity while I had the chance.

Just as I closed the stall door, I heard the main door open. Ever cautious, I checked under the door and saw a rather boring pair of stacked brown heels. It was Melissa's voice that I recognized, however. I jerked upright, but then realized she wasn't addressing me.

"Mr. Arden? It's me, Melissa Winters, from art class, remember?" It was obvious from the way she talked that she had reached voice mail. "I am. . . I was a friend of Rebecca Beatty's and Esther Hanks. I really need to talk to you. It's awful important. I know you're in the hospital and all, but when you can, please. . ." She gave her phone number.

She sounded as if she might be crying. I hastily righted my clothing and was just about to leave the stall when I heard the main door slam open. Restroom doors are usually on hinges that close quietly. Most people would have to be furious or very strong to pack enough power to slam one—which screamed *danger* to me.

I hastily climbed onto the toilet so my feet weren't visible. I expected angry shouts and weeping arguments and maybe an insight into Melissa's life with Ed.

I got two pops and a gasp.

It took me five seconds to get past the shock of my shattered expectations, wrap my head around what actually happened, and leap into action—five seconds too long.

The heavy restroom door closed. I didn't hear anyone leave, but I hadn't heard them enter either. I pulled myself up on the top of the stall and saw no one. I jumped down and pushed open the stall door.

Melissa lay sprawled, face down, on the tile floor, two holes oozing red from her back.

In emergencies, all my instincts shut down, and I go into robot mode. My head ticked off everything that I needed to do, but first, I crouched beside her to take her pulse. Her eyelids fluttered. "Tell the reverend," she whispered. "Tell him. . . George did it."

Since George Paycock's skeleton was currently in the police morgue, I had to assume she wasn't telling me he shot her. I was holding her hand and texting Nick and Patra with the other. They were closest and could come fastest.

"George did what?" I looked around for something to pack into her wounds. They weren't pumping much blood. I had a nasty feeling that wasn't good.

"George killed Esther." Tears were running down her cheek, and she shuddered and clutched my hand. "And probably Owen."

"Who shot you?" I asked, because I couldn't be in two places at once, and I was too human to leave her here alone while I chased a killer.

"GenDef—"

Patra and Magda burst into the room just as the light faded from Melissa's eyes and her last words died on her tongue.

Magda swore a blue streak, grabbed the fancy towels from a basket beneath the vanity that I hadn't even noticed, and flipped Melissa over. I was punching out 911 when she began applying pressure to Melissa's blood-covered chest.

No wonder there hadn't been blood on her back. The exit wounds from some really nasty bullets were in her front.

Patra was nattering into one phone and texting on another. I could hear Nick ordering people away outside.

"We have to get you out of here before anyone realizes you were in here," Magda said, grabbing my phone before I could talk to the dispatcher. "Call Graham."

My phone started ringing the instant she disconnected my call. My formidable brain was shutting down. I knew I needed to go after the killer. I needed to report to the police. I needed to tell Graham what I'd learned. But a nice Sunday school teacher had been *murdered*. And all I wanted to do was listen to my mother and run and hide.

It was too much. I was freezing up inside.

I'd seen dead bodies before, but no amount of experience can protect against the shock of watching someone die, especially if it's someone you know.

Dazed, I answered my phone.

"Get out," Graham ordered in my ear. "I'll give the video to the cops. Get out now before the killer realizes his mistake. My guys are already after him. Sam is at the door and will drive you home."

The line went dead.

I'd forgotten the damned camera and recorder on my head. I snatched it off and flung the fascinator in a corner like a snake.

To my eternal shame, I let my mother throw me to Graham's goons.

Twenty-four

Juliana discovers the secret

JULIE WOKE WITH A snort, straightened too quickly, and almost toppled over. Fortunately, the bed was large. She grabbed her laptop before it hit the floor.

She remembered someone waking her downstairs in the library and leading her to her room. She must have brought her laptop with her and continued working in bed, then fallen asleep again, sitting upright. She clicked the computer open to see where she'd left off, and the battery manager gave her a notice of imminent demise.

Dragging herself from the warm bed, she tottered to the tiny bathroom, splashed water on her face, and finally recalled what she'd been working on—the videos, the months of appalling videos.

Drying her face, she ran back to her phone and checked her messages. Last night, she'd hated texting the *dwankie*, but Lucas was the only person crazy enough to go back to the park. She wouldn't send Zander.

This morning, Lucas had sent her an image of a blueprint from Gregory's office that meant nothing. . . .

Jislaaik! She widened her eyes as she understood what he was telling her with this complicated image. She needed tea. Her mind was working too slowly. Without changing from yesterday's clothes, she dashed into the hall to check Zander's door, but the overachiever was already up and about. Since she was safe now, he had no reason to be working so hard, but he'd dug his teeth into the park puzzle and wouldn't let go.

She was grateful, because the authorities were certainly operating on backward time. Lava couldn't move slower. She ran downstairs to find Zander in the library.

He had acquired another monitor and computer. He glanced up from his eternal spreadsheets in concern when she rushed in. "You should still be sleeping!" he scolded.

"So should you." She slapped her phone down in front of him. "Tell me what this looks like." She opened the blueprint image first, then the image from her video camera that she'd sent to Lucas last night.

Zander shook his head. "Big room," he said, shrugging at the drawing. Flipping to the shadowy night photo she'd clipped from the video, he wrinkled his forehead. "A pallet of crates."

She zoomed up the image to show lettering on the crates. "This comes from my camera at the back of the park, near the Jesus cave, where the park has no security cameras. I thought the cave would make good footage, but I think I've caught thieves. These crates are being transported by forklift—at night—on the video. The park is supposed to be closed at night."

He studied her phone some more. "I see a large G and a large D but I cannot read the small letters in between."

Clenching her teeth to keep them from chattering, she sat down at the table, fiddled with his computer, then called up the cloud account where they'd been storing images for everyone's use. "Patra and Graham were working on General Defense's warehouses yesterday. Here's a shot from there."

He turned the monitor so he could see what she'd called up. "This shows large crates prepared for shipment," he said, not understanding. "That is what factories do."

She pointed at the extra large G and D imprinted on the sides of the crate.

Zander flipped back to the night picture from the park. "They're storing weapons underneath Jesus?"

Ana wakes in a strange bed

I WOKE UP BENEATH Graham's suffocating—naked—weight. A warm, strong body in my bed felt so good that I chose to wallow in sensation for a moment. He had one arm over my—bare—breasts and a leg pinning my thighs. I was pretty certain I had been dressed the last time I remembered being awake—in the bathroom of the 701. I blocked that and returned to enjoying naked pleasure.

I thought I'd remember being ravished, and I didn't. That was a shame. Graham and I had never slept together, but I was willing to have my space invaded if this was the result.

His breathing changed, and I figured he was waking up.

I opened my eyes to check, and the first thing I saw was a ceiling made of midnight with galaxies swirling across it. I was in Graham's bed. No wonder I was comfortable. My futon left a lot to be desired in comparison to his cushy mattress.

"Why am I here?" I asked aloud, just because.

His big hand played an amazing tune on my breasts. He lifted himself over me so all I could see were wide, muscled shoulders and pectorals—and his perpetual scowl. Then he kissed me, and I forgot the question.

I lost track of time as well. At some point, I became vaguely aware of an occasional pinging chime, but not until we were fully satiated and sprawled amid the twisted covers did the noise begin to annoy. I lay there in almost contentment and admired the ceiling again.

Graham growled and sat up. "Four. They're all loose in the wild."

I considered that, but thinking meant remembering last night, and I wasn't ready yet. "Not computing."

"Your family." He dragged the sheet off and wrapped it around his waist, not out of modesty but because it was cold up here. Leaving me the comforter, he stalked like a lion toward the bathroom. "Every one of them is out of their cage and roaming free."

"You track when my family leaves their rooms?" I asked in incredulity, flinging a pillow after his broad, scarred back.

"Servant bells, so they know when to make up rooms," he called over his shoulder. "The attics used to be for servants. That's the original purpose of the hidden staircase. It has a door in Max's old room if you don't want to be seen."

Really, the man needed to be put out of my misery. He had just given me the most incredible sexual experience in my life—not that we're saying much here—and then he walked off as if it was nothing.

I'd take an ax to his head, except I was pretty sure he had brought me here last night to comfort me, so I didn't have to be alone with my horror.

Curmudgeon that I am, I preferred to be distracted by irritation. Yanking on last night's little black dress, I gathered up the rest of my clothes and sauntered down the hall to his office. It was good to know that Graham actually slept occasionally.

I could hear voices carrying up the main stairs, but I was more curious about the hidden exits.

I knew that the spiral steps behind the office wall went down to the closet in the bedroom Magda was currently occupying, two floors below. It made sense that the stairs would also connect to a room on the level in between. I just hadn't realized it, and Graham had never told me. I was so going to kill him—or I would, except I was pretty sure the stairs didn't connect to the study I slept in. Score one for me.

I took the stairs down, found the door, and entered Max's old bedroom from behind an ancient wardrobe, of course. I didn't emerge from a snow-covered Narnia, but this uninhabited room was close enough to a dusty old attic. The wardrobe hid the sliding door but someone had conveniently left enough space between the wall and the wardrobe for me to get out.

My grandfather's chamber was stuffy. The ancient bed probably could use a new mattress, and the fading gray covers were moth-eaten. But it was private, and no one saw me make the walk of shame to my own room in the adjoining study. Nice.

As I showered and regained a few of my neurons, I let last night creep back to me. Melissa and Rebecca had deserved better, much, much better, than ignominious death by greedy thugs who treated them like disposable napkins. My guess was that it wasn't the *hired help* who'd killed Melissa last night in that fancy venue, not by a long shot. But no matter how wealthy their killers might be or what justified their actions, they were no better than common criminals. I couldn't bring the women back to life, but I could avenge their deaths. Anger felt better than grief and shock. I knew how to use anger.

I stepped out of the shower, knowing it was already too late to see EG off to school. I was pretty certain she had only half a day of school today, and then she was on vacation until after New Year's Day. I had to solve this mess *now*. Melissa's death, practically in my arms, had made it personal.

Downstairs I grabbed tea and toast, waved at a groggy Tudor, looked in on Julie and Zander safely bent over their computers, and dashed down to my office. I needed to see what had come in last night, if anyone had chased the shooter.

I read through Nick and Patra's reports, combed all the videos, read the police reports, and sat up, more furious than ever.

The police didn't have bullets for George Paycock or the woman we were assuming to be Esther, so they were operating in limbo.

Lacking our information about CAD, they had no reason to associate those bodies with Melissa's murder. *Yet.*

Whoever Graham's security guards had chased had escaped before they could catch a look at him, or her. Witnesses had reported that the shooter hadn't been large and had blended instantly into the fleeing crowd. The cowardly guests had panicked the instant they'd heard a commotion and left the building.

I thought the size of the shooter might eliminate most of the armed security brutes I'd noticed around the room. A man using the women's room might have been noticed, but I couldn't be certain of that. That the shooter had blended so well into the crowd indicated he or she was most likely one of the rich party-goers. The catering staff would have been noticeable shoving out the door. I needed to know if security had identified those allowed to conceal carry. I shot a note to Graham.

Family/spouse/lovers were usually first to be suspect in any murder. According to these reports, at the time of the shooting, Melissa's *sponsor*, Ed Parker, had been talking to Hammond, the oil magnate, in full view of the entire room. I'd seen them myself. I doubted either of them would have had time to make their way through the crowd to the women's restroom. And if Melissa really was just Ed's beard, then there was no emotional involvement to elevate him to any special status.

I continued hunting for names of others associated with CAD. Tony Jeffrey had been surrounded by Paul Rose and his entourage. Even Rose had been in full view, much as I hated his manipulative guts and wanted him behind bars.

With her dying words, Melissa had mentioned George Paycock, who was already dead, and GenDef. General Defense is a company, not a person, and couldn't kill anyone—not point blank anyway.

The JACAD contractor's employee who had confronted me at the hospital had been arrested. I verified he was still behind bars. That had been about my visiting Arden. I couldn't see how artistic Melissa fit in with skinheads and construction workers.

I checked police files on Tony Jeffrey's skinhead bodyguards, the ones who had attacked Julie and her friends at the hotel. The punks had been let loose on bail. *Excrement.* GenDef's good lawyers had reduced their bond, thus verifying the thugs had been employed by the weapons manufacturer. They could have been among the hired brutes circling the room last night, and I might not have noticed. I trusted Graham to review the security camera videos because I didn't have time or his obsessive acuity.

George killed Esther. . . and probably Owen, Melissa had said.

I ran a search on my files in the Jesus World folder and found Owen Black, the construction worker who had died of a broken neck last spring and whose body had been found in a shallow grave in October. The police case had gone cold, with some speculation that he might have fallen or been shoved and someone covered it up.

George Paycock had been a highly paid CFO, an embezzler, and a womanizer from all reports. Why on earth would he kill a construction worker? How would Melissa know that Paycock had killed Esther? The police hadn't even confirmed the identity of Esther's body yet.

So many events were tied to October. . . .

I began another spread sheet. Owen Black died of a broken neck, approximately in April, about the time Melissa left school to live with Ed Parker. Melissa must have known Owen to mention him in her dying words.

I added Mrs. Overcamp, the school's marketing administrator and mother of William Gregory, the general contractor, to my worksheet. She had introduced the school's second year students to predatory board sponsors like Ed Parker and George Paycock. Julie's overheard conversation indicated Gregory was somehow getting kickbacks from the party arrangement and Overcamp knew about it. Or the school received *contributions*, not kickbacks, that paid the contractor—the more likely scenario. The women would chat up rich old men and the old men would pull out their checkbooks to impress them—morally deficient but not much different from lobbyists promising legislation, sports tickets, or other perks for contributions to their candidates.

Back to my chart. Sometime after Owen Black disappeared from the picture, Melissa hooked up with Ed, Esther connected with George Paycock, and Rebecca was chumming with William Gregory. The three women rode high all summer, escaping the school slum of a trailer park to live in fancy digs and attend parties with the likes of Tony Jeffrey and other wealthy corporate types.

Then their high life came tumbling down in the fall. In October, Owen's body was found in a shallow grave, and George Paycock was accused of embezzling from GenDef. Rebecca's body was found in the Potomac.

In early December, Paycock went missing, and Julie captured the image of man's body being bulldozed. I was uncertain of the timeline on Esther's disappearance. Julie had said she'd left the school in September. I should have asked Melissa when she'd last seen her friend.

In late December, Joshua Arden was shot at, Julie and Maryam were threatened, and I was accosted by an idiot at the hospital, outside Arden's room. And just a day or two ago, Paycock's body was found buried in the park, along with a woman who might be Esther. The DNA and dental reports were still out.

But Ed and Melissa had safely been an item until now, until I started interfering. Anger nicely squelched my guilt.

I pulled up Zander's financial spreadsheet. He'd started tracing the companies receiving large funds from the park. Gregory's construction company received an extortionate share. Could rusted dinosaurs or giant holes in the ground cost that much?

Zander had dug into the construction company's expense accounts, good boy. My eyes almost popped as I recognized the lobby groups and super-PACs Gregory was paying into. No wonder the guy was going bankrupt! Million-dollar political donations made no sense for a construction company barely keeping its head above water.

It only made sense from the standpoint of the park's sponsors: *Gregory's construction firm was no more than a money-laundering account.*

My guess was that Gregory didn't even control his own funds.

GenDef, Hammond Oil, Goldrich Mortgage, et al, contributes huge sums to JACAD, a charitable organization promising to build schools in third world countries. Their boards approve. The IRS approves. Everyone is happy.

JACAD turns around and invests in charitable projects, like the schools and park construction. The IRS again approves because the money is going for the non-profit's stated cause. Nice. They're not about to audit the value of rusted dinosaurs. That was the duty of JACAD's board.

But JACAD's board of directors was made up of officers from the same companies contributing to the park. And the board approved expenditures and financial statements and never questioned exorbitant invoices—probably because they had undercover deals that bloated them on purpose.

Gregory's construction company probably wasn't the only one receiving large sums for services not performed. I assumed the modus operandi would be the same for the others. The smaller, non-public companies the park was paying for catering or lumber or construction equipment turned around and donated the excess to super-PACs supporting Paul Rose, the park board's candidate of choice. Such political donations would never have been approved by the boards and stockholders of the large, for-profit companies the park board represented. But these small, non-public businesses and private persons could pour money into lobbies to their hearts' content. No one would be irate to see a small firm like WGCI contributing to the gun lobby's PAC. No one knew who the heck they were or cared.

Jesus World was just a funnel for lobbying money. A few stray dollars occasionally got spent on the intended purpose of the amusement park and schools.

Josh Arden was an idiot.

He was also a sitting duck, if the police reports were any indicator. On the surface, the only person benefitting from the cooked books would be Arden—he was getting a park out of the subterfuge. Paycock would have known what was happening, could possibly have objected, so his death could be attributed to Arden. The police would automatically associate all the deaths they knew about at CAD to one killer—leaving out Melissa and Rebecca because they wouldn't grasp the connection to CAD.

Until Arden was shot, he'd been their main suspect. He might still be, for all I knew. That old "falling-out among thieves" cliché worked to cover his shooting.

Arden probably *should* have shot Paycock and most of his thieving board, but I was pretty sure he hadn't. His kind prayed, then called the law, instead of seeking revenge.

And that was probably a clue right there—had Josh Arden threatened to call the law and got himself shot? Who had he threatened? Unless I was missing something here, he hadn't reported anything to anyone before or after the shooting.

I checked my email box. Magda, of course, had sent me nothing.

In typical Magda fashion, she'd jumped in when she'd seen one of her offspring threatened, handled last night's adventure by covering up everything, and then vanished into the mist. I was accustomed to benign neglect and expected no more.

My mother worked alone—or occasionally with the CIA or other shady organizations, I suspected. I didn't know how I felt about her shoving me out of trouble last night. I can take care of myself pretty well, but I'd been pretty shattered. Calling the cops had been my honest reaction, but maybe not the smartest move. I didn't want to have to hide in Graham's mansion fortress until the killer was found.

So for my anonymity, I was grateful.

The police were happy with the grainy video and recording from my fascinator. It only showed the toilet stall, but it had picked up Melissa's message to Arden before the two pops. That gave them direction—probably a wrong one, again. I couldn't have told them any more than they knew—except maybe her last words. The whisper had been less than clear on the recording.

The police were still scouring Melissa's apartment, looking for anything she might have on Arden. They'd probably find my Linda Lane card. I forwarded the phone number to an answering service in India. That would take them a while.

Judging from the frustrated reports obtained by Graham's inside police contact, Ed Parker had hired a lawyer to guard the apartment while the police searched it. I wished them all well. Given the level of chaos Melissa lived in, they'd be lucky to find her car keys.

I did stumble across one item in the file—a photo of Melissa with a young man in jeans and t-shirt. They had their arms around each other and looked blissfully happy. His face seemed familiar. I have a retentive memory when it comes to faces but not names.

But I'd just drawn up a timeline with the name Owen Black. . . .

I dug deeper into my folders and came up with the police report on Owen. There was his high school photo. He was younger, leaner, with longer hair, but I was pretty darned sure that this was the man in the photo with Melissa.

Damn.

Ed Parker had probably been a rebound after Owen disappeared off the face of the map. Given her lack of news knowledge, when had Melissa learned they'd found his body? Last night? I could very easily imagine grief rocking her world. So, what had she done to get shot—blackmail? Revenge? Blind fury? All of the above?

I didn't have time to dwell on what I might never know. An email from Patra joined the others streaming in. Wanting to find out what she'd learned about Tony Jeffrey, I opened hers first.

It merely contained a domestic violence report on William Gregory, the park's general contractor. Charming jerk. His first wife had taken a restraining order out on him. He'd been convicted of assaulting a girlfriend and spent time in jail for threatening a police officer afterward. And he was working with Jesus World, how?

Because no one else would hire him, because his mama worked with the board, and *he would agree to anything to keep his daddy's company open.*

I didn't think I was making too far a leap in that judgment.

Julie had said the construction trailer on site seemed to be his only office. Which meant the accounting books Zander was accessing weren't there, since the trailer had contained no computer. More evidence that Billy-Boy didn't control his own funds, just the bulldozers.

And then I remembered poor Rebecca, the strangled girl in the Potomac, last known as a companion of William Gregory. *Bingo.* Bully-Boy had just become a major suspect. I ran a search and found a William Gregory with a boating license at the same address as the construction company. Melissa had said Rebecca's boyfriend had a boat—and Rebecca had ended in the Potomac. All signs pointed to a fight on board that led to Rebecca going over the side. I sent the domestic violence file along with my notes about Rebecca to Graham. He could feed them to the police.

My gut was churning. Would a man who beat his wife and assault his girlfriends shoot a powerful executive like George Paycock? The police reports showed a brutal man who liked to use his fists. Shooting didn't seem to be his routine. And he'd have no reason to shoot at Arden—his bread and butter. Or poor Melissa.

But he controlled the bulldozers and could very well have *buried* Owen and George and the unknown female, if ordered to by the man or men writing his paycheck.

Realizing none of the email filling my box was from Zander or Julie, I dashed up the stairs just to reassure myself of their safety.

The library was empty.

Twenty-five

Juliana follows the leader

"YOU SHOULD HAVE STAYED home," Julie whispered at her brother. "It does not take three of us to look for doors in dirt." As far as she'd been able to tell from Lucas's explanation, there was a concealed door in the back of the artificial hill that disguised the workings of the Jesus Cave, one of the park highlights.

"I wouldn't trust that *skelm* with a blade of grass," Zander muttered as they followed Lucas along hedges in the direction of the back of the park. Under heavy clouds, the late afternoon light was gray enough to turn them into shadows. "For all I know, he's a killer. Do we know where your FBI informant was last night?"

"Not attending an invitation-only party for the rich where Melissa was killed," she said scornfully. "They murdered his *sister*. He's on our side."

"What exactly is our side?" Zander asked in exasperation as Lucas halted to peer through the sticks of the winter-barren hedge.

"Reverend Arden, of course. He is in danger, and so is his school program. And now, Ana may be in danger as a witness, just the way I am. We must stop this killer."

"For all we know, Arden is a criminal who is hiding in a hospital bed," Zander said with scorn. "You are too trusting. We should just tell the police what we suspect and go home."

"The police have been all over the park and have not found this room even though they had the blueprints. Lucas is the one who is helping!"

"That is because there are two sets of blueprints," Zander argued. "We should show the police the ones we found in Gregory's files."

"Too late. They should have found them on their own. I bet they didn't even know what they were. Lucas does." Julie picked up speed when Lucas waved at them to proceed. She was being defensive because she was starting to feel the same as he. . . that they were doing something dangerously foolish.

But Ana had already risked enough for them. Julie needed to learn the same courage.

"The blueprint shows a door in the hill behind the cave," Lucas said when he caught up with them. "We'll need to go around the high side of the mound, and it would be best to stay off the road." He pointed to the tractor path on the lower end. "We'll have to go to the left to stay out of sight."

"All I see is a mound of dirt piled over a concrete arch," Zander complained. "How can there be a door? And even if there is, how would we unlock it?"

"I have Arden's keys, but we won't know what we can do until we find it." Lucas began easing through the overgrown bushes surrounding the mound.

Julie thought there might once have been a lovely hedged garden here. The digging had destroyed all but the remnants.

Zander had his phone out. "We should call the police."

"Not until we have something to show them." Lucas held up his hand to halt them.

Julie peered around his shoulder. From their vantage point on the hill, she could see two men using a forklift to load a crate onto a rental truck on the far side of the mound. She zoomed up and took a quick photo but didn't have time to do more before they climbed in the cab and drove off.

They waited, listening, but Julie only heard the wind rustling in the hedge. Lucas slid out from under cover and started down.

Cursing, Zander trotted off after him. With trepidation, Julie did the same, scrambling around the mound with thick brambles to conceal them.

They found the door in the mound easily. Tire tracks led straight to it, although the door itself appeared to be solid rock. They eventually located a concealed hinge that hid a keyhole behind a rock-like plate. Lucas jiggled through his keys until he found the ones he needed. After a few attempts, the lock clicked.

Handing Julie the keys, he used both hands to tug the heavy door open. "It's built strong enough to keep out an army," he complained. "What the hell do they have in here?"

He pulled out a flashlight and beamed it into the opening. "Shit."

Zander pushed past Julie to peer inside. His response was the same, only in a more familiar dialect. "*Kak.*" He began snapping photos with his phone.

"Wait," Julie said, grabbing his arm in panic. "I hear something."

The low roar of a heavy motor rumbled closer. Zander and Lucas repeated their imprecations.

"If there's evidence in there, I need to find it. I'm going inside. You two lie low." Lucas jogged into the interior, taking his flashlight with him.

Before Zander could imitate that macho stupidity, Julie grabbed her brother's arm and tugged him toward the safety of the leafless hedge on the hill.

The cave had been filled to the two-story ceiling with crates labeled *General Defense*. She had a very bad feeling deep in her belly as she started sending messages to Ana.

Ana goes visiting

I WILL NOT WORRY, I will not worry, I chanted inside my head as I once more caught the Metro for Alexandria and Arden's hospital. He was still heavily guarded but no longer in intensive care, so I'd been given permission to visit again. I wanted to know how much he'd known or suspected about his board's operations, but the visit would also put me closer to the park, where Julie and Zander had apparently gone.

I didn't like what they were up to, but I understood the urgency. I'd skimmed over their messages, knew what they were doing, and agreed it should be done. A large room under a make-believe mountain where gun crates had been unloaded sounded suspicious to me. I just didn't want the twins looking into it, which was why I was trying to dial back my mother hen instinct.

I was back to my normal invisible self, wearing my army jacket and my hair in a braid, when I walked down the hospital corridor toward Arden's room. Approaching me was the beige blonde I'd met last night—Laura Jeffrey, Tony's daughter.

I'd read up on her this morning. She was GenDef's new CFO, taking Georgie the Embezzler's place. She was a chip off the old block, quietly working her way up through the corporation, hobnobbing behind the scenes with powerful politicians and gun lobbyists, not spending much time on a social life, if the society pages were any indication. Never married, no hint of anyone but her immediate family in her life. She appeared to be a hard-nosed career woman.

And she'd told me she didn't agree with her father's policies? I wondered which policies those were, since moneymaking and wielding power seemed to suit them both. Or maybe she just meant she was a feminist, and he was a sexist.

She walked right past me without blinking an eye. Okay, so we were both invisible. I was good with that. Had she been visiting Arden? If he was a friend of her father's, it made sense they knew each other.

I showed my ID to the guard at the door, and he let me in. The good reverend was sitting up in bed, still looking pale and tired. His golden-boy good looks faded when he wasn't smiling. The bandage hiding most of his pretty hair didn't help. He shoved away his half-eaten lunch and picked up a Bible from the side table.

"Good morning, Miss Devlin," he said formally. "Thank you for sending your mother by to see me. It was good to catch up after all these years."

I took a seat in one of those uncomfortable plastic hospital chairs and snorted impolitely. "You're probably the first person besides Mallard who has expressed happiness at seeing my mother when she's on a mission. Did she grill you unmercifully?"

He shot me a glimmer of his old smile. "Of course, but not any more than Laura did. I seem to be attracted to strong women."

"Laura? Jeffrey?" This was not the direction I'd planned to take this conversation. "You're an item?"

"Once. But I'm devoted to my work, and she's devoted to hers, so there really wasn't much point."

"But she was in here grilling you instead of asking after your health?" Not that I was doing anything different, but I'd never expressed any other interest in him.

His smile faded. "She's upset that I'm considering closing the park. I hadn't realized her faith was so deep. She even offered to straighten out the mess George Paycock has made of our finances."

"That's generous of her, but I think you should hire an outside auditor instead of relying on friends if you go that route," I tried to warn him politely. I wasn't in any position to order him to do anything. That was a job for the feds.

"That's what my father says, but to put it politely, he's not a friend of the Jeffreys. We don't agree on the gun control issue, so I avoid that topic when we're together."

So would I, then. "My issue, and probably the cops', is with your board's accounting. You sign off on the invoices. Who explains them to you?"

"George handled it until he died," Arden said, rubbing wearily at his temple. "I haven't had time to find anyone else to step in yet."

I wanted to feel sorry for the former football hero, but I was too angry. "Whose idea was the park? You don't seem to have much interest in the details of an undertaking this large."

"I'm only interested in the school," he said, sounding a little more spirited. "Spreading education and the Lord's word is my mission. Laura suggested we could raise more funds with a theme park. She and the rest of the board have been there from the first, helping build support. And they're right. People want to contribute to the park more than they do for education. We've been able to build twice as many schools as previously."

I didn't want to argue with education and the Lord's mission, but I danged well would like to argue about his old flame, Laura and the "people" who were contributing to the park. But I couldn't slap any evidence on him, especially when he looked as if he was doped to the gills. He hired people to handle finances. They'd let him down. So I went back to his *mission.*

"I came here to talk about Melissa. Did you know her?"

He looked even older and grayer. "I wish I understood what was happening with those girls. They seemed such good, responsible young women. How did they end up with mobsters?"

"*Mobsters*? Who told you that?"

"Laura. She said they'd fallen in with a bad crowd, and there wasn't anything I could have seen or done. But I feel as if I've shirked my responsibility to their parents and to them." He frowned and flipped the pages of the Bible in his hands. "I have thought of myself as their shepherd, but that is arrogance, I suppose. I must put my faith in God, and trust that He knows what is best."

"Looking after young students is *not* arrogance," I practically shouted. "Isn't there a verse about God helping those who help themselves? You can't ask God to do your job! I'm not a Bible student and not much of a believer in omnipotence unless there's a verse about us acting as His hands and eyes. Melissa was *not* living with a mobster. Did you never inquire about those concerts and parties your students were attending?"

Arden looked surprised at my vehemence. "The concert tickets were merely donations, unused seats that our generous sponsors gave to the school. I wanted the students to have as well-rounded an experience as possible. Some of them come from very rural areas and have never seen an orchestra. It was good for them to rub elbows with the people who build our schools. What do you mean, Melissa wasn't living with a mobster?"

Lord, save me from naïve do-gooders wearing rose-colored glasses. "Melissa was living with one of your sponsors, Ed Parker, a perfectly respectable gentleman and a member of your board of directors. Admittedly, his support of the American Gun Association puts him in the creep department, but that doesn't make him a mobster even in my eyes." I waited to see his expression on the topic of guns.

"Even my father gave up fighting the AGA," he said, shrugging, revealing nothing. "As much as I dislike violence, I cannot turn my back on so many of my flock who believe guns are their God-given right. I agree, AGA membership does not mean Ed is a mobster." He frowned in puzzlement, finally.

"Then who does she mean? Esther was dating George Paycock, another AGA member who, given his embezzling tendencies, may have been a mobster for all I know, but he worked for General Defense and was on your board too. Maybe Laura knows something we don't."

Squirming uncomfortably, he wiped at a bead of sweat on his forehead. "Months ago, Esther tried to warn me that the books were 'cooked,' I think she called it. I talked to George about it, but he said she was just an angry young woman and said he'd have the books audited, if I wanted. Only audits are rather expensive, so I hesitated. I trust my board." He rubbed at his middle. "Money has never been my interest."

Yeah, I was starting to see how that could be a bad thing. "Rebecca was another of your missing students. But she was unwisely dating your general contractor, a violent man who beat his wife. I'm not sure that qualifies him as a mobster, but he seems an odd choice to be allowed around a crowd of young students."

When he merely looked sick and didn't reply, I threw in my zinger. "Surely you had your suspicions about Gregory's construction work."

He closed his Bible and his eyes. I thought maybe he was praying. And then he turned a ghastly gray, clutched his chest, spewed his breakfast across the covers, and began twitching spasmodically.

I'd pushed too hard and *I'd killed him!* I screamed for the guards. I slammed the nurse's alarm button. That hadn't been guilt on his face, but pain. I panicked at my helplessness and watched a decent man writhe in agony.

The room filled with more useful people, who shoved me aside. For a moment, I thought Arden's eyes lifted beseechingly to me, and he tried to speak, but a nurse was pressing something between his lips and a doctor ordered us all out, and I fled, shaking. Had I really done that? What had he been trying to tell me?

I might never know, I realized, gulping back tears and a bucket of horror and guilt. If I knew how to pray for him, I would. If he died. . . Two deaths in two days would seriously shake my world.

I leaned against the wall, trying to pull myself together. An orderly rushing down the corridor with a gurney brought back my last deadly encounter in these halls. Hospitals were not a safe place for me. I needed to leave.

I avoided the public elevator and fled down stairs in the wake of a janitor. I followed an aide to a staff elevator and escaped out the back. Still rattled, I hid behind some dumpsters and texted a message to Graham about Arden. Did people throw up if they had heart attacks? I really didn't think Arden could fake that act to avoid questioning.

Trying to control my shredded nerves, I scanned the messages on my phone.

IS STORING CRATES OF GUNS ILLEGAL? That one was from Julie.

Zander was more dramatic. GUN SMUGGLING INCOME PART OF PARK DONATIONS?

I couldn't see any way that could turn out good. They'd also sent me photos they had taken of a forklift loading crates into a rental truck. I couldn't read the writing on the crates, but more photos showed a door inside what looked like a dirt mound with more crates inside. The GenDef insignia was clear. The park could be supplying terrorists or local gangsters with weapons for all I knew.

Mobsters. Laura Jeffrey had called Arden's board of directors mobsters.

Paul Rose had been known to hire local gangs for his dirty work.

I swore and sent an all cap message to both of them. GET OUT NOW!

Not enough suspects. I didn't have enough suspects. Where was our brutal contractor right now? Driving forklifts? But he couldn't have murdered Melissa. No way that crude brute would have showed up at a party in a tux and not been noticed.

My phone rang and I nearly dropped it in surprise. I punched the screen and Graham shouted, "Gunfire at the park now! Get those idiots out of there. Limo will meet you at the bus stop. Crash the gate. I'm on my way."

Heart pounding, I dashed toward the street and the waiting limo. I couldn't find my twin siblings and lose them only a few days later. I just couldn't. Their family would declare war on Washington and behead me and everyone else involved. We were rich now. Everything was supposed to be hunky-dory, copacetic, and Andy Griffith idyllic.

And then I noticed the limo was parked the wrong way for this side of the street. Sam never did anything improper. Like Mallard, he was old school. Ergo, either that was a space alien behind the wheel or Sam was in trouble.

I swung around and shot off across the parking lot, away from the street. "You still there?" I called into the phone. I heard a car door slam. I didn't have time to look over my shoulder.

"On the roof. Out of contact shortly," Graham said, sounding as if he were talking into a mouthpiece.

"Someone may have Sam. I'm not taking the limo." I would tell him to send help for Sam, except I suspected the space alien had abandoned Sam and was running after me now. "Meet you at the park." I turned off the phone and scrolled across my screen, looking for my Uber app.

I raced through a crowded parking lot, heading for the opposite street. Hospital parking lots are acres of bad hiding places and excellent visibility, so anyone following me could easily keep up. On the positive side, hospital visiting hours made for traffic jams and way too many people dodging cars. Whoever was behind that slamming door and badly parked limo probably wouldn't dare fire— yet.

I poked my favorite app as I ran, darting in between the tallest vehicles I could find and ducking behind short ones. I lucked out. A low-rider pickup truck carrying lumber with its tailgate down had just started pulling out of a spot. I leaped into the bed. The driver may have looked up at my thump, but I was already down flat, and he probably didn't see me. Being small is occasionally useful.

As the truck took a curve, I clung to the tool box fastened to the truck bed and peered over my shoulder. More people were pouring out of the hospital into the lot. No one was overtly waving a weapon.

But I could have sworn a woman in a fur coat raised a middle finger at me.

My mind raced furiously as I slid out of the truck bed at the first stoplight. Dodging traffic, I ran for the coffee shop where I'd told my favorite Uber driver to meet me.

Hiding in the crowded coffee line, I called Sam, the limo driver. "Are you okay? Did you have a passenger or am I crazy?"

He greeted me in relief. "A lady in a fur coat. I thought she was a friend until I saw the gun. Thank goodness you understood my message. Shall I pick you up now?"

"No, the limo is too conspicuous. Be available in the vicinity of the park. I'm afraid the hornets have been stirred."

A lady in a fur coat. . . As far as I was aware, the only females left alive in this sorry affair were my mother and Mrs. Overcamp.

Or Laura Jeffrey. She'd seen me in the restroom before Melissa entered.

She'd passed me in the hospital corridor this morning. Maybe I wasn't as invisible as I thought.

Juliana panics

"Lucas is *trapped* in there." Julie hated herself for sobbing as they edged further down the hedge row, away from the activity below.

The trucks they'd heard had carried construction equipment. While she and Zander had darted up the hill, Lucas had shut himself inside the cave, proving he was *bosbefok.*

They hadn't been able to reach him since the door shut.

When the men in the trucks hadn't been able to open the door, there had been a lot of shouting and cursing. Lucas must have jammed the lock from the inside.

And now, the mean-looking *skebengas* were ramming a bulldozer against the back door into the Jesus Cave. Julie wanted to weep, but there wasn't time.

"His own fault for going inside to explore first," Zander said. "We can't do anything against a dozen men with machinery. I have called the police, but the dispatcher thinks I am a prankster. I don't know if they will arrive or if they will send enough cars."

Julie had attempted frantic calls to Ana and Graham but received only voice mail. "Distraction," she said. "We could stage a distraction to lure some of those men elsewhere. There may be other ways to escape if he just has time to find one. What can the police do when we're the ones trespassing? Those men could just say there's a problem with the door."

Zander hesitated, studying the fleet of construction machinery and trucks parked in the back lot. "I am not an engineer. I have never driven so much as a forklift. I drove a *bakkie* once. It is not much different from a car, if these are like the one I drove."

"Would they leave keys in the ignition?" she asked dubiously, studying the lot of equipment. There were several small white *bakkies*—pickups—down there. She'd seen the contractor driving around in a monster version, but his vehicle wasn't in the lot.

They both peered over the shrubbery. The forklift drivers were now employed in attempting to pry open the door. Could Lucas hide once they did? Did the workers know the door had been deliberately jammed?

The parking lot was empty and on the far side of the hill from the angry workers. Zander slid from the shrubbery and down into the gravel lot. Julie followed on his heels.

"Let me see the keys Lucas gave you." Zander held out his hand.

She'd almost forgotten she was clinging to them. She handed them over and let him sift through them.

"*Bakgat*," he said softly, holding up several of the keys. "Ford."

Cool, indeed. The pickups were all Fords. They tested truck doors until they found two that opened with the keys. Zander slid one key off, kept it, and handed the ring back to Julie.

She climbed into the interior of the second truck. Now what?

She was a photographer, a filmmaker, not a terrorist. What could she do to distract the bad guys?

Zander discreetly rolled his truck downhill out of the parking lot.

Julie wished for a big video screen. . . . Wait a minute! The park had a sound system that played anthems in the morning before class and gospel at the end of the day. The ancient system was rotten, but it could be heard all over the park. They even occasionally used it for *announcements*. Her mind spun with possibilities.

She couldn't think fast enough to text. Starting the truck, she punched the phone for Ana's number but only received voice mail again. As she rolled out of the lot, a man ran over the hill, shouting, and she hastily hung up. She thought she heard shots. Glancing in the rearview mirror, she saw dirt fly up from the road. Her heart thumped in terror, but knowing she might be able to help Lucas kept the adrenalin pumping and her foot on the pedal. She was around the bend before he could aim better.

Zander veered off toward the pathetic excuse for a Ferris wheel. Julie hit the gas and aimed for the market coffee house. Lucas's keys might open more doors. If so, she could access the audio equipment.

With the park and school closed until after the new year, no one was about as she pulled up at the back door. There might be a few students holed up in the trailers. She hoped they stayed inside, if only for their own safety. She glanced over her shoulder, but no one seemed to have followed.

Turning off the truck, she could hear the roar of the bulldozer ramming the cave mountain, slamming against metal and concrete. The beep, beep as it backed up to try again kept her heart pounding. She prayed the door was as solid as Lucas had said.

It took a few frustrating minutes to find the right key. She was almost in tears before she had the latch open. She locked it behind her and shoved a chair beneath the knob.

More precious time was lost while she located the sound equipment and figured it out. Like everything else, it was dated, but that made it simpler. She found the microphone, heard the familiar buzz when she flipped the switch, and took a deep breath as she pondered what to say.

"*Police*, stop in the name of the law," she cried, turning the volume up to *boom,* and striving for a voice of authority. "Weapons down. We have you surrounded."

She had no idea if anyone was paying any attention. She located the switches that turned on the security monitors and flipped through them. There was no camera at the back of the mountain where the bulldozer operated, but she found the monitor overlooking the construction road to the back exit.

A rental truck rolling slowly down the rutted road picked up speed as she watched.

"Stop that truck right there, young man," she shouted into the microphone. "Freeze where you are."

Instead, the truck driver hit the gas, veered off the road, and aimed for a broken gap in the chain link fence.

Well, she shouldn't have expected criminals to listen to the law.

She tried Ana's phone again and told voice mail what was happening while she flipped through various cameras until she found Zander. The camera showed that he was out of his *bakkie* and examining the machinery that ran the ramshackle Ferris wheel. She remembered the reverend crowing happily over the gift of old amusement park rides. He'd had the engineering department working on them in their spare moments. She'd seen some of the rides running when they first arrived but not since. What did Zander think he could accomplish?

He fiddled with a box, and the wheel suddenly lit up in a colorful array of lights against the gray clouds.

She bounced happily in her seat. A twinkling amusement park ride ought to startle a few people into looking up. The criminals had to know they were being watched. Was that enough to make the rest flee? Only if they realized cops might ask to see what was behind the locked door.

She wished she had a camera behind the mountain to see what the bulldozer was doing. She flipped to a view of the front gate to see if anyone was leaving that way.

A fancy black sedan had stopped in the entrance, and a chauffeur was unfastening the lock. Reverend Arden drove a white *bakkie* like the one she'd stolen, so the sedan wasn't his. Who else would have a gate key? All the teachers? The board?

She checked her phone. Had their frantic calls to Graham and 911 been heard? They hadn't had time to do much more than cry for help and give a location. She couldn't hear sirens from this sound-proof booth. Would police use sirens for runaway bulldozers?

The Ferris wheel began to creak into jerky motion in a bright glow of red, white, and blue. Cheering at this most excellent diversion, terrified for Lucas, Julie added her own touch. She slid a

CD into the slot and played the gloriously dramatic tribute—"The Star Spangled Banner."

Into the microphone, she announced the only other phrase she remembered from the dreadful American TV shows Zander liked. "Put down your weapons and come out with your hands up."

She'd almost forgotten the rental truck racing for the fence. At least that driver believed her announcements. She caught its motion on the screen when it hit a fence post near the gap it had aimed for.

The image on the screen exploded in fire, flying mud, and truck parts.

Twenty-six

Ana gets personal

MY BLESSED UBER DRIVER hit the gas as we reached the rural road leading to the park. I couldn't reach Graham. Julie's frantic messages about bulldozers and Lucas filled me with confused horror. I checked over my shoulder but no one was following.

That was because they were ahead of me, I realized with shock, looking out the front window as the park gates opened. A woman in a fur coat stepped from a high-end Mercedes limo.

"Turn around!" I screamed at the driver.

My ex-vet driver performed an acrobatic U-turn in the middle of the narrow road. That maneuver earned him a tip of every bill in my purse. "Is there a back entrance?"

"Construction road," he said tersely. "It's likely to rip out the suspension."

"Just drop me off near it. I can climb fences." I emptied my wallet on the front seat. "I don't have enough in here to buy you a new car."

He glanced at the cash, then at me in the mirror. "What's going on out there?"

"I don't think Arden is running the show anymore."

Before I could say more, the earth shook and flames shot in the air from along the fence in the field. My driver hit the brake and ducked. "IED," he shouted with the lungs of experience.

I mentally repeated every curse word I knew—in twelve languages. He wasn't kidding. Either the truck or the fence had been booby-trapped. As the car stopped, I opened the door and shot out, keeping low.

Insanely, a loudspeaker blared "The Star-Spangled Banner." *Bombs bursting in air* was not a peace anthem or even an appropriate metaphor at the moment.

Flames ate at the sky. That was more than an IED. That had been a truck full of explosives. I'd seen them before and had hoped never to see them again. What the hell had Julie got into?

A rusty creak dragged my gaze upward. In the far distance behind the flames revolved the skeletal Ferris wheel, its garish lights blinking weakly against the winter-gray clouds.

In the distance, a police siren finally screamed.

I leaned in the passenger window. "Go find a safe place and have a cup of coffee. The cavalry is on its way."

"You're some kind of crazy, lady," he said in what sounded like approval. "You're sure? I've seen worse in the war. Maybe I should go with you."

"These are homegrown terrorists. You've done your duty for the country. Let the locals handle this one." I hit the roof of his little car, and heart in throat, trudged into the underbrush around the construction fence—in the direction of the front gate and my family.

If paranoids had planted booby-traps around the perimeter, I didn't mean to find them by going in the back. I'd rather take on the fur coat lady.

My ride lingered until the driver saw my direction. Then with a wave, he drove sedately away from the park, in the opposite direction of the approaching sirens. Smart man.

I don't carry guns, but I do carry a few other weapons in the capacious pockets of my army jacket. With Julie and Zander trapped inside the park, presumably surrounded by explosives, arsenals, and terrorists, I had no compunction about using what I had, if necessary.

The whole park puzzle was coming together in my mind. We'd been approaching it from the financial angle, silly us. Crazies may like money, but only because it buys them power. The paranoid like control and require lots and lots of security. Things that go bang in the night apparently let them sleep well. It wasn't a mindset that I understood, but I'd had lots of experience with the build-a-better-arsenal mentality in my travels.

Paycock, Parker, and Gregory were *all* gun enthusiasts. A blue collar wife-beater like Gregory fell into my admittedly biased image of the usual AGA supporters. I'd thought wealthy CFO Paycock and Harvard alum Parker's enthusiasm was all about lobbying the AGA members to support Paul Rose's candidacy.

I'd forgotten the other end of the stick—they supported Rose because he promised them a gun in every closet. An explosive arsenal in a Jesus theme park carried that capacity one step too far.

As I walked toward the front gate, fur coat lady was nowhere in sight. The driver of her Mercedes was smoking a cigarette. Obviously not a bodyguard, he just watched me trudge in. He may have called a warning on his phone. I wasn't trying to be invisible.

The sound system now played what sounded like a dirge, presumably for whoever had hit the IED. My heart thudded in dread at the possibility that Julie and Zander had been the ones attempting to break the fence, but I didn't think so.

The Ferris wheel and sound system actually gave me hope. My family tended toward purposeful, creative lunacy.

I might have short legs, but I walked with fury in my heart. I caught up with fur coat, who was sauntering along with her phone to her ear, giving orders.

"If you killed Reverend Arden, you're going to fry," I called after her.

She swung around, phone still to her ear—Laura Jeffrey, of course. Her pale brown eyebrows raised, and she clicked off her call. "I'm guessing your name is really not Linda," she said, irrelevantly. "Arden spoke of Magda's daughter, and I surmise that's you. Magda warned me to stay away from you, you realize."

No, I hadn't realized, and I didn't much care. "Did she also warn you to stay away from the park? That would have been more sensible." I didn't know Laura's position in all this or her relationship with my mother or Arden, so I was fishing for information.

She didn't oblige, just shrugged. "Judging by your reaction to my father's bodyguards at the hospital, you're as crazy as she is. What do you think you can possibly do to me?"

Arrogance goeth before a fall. Much as I would have loved to discover how Laura knew my mother—they vied for the attention of the same football hero in junior high would be my guess—I had to reach Julie and Zander. Fortunately, I keep my coat loaded with fun and games. I removed the grenade from a utility pocket and said, "Catch!"

I mocked pulling the pin and lobbed the bomb at her. She shrieked hysterically, dropped her phone, and stupidly did just as I'd ordered—tried to catch it.

While her hands were otherwise occupied, I pepper-sprayed her with my Mace squirt gun containing my own unique formula of pepper and perfume. The grenade rolled away as she grabbed at her eyes and screeched in decibels high enough to alert satellites. I was too furious to feel sympathy, even though I had some notion of the pain she suffered. If my theories were anywhere close to correct, she had caused far more pain and suffering than a squirt of high-class pepper.

She dropped to her knees holding her eyes with one hand and groping for her phone with the other.

"You'd be dead by now if I were as cruel as you," I said conversationally, catching her shoulder with my army boot and shoving her backward. I planted my foot on her middle to hold her down. She flailed frantically, but she couldn't see what she was doing even if she tried to bite me.

"I'll sue you for this!" she shouted. Unfortunately, pepper doesn't stop mouths.

"I'll make certain Melissa's family sues you in return," I said with a verbal shrug, since she couldn't see me. "What could that poor girl do to you that deserved shooting?"

"She upset Arden!" she spit angrily, wriggling harder now and pushing up. "Between the two of them—" Finally realizing she was talking too much, she shut up. "I didn't shoot anyone."

She started wriggling beneath my boot, trying to reach for her coat pocket. What were the odds that she kept a gun in here? I stomped her wrist, probably crushing bones, if her scream was any indication. "If you pull a gun, I have to pull a gun. And then if my sister shows up, she'll need a gun in case we start shooting. Then the cops show, and they all have even bigger weapons. Guns beget guns. See why it's best not to carry them?" I leaned over and yanked hers from her pocket, kicking it under a thorny bush.

She grabbed my ankle with her uncrushed hand. I'm sturdy and low to the ground and don't topple easily. I stomped her again, hopefully cracking a few ribs. She screamed and held my boot. This was one determined lady. Too bad she hadn't applied that strength to the greater good. Selfishness begets greed which begets evil. Maybe I'd get into this religion thing after all.

I didn't think I could pry any more out of her, and I was still worried about the twins. I could hear machinery running in the distance.

I breathed a small sigh of relief as two police cars and an ambulance squealed through the gates.

At the arrival of the screaming sirens, the loudspeaker blared a triumphant "We are the Champions."

***

Julianna to the rescue

WATCHING HER SECURITY MONITORS, Julie saw Ana arrive after the Mercedes lady, and the police racing toward the cave and bulldozer. With reinforcements on the ground, she felt comfortable leaving her post to join Zander at the Ferris wheel. She left the loudspeaker booming, slipped out the back, and drove the little *bakkie* up the hill to the side field. Parking off the dirt road, she scanned the winter-sparse shrubbery until she spotted her brother knotting an old piece of twine. He was making a sling. *Ag man*, the boy never grew up.

He twisted the final knot just as she crouched down beside him. "What do you do?" she asked in irritation. "How does this help?"

He nodded at the road. "They only sent one man after me. I took him down with a stone to the back of his head, but that requires being too close. A sling will give me distance and more power if others follow."

"You knocked a man out?" she asked in incredulity, peering over the bushes. "I see nothing."

"I tied him up with some wire I found in a pile of construction material. That's what gave me the idea for the sling."

"You think quickly under pressure," Julie said in admiration of her nerdy brother.

He shrugged off the praise. "Look, here comes a truck. Did you see where the police went?" He tested the strength of his rope sling, then picked a rock from a stack to set in the cradle he'd knotted.

"One police car headed toward Lucas. The other is with Ana. She's standing on some woman bigger than she is."

Zander raised his eyebrows in surprise, but the big truck barreled closer, erratically careening from side to side.

They ducked down. Not daring to make a sound, Julie texted Ana of their position and asked about Lucas.

The roar of a helicopter overhead drew her attention skyward. Did police send helicopters?

"Gregory's truck," she whispered as she recognized the monster white truck approaching up the hill.

Zander nodded his understanding. Gregory had the authority to order the bulldozer to slam into the mountain. It paid to be wary of him.

Gregory's truck stopped before it reached the Ferris wheel. It looked as if the man behind the wheel was using binoculars to survey his surroundings.

"Looking for snipers maybe," Zander said with a snort of amusement. "There are only three seats on the wheel. They'd be ideal for peppering the park if I had a rifle."

Julie didn't find any of this amusing. She swallowed hard and prayed.

She prayed harder when Gregory climbed out of his truck in camouflage suit and heavy boots, looking like a soldier. He opened the massive tool box in the truck bed and removed something long and dark.

She gasped when he turned around, cradling an assault rifle.

Zander muttered a bad word. "Lay flat. Don't move." Frantically, Julie texted a warning to Ana. Perhaps Ana could steer the police here before the madman realized the pretty park ride made an ideal sniper's nest.

To her surprise, Lucas texted her. WHERE ARE YOU?

Lucas was alive! And out of the cave! Fingers flying, Julie explained their predicament.

GOT IT. COMING.

She showed the phone to Zander, who just nodded tersely and watched Gregory.

"He's looking for an offensive position," Zander whispered as the contractor examined a pile of boulders left from one of the unfinished exhibits. "He has to know the police will see his truck and come looking for him. He wants a fight. Why?"

"Because he is *bosbefok*? Or just drunk," Julie suggested. "Lucas can warn the police away, can't he?" she inquired anxiously, texting the new horror to both Lucas and Ana.

Gregory turned in their direction, and she shut up.

A motorcycle roared up the hill in their direction. Lucas had arrived at the park on a motorcycle.

Julie covered her mouth as Gregory swung to face the road. Zander set his mouth in the grim, stubborn look directly reflecting their father's fierce warrior heritage.

Gregory aimed his rifle as the motorcycle came closer. *Was Lucas suicidal?*

The helicopter dropped lower, startling Gregory but not the

motorcycle rider. The rifle rattled off gunfire, just as the cycle deliberately veered off the road at a sharp angle.

With Gregory concentrating on the bike, Zander loaded his sling, stood up, and swung with all the force of his well-trained arm, hitting the gunman on the temple.

Gregory toppled. His rifle shot aimlessly at the sky as he fell.

The helicopter rose and flew away.

Ana runs for the hill

I WAS ALREADY TROTTING toward the Ferris wheel when all hell broke loose. I nearly expired on the spot at the rattle of high-powered weaponry from the hill where Julie and Zander hid. In the distance, from behind Jesus Cave, more explosions lit the sky, and a helicopter zipped in overhead.

I had no doubt that Graham was in the 'copter, directing operations from a visual advantage. I just didn't know what the devil he was doing because the bull-headed man didn't *communicate*. He gave orders, not explanations.

I kept heading toward the twins, even though I had next to no cover. As Maryam had said, this was an excellent field for seeing stars—and anything approaching.

Heart in my throat as the gunfire broke out again, apparently aiming at the helicopter, I dropped to the ground and studied the situation. Julie had said Gregory was up there with an assault rifle, and they were hiding. Who was he shooting at?

The gunfire stopped. A motorcycle started. And the helicopter bobbed, hovered, and flew toward the back of the park. Mission accomplished?

I didn't know whether to curse Graham or thank him.

A text came through from Julie saying only HURRY.

Trying to breathe a sigh of relief that my siblings were alive, while imagining blood and gore, I trotted up the hill. I didn't know whether to expect dead bodies, the walking wounded, or Disney fireworks. The Ferris wheel was still running. Half of its brightly colored lights were out and more were blinking erratically. I realized the time had got away from me, and it was late afternoon because the sky behind the lights was almost black. The shortest day of the year had been yesterday.

EG would be home. Mallard would have to look after her.

The shooting began again. This time, I could see the laser light and spit of fire—from the Ferris wheel. As the ancient wheel turned, so did the gun.

I crept up the back of the hill hoping the growing darkness provided cover. Below, more police cars were arriving—an entire SWAT team from the looks of it. Man, we'd really stepped in a fire ant nest this time.

Authorities took too long. My family was trapped up there, and that freakin' gunman was going down. Well, literally going down right now as the wheel swung his seat away from us and toward the ground on the far side. The blasted ride had only three seats and he'd claimed one of them.

Finally finding Julie's ugly pink coat behind some ragged weeds, I belly-crawled up behind them. Julie poked the long, lanky body lying beside her, and Zander turned. He held up his sling shot and shrugged, indicating their helplessness.

"Zander knocked him down with a stone," Julie whispered proudly.

"And then Lucas arrived, and Gregory got up and ran," Zander explained in disgust. "The wheel is slow, so he can climb on and off easily, but he just sits there, shooting at anything that moves."

"A dream come true for a real sportsman," I said sardonically, judging the angle of the wheel and our hiding place and deciding we were safe enough if we kept our heads down. "Where is our super-genius FBI informant?" I didn't know Lucas, but in my opinion riding up on an assault rifle was not a good tactical maneuver.

"He learned Gregory killed his sister," Julie whispered in a voice full of horror. "Lucas has been trying to confront him, but Gregory is always surrounded by men, until now."

Since they all had access to my findings about Gregory's prison record and theories about Rebecca, I didn't even bother asking how Lucas knew. With the FBI at his fingertips, he probably had access to more records than I did.

I wondered if Laura Jeffrey had bothered sending Gregory a warning, and if he knew the jig was up.

I pulled out my phone and showed the twins the air-to-ground photos Graham was sending me of the cops in a stand-off with the bulldozer guys at the Jesus Cave. "Looks like they're holed up in that cement bunker with an arsenal. Gregory must have decided he'd rather die on high ground than starve to death with Jesus."

Zander snorted. Julie glared at my disrespect. The assault rifle continued spitting fire but mostly as laconic warnings. Or *look at me, I'm up here, pigs.*

"You can't touch me," he slurred as the wheel circled downward. "I have a second amendment right to bear arms and protect myself from a government I don't recognize!"

Oh yeah, here came the drunken justification. A man who beats up his wife and murders his girlfriend, probably hadn't the ability to calculate any further than a grandiose super-stud ending like in the movies. The news was filled with idiots like that.

"I ain't goin' back to prison," our bright bulb shouted.

If he thought we'd respond to that and make targets of ourselves, he'd seriously underestimated the enemy. Of course he had.

Julie nodded worriedly in the direction of the road. "Lucas is armed, too. He has a rifle."

"Oh, for pity's sake," I said in disgust. "Stay here."

I gauged the distance to Gregory's monster truck where it blocked the road, then found the shadowy figure kneeling in a pile of boulders with his rifle in the ready position. When Gregory's amusement park seat revolved down the far side of the wheel from the road, I darted out of our hiding place. He might see my movement, but he'd have to shoot through the wheel supports and his truck to reach me.

Lucas heard me coming, swiveled, rifle ready, then made a gesture of disgust, and returned to following his target like any good sniper.

In my fury, I felt his disrespect justified my reaction. I picked up a good-sized rock, smashed it against his trigger hand, kneed him in the back, and ripped the rifle away. Half of my success is surprise. No one expects a shrimp to attack. I heaved the weapon down the hill as he turned to grab me.

"Don't make a bigger asshat of yourself by hitting me in front of Julie," I warned. "Going to jail and ruining your career for revenge is the act of a temper-tantrum-throwing toddler."

"How many more people does he have to kill before I'm allowed to take him down?" Lucas asked angrily.

"You are *not* judge and jury. The cops will be sending in experts shortly. It's just you down here wanting to kill right now, which makes you as bad as him. You and the twins could drive away, and he'd be up there all by his lonesome. How long do you think that would last?"

He growled an expletive and glared at the sky. "The cops will let him surrender when he gets tired. He'll lawyer up. There won't be enough evidence against him. He'll get away to do it again."

Possibly, but I could not condone his testosterone-addled version of justice. Young men simply did not have the brain wiring to think through the hormones, which probably explained half the world's problems. Still, I had enough experience to sympathize with his frustration and the need for release. "If I bring him down, will you promise not to kill him and to keep me and the kids out of it?"

I was hoping Graham's men were handling Laura Jeffrey and any other killers on the premises. I could manage only one situation at a time, and the twins came first. I would not let them think it was okay to kill, or take justice into their own hands. But I wasn't averse to teaching lessons.

If laughing wouldn't have drawn attention, Lucas probably would have rolled around and howled at my suggestion that I could do what he could not. Instead, the snot looked me up and down and made a rude noise. "Sure, knock yourself out."

After that, I had enough rage to knock *him* out. Instead, I pointed at the boulders we were hiding behind. "At the count of three, push." I placed my palms squarely on the top rock.

I couldn't see his expression in the dark, but he caught on quick. He raised his head above the rocks, gauged the angle of our target, placed his greater muscle power in a strategic position, and we rocked and rolled.

The first boulder bounced off the rest of the stack and only rolled half way toward our target. Gregory shot in the direction of the noise, and fragments spattered.

"What did Rebecca do to you that she deserved to die?" Now that he knew our position, I felt free to shout at the wheel as we rocked another boulder.

"I didn't kill her!" Gregory shouted. "She couldn't swim. That ain't my fault."

"It's hard to swim if you've been strangled to death," Lucas roared at his sister's killer.

Gregory answered with gunfire. So much for making him talk

like they do in the movies. I didn't expect to get sense out of him anyway.

Having a better idea of how much strength we needed now, we gauged the next boulder better, and the one after that. They bounced and rattled and flat-lined while Gregory emptied his ammo using them for target practice. Eventually, a boulder slammed into the Ferris wheel mechanism.

The wheel slowed down.

"Ancient engine," Lucas said in satisfaction. "We've got him."

"Remember, you promised to keep us out of this. You can have all the glory," I warned before pushing the next rock.

He didn't argue but shoved.

Sure enough, the next rock bounced off the others, arced through the air, and smashed into the lever that operated the engine. The wheel shuddered, groaned, and Gregory—standing up to better aim at us—flew over the back of the seat. Fortunately for him, he was on the downside roll. His gun went one way, he went the other, hitting the ground hard enough to knock the breath from him.

I ran for the rifle. Lucas ran for the man.

It might have been better if Gregory had fallen while the wheel was at its height. Then he could have broken his neck and not known what hit him.

Colored lights flashed across his stunned expression as Lucas grabbed his shirt, hauled him to his feet, and slammed a fist into the gut of his sister's murderer.

I walked away from the one-sided battle. Cop cars were on their way up the hill. I'd done what I could. Let them handle the rest. The twins and I were outta there, escaping authority—as Magda had taught me.

Twenty-seven

Ana takes the limo

SAM WAS WAITING AT the gate to take us home as ordered. Silently, Julie and Zander piled in after me, apparently shocked senseless by their recent violent experience. Chaos takes time to process, but I was proud of how they'd held up.

When the limo finally deposited us on our doorstep, Magda was there, helping EG string popcorn around a tree blinking in lopsided glory. The domestic scene, alone, after the gun violence was sufficient to push me into overload. Mallard hanging tinsel had me toppling in shock.

I grabbed a wall, and our little family waved in welcome. Shaking my head to clear it, I followed the twins and staggered toward the stairs and showers.

At that point, I really didn't care what Laura Jeffrey had to do with a wife-beating killer, a bunch of AGA thugs, and Arden's board of directors. It would no doubt make more sense when I read the police reports in the morning. For now, I was home, my family was safe, and Graham was landing his damned helicopter in his private heliport. I hugged safety around me like a cozy sweater and abandoned the outside world.

Graham didn't come down for dinner, but he sent me Arden's hospital report. Our favorite preacher was recovering after having his stomach pumped for poison. Nurses reported that Laura Jeffrey had arrived during lunch and had been the last person to see him before me. Josh had cleared me because he'd eaten nothing while I was around—I do that to people.

The police had Laura in custody, but she would be circled by lawyers.

One could hope Arden would finally report everything he suspected about people he could no longer trust, but I wasn't holding my breath. He was probably praying for them. If he'd reported his suspicions earlier, Melissa might still be alive.

Nick and Patra came over to celebrate with us—and to collect information the media didn't have yet.

"What will happen to Jesus World?" Patra asked, not out of any concern for the park and its supporters but planning her next story. I knew my sister well.

Magda actually sat at the table with us. With a nonchalant wave, she answered with assurance, "Arden's followers will be praying for God's will. That should provide all the funding he needs to rebuild."

Yeah, she'd probably have the CIA secretly fund overseas schools. I gave her the stink eye but kept my mouth shut. My concern was for Julie, who was looking intensely thoughtful. I had about decided that was a dangerous thing.

After dinner, we carried our drinks to the parlor, much to Mallard's immense dismay, and admired our first family Christmas tree. EG insisted on carols. We didn't know any. Julie gallantly sang some South African hymns. We bumbled through "Jingle Bells." I pried EG away from package sorting, and called it a night. That was enough family togetherness even for me.

Finally, I was able to take the hidden stairs from the room next to mine up to Graham's lair to see what he was doing. To one side of the wall his monitors displayed the park, but it was too dark and potentially dangerous for the cops to explore it tonight if there were any more booby-traps than the ones on the fence. They'd installed lights and guards and had the place under surveillance.

Graham had some new activity rolling across the other screens. I wasn't interested.

Instead, I wrapped my arms around his neck from behind and leaned over and kissed him. "Thank you."

"For what?" He hit his keyboard and changed the monitors. One showed Julie slipping outside to meet Lucas in the barren grape arbor behind the mansion. . .

"I knew you'd have the arbor bugged," I complained, switching off that screen. "Leave her be. She's old enough to make her own bad choices."

"He's not bad, just inexperienced. Your sister is the crazy. Once you give her her share of the money, she'll give it away, probably to Arden."

"Her choice. It's allowed. EG and Tudor are the only ones who need real guardians right now. I can handle that."

He snorted. "You haven't a clue what Tudor is into. And EG will be worse in a few years."

EG was pretty bad now, so I didn't argue. "I just need to steer them down the right paths. It will be easier here than wandering the back roads of the Middle East." *As our small family had done in Magda's misbegotten youth* went unsaid.

He couldn't argue that either. "Keep an eye on Magda."

My turn to snort. "Like that's happening in our lifetimes. I'm guessing she won't stay long enough to enjoy a gift of wine. So I bought her a red emergency phone with all our numbers in it, and I'm giving the phone number to the kids for Christmas."

He chuckled. "You're mean. Did you buy Mallard his wine?"

I nibbled Graham's ear lobe before answering. "I bought him shares in his favorite Irish pub. He'll be paying himself when he runs up his tab."

Graham stood abruptly, grabbed my waist, and pulled me hard against his hips. The heat of his kiss was worth the aggravation of dealing with his insanity.

Juliana talks to her mother

ON THE NIGHT BEFORE Christmas Eve, Julie waited until the house settled down, and carried her stack of presents downstairs. She was still a little uncertain of her place in the family, but she enjoyed gift giving.

To her surprise, their mother was sitting in the ugly Morris chair, sipping a glass of wine and watching the lights on the tree. She looked up with a smile as Julie set her colorful stack on the floor. In the dim light, lines of weariness formed around Magda's mouth and eyes, but her sleek blond hair was as elegantly styled as her ensemble of form-fitting red sweater and wool slacks.

"I am glad we had this chance to meet," Magda said in a low voice that wouldn't carry far. "Your father would be so very proud of the two of you."

Delighted with this opportunity to know her mother better, Julie sat cross-legged at her feet. "We've always understood that you and Father had a higher calling. I'm not sure I've found mine yet, but I hope it is one that will allow me to visit often with family. I feel accepted here as I do not always elsewhere."

Magda laughed softly. "You were all born with rebel genes and excellent brains. You will never fit in with flocks of sheep. The world needs more people like us. But you will find unique friends who will be as close as family someday."

Julie nodded. "I think this is so. Where do you go from here?"

"It's best if you do not know. But Ana will be distributing your funds soon, so you may travel where you will. Let your brother handle your money so you never go hungry. When I was your age, I didn't realize how harmful poverty could be, and Ana and Nick suffered for it. Keep enough to care for your children."

"I do not know if I shall have children, but you are correct. I should keep emergency funds. Our father would hope that we would always have a home for you, should you need one."

Magda leaned over and patted her cheek. "Ana would argue with that, and rightly so. I am dangerous, but I appreciate your compassionate heart. You inherit that from your father's side of the family. Have children. Create your own dynasty and save the future. But for now, go on back to bed. EG is up in her room, plotting our entire weekend. You will need your rest."

Julie did as told, fearing her mother was saying good-bye. She did not completely regret losing a chance to know her better. In her own odd way, Magda had given a legend to all her children, so she was always present wherever her family was gathered.

Ana plays Santa Claus

AFTER A DAY OF EG's idea of a family Christmas Eve—visits to the White House lawn to see a *real* Christmas tree, more shopping with carolers, hot cider, and of course, watching *A Christmas Carol* production—I was wiped.

But I'd finally finished my Santa shopping and, with everyone in bed, I needed to fill EG's stocking. She'd found an enormous red furry one and added more glitter to the glittery stars already there. The stocking was large enough to hold a library. I added books and a paint set and some chocolates and still had room left over.

I stopped to admire the tree before turning off the lights. Among the branches, I found a new ornament—a tiny crystal cherub with a gold base. Curious, I turned it over. On the base was inscribed: *In memoriam, Marie Hostetter, 1991*. Magda must have hung it there.

Marie was my baby sister, the one I couldn't save from bombs. Apparently, Magda hadn't forgotten that painful time, although she'd divorced Marie's father shortly thereafter and moved on with her life—to Africa, to be precise. I'd never forgiven Magda for the baby's death. Maybe it was time.

Distracting myself, I watched the snow starting to fall out the front window, coating the historic street lamps and creating a Victorian panorama.

I gave the stacks of gifts beneath the tree one more glance and frowned. They'd been rearranged. I sat down to examine tags, like the child I'd never been. Nick and Patra had been smuggling in gifts from their respective abodes, so the stack was acquiring mountainous dimensions. They'd promised to show up early in the morning to watch EG tackle the motherlode. I didn't have to shake the box labeled from Nick to me. I knew it would be clothes. I just prayed they were something I dared wear.

Then I noticed that the gift I'd wrapped in elaborate velvet and gold for Magda wasn't there. I shoved larger packages aside but the square phone box had vanished—and so had all the other packages addressed to her.

She was gone.

At least she'd taken her gifts with her.

I can't say that I felt surprise or even sadness, except for EG and the twins, who would have liked pretending they had a real mother. But it was hard to miss what you'd never had. I'd long ago accepted that—whatever her reasoning—Magda loved having children. She took pride in our achievements. She simply didn't have the patience for tending us.

I didn't know if her departure meant I'd won Patra's wager and got to keep my fake Birkin bag or not. Our mother *hadn't* overwhelmed us with extravagant gifts to make us look like pikers, then run. Instead, she'd left each of us identical, small, rectangular packages.

I opened mine just to be certain it wouldn't explode.

Inside was a box from a leather store. Gingerly, I lifted the lid. A sleek black leather case larger than a wallet but smaller than a clutch lay nestled in protective paper. An emblem of some sort was embossed into one brass-protected corner. The case snapped together on nearly invisible edges. It looked like an extremely expensive day planner, which would be typical of Magda's non-technical mindset. But I was pretty certain it wasn't a calendar.

I unsnapped the case, and with one finger, lifted the top edge.

A photo of my father, Magda, and me as a toddler stared back at me. I studied it for a long time. I couldn't remember ever seeing Brody Devlin's image, although, since I recognized his devastatingly handsome face and daredevil smile, I must have seen photos at some time. I was only four when he died. Could I be remembering him from all those years ago? I had no childhood scrapbooks to call up memories, but this image of me with long black hair and a fringe across my brow was unmistakable. I didn't look particularly happy to be posing, but I was wearing a frilly dress and hair bows. That would make anyone frown.

I turned the vinyl page and found a photo of Nick and me next. He was probably two, so I must have been seven. He was a grinning golden-haired imp in cute overall shorts. I was a scowling, black-haired guard dog in torn denim.

I don't know where Magda had found these photos, but I was misty-eyed by the time I flipped through images of me with my siblings at different ages. There was even one of the twins playing with a lion cub while I stood to one side, holding a big stick. She'd chosen photos that displayed all my best and worst traits. I wanted to hate her for understanding me so well.

But she'd gone to a lot of work to prove she cared.

Shattered, wiping back tears, I wrapped the box back up again and returned it beneath the tree. I might have to order everyone to save Magda's gifts for last or we'd all weep through our first Christmas together.

I turned off the lights and trudged upstairs. Graham met me in my room. Graham never showed himself in public spaces below his attic level. I would have been worried, except he held out his arms as he never had before. It was all the encouragement I needed. I fell into them, weeping. I never cry. It's a policy of mine. But for just this moment of weakness, I poured like a teapot.

He held me against his muscled chest until I recovered.

"Like Max, and you, she hides the soft bits," he murmured.

"And maybe, like you," I suggested, wiping my eyes.

"Don't hold your breath on that one," he said dryly.

He led me up the secret stairs to his war office, where he

punched a few keys and set up a video on his biggest monitor. When he pushed the forward button, I knew this was a recording, not real time. The camera view of Jesus World being lit by police lights unfolded.

The police and feds had been busy over the past few days while I hadn't been watching. There were now gaping ditches and construction equipment everywhere.

I knew from Graham's missives that, so far, the police and the feds had dismantled strategically planted IEDs under fence posts and uncovered stashes of weapons and explosives, all in GenDef crates. The entire park was riddled with hiding places.

The complete paper trail didn't exist yet, but forensic accountants were working on it. They already knew that George Paycock the Embezzler had been siphoning General Defense's funds into the park. The feds had been assuming he was stealing money, but the motive was no longer as clear as they'd believed. With Zander's and Graham's help, the authorities were far down the trail of proving the park board had been transferring the stolen funds to Paul Rose contributors, who then gave it to Rose PACs.

GenDef was essentially buying themselves a presidential candidate who would support more wars and promise not to ban guns, thereby assuring their existence for another millennium or two.

But along with funds, the park board had also been accepting, and concealing, shipments of *weapons,* with the aid of Gregory's construction company.

Tony Jeffrey was on the park board and had to be aware of what was happening. Laura Jeffrey hadn't been a director, and she was claiming the shipments were perfectly legitimate from the company's end. But either she was lying or Georgie had been shipping weapons even after his death. And that didn't even touch on the illegality of unlicensed weapon caches.

Now that the police had enough evidence to convict Laura of poisoning Arden and shooting Melissa—she'd kept the gun she'd used in her bedroom drawer—they weren't much inclined to believe her protestations of innocence. Tony had lawyered up. We weren't hearing much from him.

"They've found shipping manifests," Graham said, halting the film to show the peaceful park in a light layer of this evening's fresh snow. "The weapons and explosives were leaving GenDef's warehouse as defective materials scheduled for recycling. The park has no record of receiving them, but enough of Julie's film shows trucks arriving at night, after the gates were secured."

"Gregory allowed them in the back gate, where there were no security cameras," I suggested. "They didn't know about Julie's cameras. They stored the weapons—for what?"

"Some of them went to domestic paramilitary wingnuts willing to pay outlandish prices for arsenals to save them from our own government. The majority, however, appear to have ultimately been sold at hugely inflated prices on the world market, to terrorists on the banned list. GenDef more than covered the donations they made to the park."

"Then George Paycock started blackmailing Laura?" I guessed.

"Eventually," he agreed. "They've finally found a bullet in the foundation where they found George. It matches Laura's gun—not enough for conviction but telling."

"What about Esther and the other guy buried there?"

"Owen was working on the underground bunkers. We found texts on his phone asking his boss pointed questions. Gregory claims he forwarded those questions to the board, and his phone reflects that."

"So we'll never know who killed Owen and Esther unless someone confesses?" I kept staring uneasily at the peaceful park scene on the monitor, looking for answers.

"George Paycock was Laura's lover," he said baldly. "We have evidence and witnesses."

"Uh oh." I sighed and leaned back against him. "The plot thickens. Laura got tired of George and found someone new. George started blackmailing her about the weapons."

He nodded against my head. "Among other things. But while they were still happily together, they discussed the problem of Owen being too smart for his own good."

"So Paycock promised to answer questions and met with him at the back of the park, out of sight of the cameras. Shoving Owen over the brink of one of those holes could have broken his neck." I hated having an imagination. I could almost visualize the whole scenario.

"That's the most likely story. We have evidence that George was Laura's go-to guy for anything she needed done, but I don't know if we can pin Owen's death directly to her."

No wonder I had more bodies than suspects if the killers started killing each other. "Owen may have talked about the bunkers with Melissa, who could have said something to Arden."

"She was a particularly clueless young woman, but you're right, she told Arden. He's starting to talk. He could turn out to be a key witness," Graham said. "Ed Parker swears he was merely supporting Melissa's art and knows nothing of anything, but they've searched his hunting lodge and found more crates of weapons. He might not have killed anyone, but he knew what the board was doing. He'll talk too."

"By eliminating Owen, and passing Melissa on to Ed, who may actually be supporting her career. . ." I pondered that, decided my head might explode, and gave it up. "Without Owen, Melissa shut up, and Arden wrote her off as just another crazy who disappeared from his radar. Cover-up continues as planned. But then Georgie got greedy, right?"

"Keeping both a wife and two mistresses is expensive," Graham said, hugging me tighter. "He wanted a bigger cut. Laura probably broke off any relations with him when she learned about Esther. But what really undid him—and Laura was spitting mad when she told this—was that Esther learned about his embezzling. When she and George had a fight, Esther reported it to Arden. Laura says Arden told her he'd been *praying* over what he should do."

"Which was why Esther had to disappear." I groaned at Arden's idiocy and Laura's arrogance in believing what she wanted was more important than the lives of others. "I don't suppose she would also admit to killing her?"

I leaned into Graham, waiting for the moment he started playing the park video again. The falling snow frozen on the screen said the film had been taken this evening. I already knew I wouldn't like whatever he was building up to.

"The DNA report verified the woman buried in the same area as George was Esther, but her wounds were from a different size gun. They found some of George's DNA beneath her fingernails. My assumption is that once Laura heard that Esther had revealed the embezzling, she would have told George to get rid of her. With Owen's successful murder under his belt, there was nothing to stop George from ending the problem of an expensive mistress and snitch in the same way. The police are going over Esther's phone records and possessions now that we have ID, but we probably don't have a case against Laura there."

I shuddered. "George had his lover dumped in the park, then Laura did the same to him? Not very creative of her."

"He'd already been accused of embezzling. He had become a liability who could easily have spilled her involvement. With him gone, she could persuade her father to let her take over his position, eliminating the middle man."

"And then Arden started asking questions, finally and at long last. The man is just too dumb or too trusting, I can't decide which."

"Whatever, he's not of our world."

Amen, I thought, before asking, "What about the yahoo who tried to strong-arm me at the hospital? Wasn't he Gregory's employee, not Laura's?"

"But he was working under orders from GenDef. He was their security guard at the gate. He just had Gregory's ID tag. Gregory might be abusive scum and willing to take money under the table and turn a blind eye, but the board—and his mother—kept him out of everything else."

"Mrs. Overcamp? Just exactly what part did she play?" I liked snuggling. I liked that he was talking instead of simply sending me police reports. I was willing to postpone the inevitable all night.

"She's been an ardent Arden supporter for years and probably the person he trusted most. If she told him not to worry his pretty little head, he believed her. She helped choose the photogenic candidates. The photos Julie found in the trailer were Overcamp's— she was once a professional photographer. Some of the men admitted she used the photos for a little discreet blackmail."

"Wow, and I suppose all in the name of Josh Arden and his holy mission. I almost like it," I said in admiration. "The rich sleaze balls had to pay for their sins."

He snorted at my interpretation of blackmail and continued. "She kept the construction company books. She knew if the students played their parts right, donations poured into the park, so she doled out the concert tickets and party invitations to those who played their part best. She had all the links to the board's wrongdoing right in front of her, but we have no proof that she understood anything beyond the money keeping the construction company and the park alive."

"She understood enough to bug Julie's phone," I pointed out. "She knew her son's history of violence. She's no innocent, but she's probably not a murderer. How did Tony's bodyguards get involved in shooting Arden?"

"Laura had her father hire the bodyguards so she had someone to do her bidding after George was gone. They're blabbing everything they know to lessen their sentences. She told the guards to get rid of Arden, and when they failed, she sent them after the witnesses. Julie's friends would probably have been killed and framed for Arden's shooting. Laura's attorneys are claiming their client is under the care of physicians who prescribed the wrong medications."

I snuggled into his arms and closed my eyes. "Who's to say that arrogance isn't a mental illness? Allowing too much power into the hands of a few leads to Caligula."

He chuckled. "Only you could make that leap of judgment."

"I'll wait for the newspapers to explain all the connections. Show me what you want to show me and then let's go to bed. EG will be up before dawn."

He held an arm around my waist as he pressed a remote. The park film flickered to life. Snow fell on the Ferris wheel and dinosaur skeletons and coated evergreens and tree limbs. A police security guard climbed into his car and drove away, heading in the direction of the market coffee house. Couldn't blame him there. It was Christmas Eve, and he had a boring job on a cold night.

The security lights flickered and died.

"Pulled the plug, did she?" I asked in resignation.

Graham hugged me tighter and said nothing. The film was short. One moment, the park was peaceful and dark. In the next, small strategic fires developed simultaneously near all the weapons bunkers. The feds had still been inventorying the arsenal and hadn't moved them all.

The bunkers, predictably, exploded.

"Timing devices?" I suggested wearily.

"No other way." He clicked off the film as sirens sounded and flashing red-and-blue police lights lit the screen.

"Magda or Laura?" I asked cynically. They were both capable. Arden sure knew how to pick them.

Graham hit the keyboard and set another film rolling.

Miraculously, he'd turned off all his other monitors so I only had to concentrate on one. It showed the exterior of General Defense's warehouse. A corner street light revealed flapping yellow police tape cordoning off the entrance.

A second later, the roof blew off the warehouse in a pyrotechnical display to rival anything the National Mall produced on the Fourth of July.

"Nice. Another weapon manufactory down the drain, and suspicion falls on the murdering arms dealer covering up evidence. Magda wins again. Can we go to bed now?"

I had no proof that my mother had blown up the factory as a Christmas gift to herself, but I could almost bet my fortune on it.

"General Defense was the company our fathers were dealing with," Graham said softly. "They've always been assassins and double-dealers."

"There is always someone to take their place. She's accomplished nothing," I argued angrily. "Don't get me started."

"Okay, I won't, not on this, at least. Want to unwrap another gift?"

I punched him for spying on me, then wrapped my arms around his neck. Ours isn't a perfect relationship, but it works for us.

Twenty-eight

Ana's first Christmas

JULIE AND ZANDER WERE wearing the Irish fisherman's-knit sweaters I'd bought for them in hopes they would decide to stay in DC. Nick had three new neckties wrapped around his neck, each one more outrageous than the next. Patra sported a red feather boa from EG and was excitedly stuffing a real Birkin bag from me and Nick. I was wearing a rather dashing black leather jacket with almost as many hidden pockets as my army jacket—Nick understood me well. Tudor and EG were already embattled in a new video game.

For the obvious reason, I'd made them all save their Magda gifts for last. Once we had all our packages to each other opened, EG passed around Magda's. Cries of excitement soon settled into silence as each of us studied the gift of our pasts. Patra swiped at her eyes as she showed me a photo of her handsome investigative reporter dad bouncing her on his knee. Like Magda, Patrick Llewellyn had spent most of his time in war zones, and Patra had known very little of him before he was killed.

Julie came over and hugged me, as if I'd had anything to do with Magda's gift: pictures of her father dancing with our mother in some gorgeous ballroom. Awkwardly, I hugged her back.

"Maryam is safe at home," she murmured. "She sent me texts. Says she met someone interesting at the airport."

"It's best that she learned what she wanted while she's young," I said in sympathy. "Perhaps you can visit her someday."

She smiled brighter and settled back in her chair with her picture book.

Tudor shrugged at the photos in his album—his father was still alive and visited once a year. The next time I looked at him, he was smothering a grin that I knew meant trouble. I leaned over his chair and discovered him holding a slender, oddly-shaped pen. It took me a moment before I recognized it from one I'd seen in the hands of one of Magda's many military contacts.

She'd given Tudor a tactical pen—one that wrote but could

substitute as a bone-breaking weapon when used correctly. Tudor innocently flashed the light that also made it useful as a flashlight—until he used it to break someone's jaw. Shades of James Bond!

He slid the pen back into the compartment hidden by the leather hinge of the album. It would most likely even pass airport security. I shuddered.

EG was already digging around in the hinge of her album. Did I really want to know what was stored there? I could hope for a unicorn-shaped thumb drive.

I explored my album and uncovered a folding finger spike baton, much more lethal than the roll of quarters I'd used in the past. I could take out eyes with the thing. I carefully re-folded it and slid it back into its hiding place. I couldn't imagine using such a weapon—or carrying a photo album around with me—but one never knew.

I'd check on EG's secret gift from Magda later, but I preferred not to know what other surprises Magda had hidden. There was still a stack of gifts left unopened, because Graham and Mallard had declined to join us, as usual. I had a plan for that.

A gift labeled for all of us with no donor's name on it still waited. I'd saved it in hopes of ending our gift exchange on a happy note.

Since EG was searching through the debris, looking for more loot to add to her stack, I gestured for her to open the rather flat package that looked as if it might be a book. I was hoping it wasn't another photo album to make us cry.

While the others were showing each other photos, EG happily tore apart the elegant gold-embossed wrapping paper. No recycling here. I hid my sigh of regret. Once upon a time, I could have had lots of fun with that paper.

The slender box held a fancy file folder which looked suspiciously as if it had come from a law office. Nick was closer and took it from her. His eyebrows practically hit the sky as he studied the documents inside. Then he offered it to Patra instead of to me.

I waited in frustration, wanting to thrash them all for bypassing me as they handed it back and forth. Zander finally looked at it in puzzlement and handed it over. My siblings waited so expectantly, that I swallowed hard and braced myself.

I skimmed the legal verbiage. Not entirely believing what I was reading, I flipped through the pages until I found the signatures and a notary's seal. I gulped, and returned to reading again from the start.

"Well?" Patra said impatiently. "Is this enough? Will you settle for partial ownership or do we still keep fighting him?"

Graham had deeded half of our grandfather's mansion to our family trust, with his half going to the trust upon his death.

Finally, and at long last, I had it all, almost. I got to keep Graham *and* my house. I looked up to my expectant family and nodded. "Graham was as much Max's family as we are, maybe more so. This makes good sense."

Six months ago, I wouldn't have agreed. Now, I almost cried again at Graham's generosity.

With that settled, Zander pointed at the remaining Magda photo-album packages under the tree. "Who are these for?"

Patra, naturally, had already studied them. "One's for Sean, the other is for Graham. We ought to open them."

Her newspaper reporter instinct was kicking in, sniffing for more insight into the mysterious past that Magda had shared with their fathers. I waited for a lamp to interrupt, but Graham apparently wasn't paying attention. I could fix that.

I gestured at Tudor, who had been waiting for this moment. He pulled a collapsible pile of plastic from behind the sofa, shook it about a bit, and produced a blinking battery-operated Christmas tree. Then I gestured at the stack of eccentrically wrapped packages left under the tree.

"If the Grinch won't come to Christmas, we'll take Christmas to the Grinch," I announced.

Gleefully, everyone grabbed a few packages, and we trudged up two flights of stairs to Graham's attic lair. I was praying he'd still be there and hadn't fled to Outer Mongolia at the first hint of my intentions.

Mallard was at the top of the stairs, behind a linen-covered table adorned with a crystal punch bowl and matching crystal cups. Crystal! Honestly, the man had gone completely mad.

EG completed a polite curtsy I didn't know she knew how to perform. She handed over her gift to Mallard, then snatched a cookie from the lovely buffet.

My siblings stacked gifts before him, and I could swear the old soldier was starting to mist up as we all grabbed plates of goodies and cups of punch. I was betting Magda had given him his photo album in private, because he was looking all smiley sentimental and had a suspiciously square bulge in his immaculately fitted jacket.

He even opened the door to Graham's office for us so Tudor could lead the parade with his blinking tree.

Only Tudor had ever been invited to Graham's inner sanctum. I'd stormed it. EG had sneaked around it. Nick had seen it after Graham had stripped and hidden everything last month. As far as I knew, Patra, Zander, and Julie had never been up here. So mostly, everyone gawked as we entered bearing gifts.

Graham was wearing a fake-fur-trimmed Santa hat pulled down over his hair and scar. But this hat was black, like his long-sleeved shirt and trousers. I was pretty sure that was a green Grinch embroidered on the front. He regarded us solemnly as Tudor set the tree down on his polished mahogany console. For once, his monitors weren't showing scenes of mayhem. Instead, he'd tuned into cameras on the Ellipse displaying the Christmas tree and crowds. There were images of skating rinks and churches too. He'd prepared for us.

I wanted to hug him, but I didn't think either of us was ready for public displays of affection. I handed him a cup of punch instead. "Merry Christmas from your extended family."

I waited for him to wince, but he was a practiced politician when he wanted to be. "Thank you, I think," was all he said.

But by the time he'd opened his gifts and was wearing a Cat-in-the-Hat scarf, while Tudor produced plastic stars on the 3-D printer and Mallard tuned in a choir singing the *Messiah,* Graham was actually smiling.

We couldn't give him anything as generous as half a mansion, but we could give him the family he'd never had. Both gifts came with passels of problems, but I figured we were up to the challenge.

Graham intelligently didn't open Magda's gift while we were present. I'd get to the bottom of the mystery of my father's relationship with him in the new year.

For now, I'd simply rejoice that I had everyone I loved under one roof.

Acknowledgments

Thank you, Tom Sietsema, the *Washington Post*'s food critic, for recommending 701 as a lovely restaurant open in 2011 that would suit my high-end gang! And as always, I could not have kept all the pieces strung together without the help of Mindy Klasky, Jennifer Stevenson, Phyllis Radford, and the BVC crew who monitor a book from a gleam in the author's eye to the final production. The publishing business wouldn't be worth the effort without the extraordinary people who populate it!

Characters

Ana's Family and friends

Anastasia (Ana) Devlin—daughter of Brody Devlin. Magda's eldest child. (Alias Linda Lane/teacher, Patty Pasko/realtor/accountant; Jessica James, attorney)

Brody Devlin—Ana's father, the Mad Irishman, killed by a bomb when Ana was four

Magda Maximillian Llewellyn Bullfinch Hostetter—Ana's mother, the self-called Hungarian princess. Ana's names for her are less pleasant.

Nicholas Maximillian—Ana's half-brother, illegitimate son of a British lord, five years younger than Ana

Elizabeth Georgiana Maximillian (EG)—Ana's nine-year-old half-sister; illegitimate daughter of Senator Tex Hammond

Tudor Bullfinch—Ana's sixteen-year old hacker half-brother; father is an Australian shipping magnate

Cleopatra (Patra) Llewellyn—Ana's eldest half-sister; journalist; dating Sean O'Herlihy; father Patrick was an investigative reporter who died when she was very young

Alexander (Zander) Khosi Kruger—Ana's illegitimate South African half-brother and Juliana's twin

Juliana (Julie) Aneke Kruger—Ana's illegitimate South African half-sister and Zander's twin

Phillip Kruger—the twin's father, diplomat, deceased

Rathbone Maximillian—Ana's grandfather, deceased

Antonina Maximillian—Ana's grandmother, deceased

Amadeus Graham—aka Thomas Alexander, security consultant; Ana's landlord or the "spy in the attic"; presidential advisor until 9/11 when his wife died

Mallard—Graham's Irish butler, former IRA general

Sean O'Herlihy—political investigative reporter; his father was assassinated at same time as Ana's and Graham's

Characters In Twin Genius

Reverend Joshua Arden—former football hero, preacher, runs Joshua Arden Community Association Development (JACAD or CAD for short)

Reverend William Arden—Joshua's father, famous televangelist and preacher

Dorothy Overcamp—manager of Arden's marketing office

William Gregory—park's general contractor

Maryam Rathore—Julie's Pakistani roommate

Rebecca Beatty—strangled and left in the Potomac; former JACAD worker

Melissa Winters—church-going Sunday school teacher and former JACAD student

Esther Hanks—George Paycock's girlfriend and Julie's former roommate

Owen Black—construction worker whose body was found in park in October

Edward Parker the Third—trust fund baby, on JACAD board

George Paycock—CFO of General Defense Industries, on JACAD board

Lucas Schmidt—a student at JACAD

Anthony (Tony) Jeffrey—General Defense CEO, park supporter

Laura Jeffrey—Tony Jeffrey's daughter

Aunt Hildegard—Phillip Kruger's sister and the twins' paternal aunt

Detective Hobbs—investigating shooting at park

Blackwell Johnson—attorney at Brashton, Johnson, and Terwilliger

Reginald Brashton the Third—executor who ran off with the Maximillian money

Arnold Oppenheimer—shark attorney hired to sue Brashton

Senator Paul Rose—running for president

SOUTH AFRICAN SLANG

Ag man—pronounced "ach;" to express dismay: oh, man!

Antie—derived from "aunt;" female of authority

Bakgat—awesome, cool

Bladdy hell—just what it sounds like

Bosbefok—crazy, mad, out of your mind

dof—dumb

Domkop—idiot, dumbhead

Dwankie—noun or adjective: uncool

Eish—expression of surprise: Wow, really, what?!

Jislaaik—similar to eish: Jislaaik, he walked off the cliff!

Kak—c'mon, you can guess this one! Probably from the same origin as caca, meaning excrement; vulgar

Mallei—mother

nè?—from French *n'est-ce pas*: don't you agree?

Skebanga—criminal, thug

Skelm—similar to skebanga

Skort—Watch out

Vrot—Bad, wrong

Yoh—similar to eish; expression of surprise

GET A FREE STARTER SET OF PATRICIA RICE BOOKS

Thank you for reading *Twin Genius*.

Would you like to know when my next book is available? I occasionally send newsletters with details on new releases, special offers and other bits of news. If you sign up for the mailing list I'll send you a free copy of the Patricia Rice starter kit. **The books average 4.4 out of 5 stars and together usually retail over $15.00 and include the first book of the Family Genius series—EVIL GENIUS.** Just sign up at **http://patriciarice.com/**

I am an independent author, so getting the word out about my book is vital to its success. If you liked this book, please consider telling your friends, and writing a review at the store where you purchased it. Reviews help other readers find books. I appreciate all reviews, whether positive or negative.

***

Sign up for my newsletter to be the first to know when about my next release! *http://patriciarice.com/sign-up*

About the Author

With several million books in print and *New York Times* and *USA Today's* bestseller lists under her belt, former CPA Patricia Rice is one of romance's hottest authors. Her emotionally-charged contemporary and historical romances have won numerous awards, including the *RT Book Reviews* Reviewers Choice and Career Achievement Awards. Her books have been honored as Romance Writers of America RITA® finalists in the historical, regency and contemporary categories.

A firm believer in happily-ever-after, Patricia Rice is married to her high school sweetheart and has two children. A native of Kentucky and New York, a past resident of North Carolina and Missouri, she currently resides in Southern California, and now does accounting only for herself. She is a member of Romance Writers of America, the Authors Guild, Novelists, Inc., and BVC Publishing Cooperative.

For further information, visit Patricia's network:
http://www.patriciarice.com
http://www.facebook.com/OfficialPatriciaRice
https://twitter.com/Patricia_Rice
http://patriciarice.blogspot.com/
http://wordwenches.typepad.com/word_wenches/
https://www.tumblr.com/blog/patricia-rice/

About Book View Café

Book View Café is a professional authors' cooperative offering DRM-free ebooks in multiple formats to readers around the world. With authors in a variety of genres including fantasy, romance, mystery, and science fiction, Book View Café has something for everyone.

Book View Café is good for readers because you can enjoy high-quality DRM-free ebooks from your favorite authors at a reasonable price.

Book View Café is good for writers because most of the profits goes directly to the book's author.

Book View Café authors include NY Times bestsellers and notable book authors (Madeleine Robins, Patricia Rice, Maya Kaathryn Bohnhoff, and Sarah Zettel), Nebula and Hugo Award winners (Ursula K. Le Guin, Vonda N. McIntyre, Linda Nagata), and a Rita award nominee (Patricia Rice).

www.ingramcontent.com/pod-product-compliance
Lightning Source LLC
Chambersburg PA
CBHW070445120726
47910CB00003B/940